THE HEIRS

a novel by

Fran Hawthorne

For more information:
Stephen F. Austin State University Press
P.O. Box 13007 SFA Station
Nacogdoches, Texas 75962
sfapress@sfasu.edu
www.sfasu.edu/sfapress

Book design: Thomas Sims
Cover design: Thomas Sims
Distributed by Texas A&M Consortium
www.tamupress.com

ISBN: 978-1-62288-230-4

Dedication:

*To my "Ritter" family: The ones who made it out of Poland,
and also the ones who bequeathed their stories and their names*

CONTENTS

Chapter One

"It was almost funny, in a way," the emergency-room triage nurse said. She even smiled.

"In what way," Eleanor demanded—or maybe she shrieked—"is my mother falling down and calling 911 *funny?*"

The nurse immediately sat up straight in her padded swivel chair and grasped the edge of her steel desk with both hands. The turquoise nametag on her pale-blue uniform said: Marion Hanks. "Well, no, not that part. Oh not at all."

Eleanor still glared at the woman. Yes, her mother had a smart, double-take kind of wit. Unexpected little pinches of humor. But Eleanor's mother was not *funny*, and Eleanor's mother did not fall down.

"I'm sorry, Ms. Hanks." Natalie's voice slid right in. It was a calm and even-paced voice, as always. Soothing. Half-apologetic. It came from all those years of practice, of being a judge and getting the parties to sit down and work out a compromise. Or maybe from not having to argue constantly with a twelve-year-old daughter who wanted to get her nose pierced. Or from living with a husband who was such a nice guy, as everyone always commented.

"I'm sorry," Natalie was saying, "but I guess my cousin and I aren't quite clear on all the details of my aunt's accident." Natalie smiled back at Marion Hanks across the desk.

Of course Judge Natalie's intervention worked. Marion Hanks nodded vigorously and picked out a manila folder from a set of metal dividers.

As the emergency-room staff had reconstructed the event, Rose Ritter probably slipped and fell in her bedroom, because that was where the EMTs had found her, lying on the carpet next to the night table with the telephone. Alternatively, there was some disarray in the bathroom, so possibly she fell there and somehow crawled to the bedroom. "The X-ray showed an intertrochanteric hip fracture," Marion Hanks continued, reading. She looked quickly at Natalie. Then Eleanor. "That's a very common type of fracture, especially for older women."

It would be at least two hours before Rose would be out of surgery and could have visitors. The doctor would explain it all.

"But—will she be able to walk?" Eleanor asked.

"How serious is the fracture?" Natalie added. "Will she be in a cast? How long will she be in the hospital?"

The doctor would explain it after surgery. It really was not an uncommon procedure. Marion Hanks's smile was slipping.

"I can't believe she didn't call me," Natalie said to Eleanor. "Or you."

"So what's the funny part?" Eleanor interrupted.

Marion Hanks gave a little cough and looked at her fingers. "Well— of course, I didn't really mean that it was funny. Or laughable in any way. I just want to reassure you that nobody took it badly."

"Took *what* badly?" Eleanor's voice was heading to a shriek again.

"Well, you see. When the EMTs were lifting her onto the stretcher for the ambulance, apparently Mrs. Ritter, ah, shouted at one of them. Called her a name."

"My mother? Shouting?"

Now, instead of hesitating, Marion Hanks wouldn't stop talking. "As it happens, that technician, that young lady, is newly arrived from Eastern Europe, so you see she recognized the language. The words. Your mother was shouting in Polish."

"Polish?"

Eleanor and Natalie said the word at the same time. Or one breath apart. Natalie repeated it. Eleanor's mouth hung open.

They looked at each other, then back at Marion Hanks.

"That's incredible."

"She hates Poland."

"She hasn't spoken Polish in over fifty years."

"She won't even talk about when she lived in Poland."

"What," Natalie asked, "was Aunt Rose allegedly saying in Polish?"

Marion Hanks folded her hands on the desk and gave a little titter.

"Well. Yes. Well, of course, it's not exactly funny but just, well, so extraordinary, under the circumstances, that, you know, you can only laugh? She called the young lady, ah, a 'Nazi bitch.'"

This was too much. Eleanor quickly sucked in her cheeks and stared raptly into her dark-green leather shoulder bag, pretending to dig for something, anything, so she wouldn't burst out laughing, but her breath still emerged in a strange wheeze.

To picture Rose Ritter, retired real estate office manager, Phi Beta Kappa in English from Hunter College, Class of 1951, with her red lipstick and silk blouse, calling an ambulance driver a Nazi bitch. In Polish.

* * *

It was like an invasion, to walk into her mother's apartment when Rose wasn't there. To see the damp, lacy bras hanging over the shower curtain rod and the copy of *Newsweek* on the seat of the rocking chair, a paper clip marking a page. The twin bed that had been Eleanor's, now covered by a blue-and-red striped spread. The blue-flowered sofa that Rose and Izzy had bought for their thirtieth anniversary, and the wooden nightstand, with a small pile of books and the Tiffany lamp that Natalie had given Rose and the white telephone that Rose must have used to call 911. She'd placed the receiver properly back on its cradle.

Plus photos. Jammed on every horizontal surface and a few mounted on the eggshell-colored walls, three-by-five, four-by-six, eight-by-ten, framed in cheap wood and fancy silver, in painted porcelain and bare Lucite. The 1950 wedding picture, of course, with Rose in a long silk gown and tulle veil, and Izzy in his rented tux. Rose variously as a wavy-haired young woman on a park bench, a new mother, a working girl at Macy's, cigarette in hand. Izzy, serious, in his Columbia cap and gown, with his parents just as serious next to him. Rose and Izzy with the baby photos of Steven and Eleanor. Steven's bar mitzvah. Eleanor and Nick's wedding. Steven and Leah's wedding out in San Diego, with the *chuppah* and rabbi and full religious trimmings. Natalie as a little girl with her parents. Natalie with Rose and Chana at her engagement party, Chana already in a wheelchair; that was probably the last photo ever taken of the two sisters. And of course Rose's five grandchildren, a cornucopia of ages, together, separate, with their parents, with their grandparents.

Nothing, however, from before her life in the United States, from before 1946. Nothing smuggled out of Poland. Nothing inscribed in Polish.

Toilet paper trailed out, unspooled from its holder, through the doorway of the bathroom where Rose might have fallen before she somehow dragged her ninety-pound body to the phone.

Could she really have managed to crawl or limp the few yards from the bathroom, with a broken hip? Knowing Rose, that was perfectly possible, but did that mean the hip fracture hadn't been serious? Or would the crawling have made it worse? Damn, how bad was Rose's situation? A person didn't die from a broken hip, did she?

Natalie was carrying a small plaid suitcase, maybe from Rose's front closet, as she walked over to Eleanor at the bathroom doorway. Briefly rubbing Eleanor's shoulder, Natalie continued on into the bathroom, tore off the dangling paper, and shoved it into the little green trash pail by the sink. "She should be almost out of surgery now. Let's finish up here so we can get back and talk to the doctor."

"What do we need to do here?"

"Toiletries. Something to read. Anything to make her comfortable. With a broken hip, she'll be staying in that damn hospital for a while." Natalie's long purple fingernails clicked on the mirrored door of the medicine cabinet as she pulled it open. "Ellie," she added, her face aimed straight ahead into the cabinet, "have you been talking with your mother about Poland recently?"

"No! Not since the whole blow-up in college. You know I wouldn't."

Okay, so that wasn't entirely true, but Natalie didn't need to know about more of Eleanor's failu and fights. For instance, wasn't it perfectly natural, when Eleanor and Nick got engaged, for the bride-to-be to ask her mother what the mother's wedding had been like? Wouldn't most brides be interested in their family's traditions? And then, um, well, wouldn't that bride also ask about the mother's parents' wedding in Poland, which must have been in the early nineteen-twenties or late teens:

How about your parents, Ma? Did Jewish brides back in Poland —

Why do you care about old Polish weddings? Isn't it enough work to plan this one?

Gee, Ma, I'm sorry it's so much work for you. I thought you wanted to make this big hoo-ha wedding for your only daughter.

Or when Kate and then Adam were born, it was worth a shot, anyway, to ask Rose if there wasn't maybe a relative she'd like to name her grandchildren for. *No.* Eleanor did it anyway. If Rose realized that her grandson Adam was named in memory of her murdered-in-the-Holocaust older brother Avram, or possibly even a little pleased by the honor, she sure never mentioned it.

Of course Eleanor's idea for Rose to speak at her school's celebration of the fiftieth anniversary of the end of World War Two had been a disaster. Okay. But the principal had invited a lot of veterans and Holocaust survivors, and Eleanor's students might learn something from Rose's mysterious history in Nazi Poland, so, well, why not give it a try? Rose had actually shouted at Eleanor. Which was probably the only time, until the EMT today, that anybody ever heard Rose Ritter shout.

"No," Eleanor repeated to Natalie. "I haven't given up on getting Ma to talk, but I haven't figured out a way that works."

Natalie didn't say anything immediately, as she pulled out a pill bottle, read the label, and placed it on the closed toilet seat.

"I had an idea the other day," Eleanor continued. Leaning against the bathroom doorframe, she started tapping the opposite jamb, one finger after another, thumb to pinkie, and then back. "What do you think about this: I could ask Ma to help me write a Polish-French dictionary."

Natalie glanced quickly at Eleanor. "What?"

"See, that would be something we could do in common. Language skills. My French training. Her memory of Polish."

"Why would anyone want a Polish-French dictionary?"

"That's very American-centric of you." Eleanor grinned. "How do you know people in France wouldn't want to travel to Poland?"

"Ellie— "

"Oh, don't worry. Obviously, I won't try to start anything now while Ma is in the hospital and we don't even know what's wrong with her." Eleanor slid her hand halfway down the eggshell-painted jamb. "But you know, now that's talking Polish? Or at least two words in Polish. 'Nazi bitch.' Do you think this might be—you know—some kind of change? She might be willing to talk about her past?"

For another half-minute, Natalie stared silently into the medicine cabinet. "A couple of days ago," she said softly, easing the door shut, "your mother said something about Poland to me."

On the floor above them, a person was walking quickly, but then stopped. Water ran through pipes.

"I told her that I was going into Manhattan, to the Met. And she said that when she was little, it was such a treat to go Warsaw." Shrugging slightly, Natalie turned toward Eleanor.

"She—?" Eleanor's voice was somewhere between a cough and a whisper. "Warsaw?"

"Yes. I was pretty astonished, too. In fact, I think that's why I kept jabbering, almost on autopilot, because it didn't sink immediately in that this was Aunt Rose talking about Poland. So I asked her what sorts of things she liked to do in Warsaw."

Rose talked about Poland?

Rose talked about Poland with Natalie.

"She mentioned the big, wide streets." Natalie's voice grew firmer and faster. "Those same streets my mother told us about, remember? And the shops—oh, yes, she said there were elegant shops along some of the grandest boulevards, with furs and the newest fashions in the windows, and ladies walking down the sidewalk dressed just like those window mannequins. You know the Twenties fashions? The little cloche hats and strings of pearls?"

No. Eleanor did not know or give a shit about fashions of the Roaring Twenties.

Rose talked to Natalie about fashions in Warsaw.

Natalie, merely to schlep to the hospital on a Saturday, was dressed almost as elegantly as those Warsaw ladies must have been: a navy blazer, a cream-colored silky blouse, tight black slacks, and black pumps.

"What else? Did she say anything else?"

"Nothing else. It was as though she suddenly discovered that she'd said a bad word, and she just stopped up her lips. And then she asked me if I'd had any interesting cases recently, and what about the hit-and-run I'd told her about last week?" As she began to move out of the bathroom, Natalie smiled and reached again to Eleanor's shoulder.

"Ma talked about Poland."

"Amazing, I know."

"To you."

"I wonder if the trauma of breaking her hip could prompt some psychological reaction that would also prompt memories of her childhood?"

"She spoke to you. She hasn't talked to me."

There was a loud puff of air from Natalie's mouth.

Eleanor shut her eyes. Okay. Okay. This didn't matter right now, who Rose spoke to. What mattered was that her mother had broken some part of her hip, and she was in the hospital, and soon the doctor would tell them how serious it was.

"Ellie— "

"It's okay. It's okay. What else do we need to get for Ma?" Turning away from Natalie, Eleanor glanced around her mother's bedroom. "Maybe the *Newsweek*?" She took a step toward the rocking chair.

"It was just lucky timing. I mentioned the Met, and that sparked something in her."

"Listen, Natalie, you know? She's talking about Poland. She's talking Polish with ambulance drivers. Who knows what she'll do next?"

At that, Natalie poured out a big laugh. "Do you think she'll swear in another language at someone else?"

"At least your mother taught you some Polish vocabulary while she was alive. Did you learn the words for 'Nazi bitch'?"

Natalie laughed again. "Sorry, Ellie. Just the same phrases she taught you, I think. The basics. 'Good morning.' 'Thank you.' Do you remember how to say them?"

"Sure. *Dzień dobry* is 'good morning.' *Dziękuję* is 'thank you.' "

"Ah. You're good with languages."

"Because I switched my major to goddam French."

Carefully, Natalie folded the pink quilted bathrobe (size petite) that she'd picked up from the foot of Rose's bed. "Ellie. Please. Don't push her again. At least not right now."

Grabbing the *Newsweek*, Eleanor walked over to the nightstand. All three books were Sue Grafton mysteries; the top one had a bookmark three-fourths of the way through, so should Eleanor take all three to keep her mother busy? Or only the nearly finished one plus one more for now? How could anyone know what Rose would prefer? "It's just— " She stared at the books. "Look, I'm sure this hip surgery isn't, like, brain surgery. You know? It's not the most serious problem a person could have. But I just— "

Natalie was standing next to Eleanor, wrapping an arm which also pressed the bathrobe into her spine. "All these years, we've held back, haven't we? Respected her privacy. Not wanting to stir up painful memories? I never even asked my mother if *she* ever talked to your mother. And now, it seems as if, exactly when she might be starting to talk, she's struck down. Is that how you're feeling?"

Eleanor nodded.

"It's okay, Ellie. It's only a broken hip. It happens all the time to older women, because of calcium depletion."

"Ma takes calcium."

"So there you are. We'll have lots of time to talk to her after she recovers from this. If she wants to talk."

Time.

Shit.

The alarm clock on Rose's nightstand said eleven-seventeen.

"Shit, I've got to—Adam's soccer game is supposed to end at noon, and a parent is supposed to be there— it's his first game this year, he probably screwed up, and— "

"Okay."

"His friend Matthew's mother took him to the game but I should really be there to pick him up."

"So go."

"But Ma."

"I'll go to the hospital," Natalie said calmly.

To be with Rose when she came out of anesthesia? To talk to the doctor? "No!" Eleanor snapped. "Look, why don't you go to the soccer game instead?"

Shaking her head, Natalie patted the bathrobe into the small suitcase and reached out for the books that Eleanor was clutching. "Don't be silly. You're his mother. You have to be there."

"And she's *my* mother!"

Natalie yanked the books away from Eleanor's arms. "So ask Nick to go to Adam's game."

"Oh, sure." As if anyone could find Nick, deep in the basement of some office building with his computers. Although he had one of those new cellphone-things that he'd also given Eleanor, he claimed the phone didn't work in most basements. Which, to be fair, was probably true if it was like Eleanor's, which barely worked anywhere. "You know the world will collapse at midnight on December thirty-first if Nick doesn't personally fix all the computer codes before then?"

"Go to the soccer game, Ellie."

* * *

She should have tried calling Nick. She should have just let Adam go home with Matthew. She should be driving to the hospital with Natalie. She could be there right now, carrying Rose's toothbrush and books, getting the information directly from the doctor, waiting for Rose to wake up from anesthesia. What if Rose wanted help, for once? What if she even started talking about Poland again? But no, Eleanor had a son with a soccer game and a husband way, way too busy saving the world's computers before the Year 2K to take a few hours off for his son on a Saturday, so Eleanor was zig-zagging down eight miles of northern New Jersey side streets to Adam's soccer field, pushing thirty-five in the twenty-five-mile zones.

There was an abrupt, loud, scraping noise, as Eleanor began a right turn. She slammed on the brake.

Goddammit. Her car was inches away from a parked, vivid-green sports car, and that car's mirror was bent forward at an odd angle. That must have been the loud noise, her car scraping against the mirror, shoving it out of position.

Still, it was only a mirror. Otherwise, the other car looked okay. She hadn't actually caused any damage. Side-view mirrors were supposed to move.

Eleanor glanced around the intersection: small front lawns, houses covered in aluminum siding of dulled blue and beige, a couple of bikes half-propped on their handlebars and tires. No one had emerged from any of those houses brandishing papers and gesturing at the sports car.. No one had seen the little encounter. It was just a stupid mirror.

Eleanor lowered her foot onto the gas pedal and, slowly, turned the corner toward the soccer field.

Chapter Two

There was no mistaking him, even from the far end of the soccer field. Small, with white shorts, royal-blue knee socks, and mascara-black hair jutting over his ears, and what the hell was he doing standing in the netted goal area—playing goalie, the most important position in the whole game, the last line of defense, after he'd missed the first game of the season and was undoubtedly the worst player on the team and couldn't even kick a ball three feet?

One big, burly dad with impossibly corn-blond hair was actually jumping up and down at the sideline just near the goal, punching his fists into his own thighs and yelling.

Eleanor had to get Adam out of there.

She ran toward the field, her leather bag slapping her jeans.

The air smelled of dirt and fresh grass, slashed by shouts from every direction. A whistle screeched horribly. Parents on the blond dad's side screamed. Parents on the other side cheered. The blond dad was shouting at a guy with curly brown hair and waving his arms and pointing at Adam, the curly-haired guy was running toward Adam, and the black-and-white ball rested triumphantly, accusingly, tucked into a corner of the goal net right behind Adam's incompetent feet.

* * *

It was Nick's fault that Adam was on the soccer field, ruining the game.

Boys have to have a sport or they will be taunted, teased, called sissies, fairies, made totally miserable, Nick insisted. Especially if they were short, like Adam. Nick had suddenly started this campaign a year and a half ago, when Adam was in the spring of second grade.

"He's only seven," Eleanor had protested. Briefly. What did she really know about such guy things? Nick had played basketball in high school in Cincinnati. By the time Eleanor met him in college, however, his hoops had been long abandoned, and he was totally immersed in his computer stuff and the Earth Day Club and the organic garden he started at his dorm.

Reasonably, really, Nick had asked what sports Adam's friends were playing.

There had been several casual, quick conversations with Adam over the next few months. He had seemed neither very eager nor fearful. His parents could have been suggesting that he might want to get a new pair of sneakers. Maybe he had been too young to realize the social pressure of holding up your part in a team. He was a good kid, not the arguing type, like Kate. Apparently he knew a few boys who played soccer and others who played softball, and his friend Matthew's mother advised Eleanor that soccer didn't require as much skill or practice time as softball.

It hadn't worked out so terribly the first year. Adam was able to join Matthew's team, and they emerged with a winning season and a pizza party at the end. He seemed to shout and clap and do some special cheer that their coach led after each game, along with everyone else. He ran out to the field without dawdling when it was his turn. He didn't score any goals, nor did he commit any disastrous flubs. It wasn't as though Eleanor or Nick had to drag him to the games.

Nevertheless, when Eleanor asked Adam occasionally over the summer if he wanted to sign up again for soccer this fall, he mumbled his answers. "Maybe. I guess."

So Eleanor had delayed and delayed throughout July and August. Adam, after all, was engrossed in art camp. Eleanor was teaching two remedial French classes at Edgewood High School. Nick might forget the whole idea for now, while he was working day and night. Adam certainly didn't ask about it. Nor did Nick. The sign-up date passed. The first game passed.

And then the night after that missed game, last Sunday, she had asked Nick to really try to be home for dinner because it was the beginning of Yom Kippur and it would be nice to start the fast with an actual family meal, even though she was the only one who sort-of fasted. And Nick asked, "Hey, Adam, hasn't soccer season already started?"

And Adam looked at Eleanor. "Mom....?"

And Nick stared at Eleanor. "Didn't you sign him up yet?"

And Kate said, "Whoa, fight time, I'm outta here."

* * *

"Who's that horrible fat, blond guy?" Eleanor asked Matthew's mother, pointing to the spot a few yards away on the grass where the guy was standing, thrusting his arms into the air and talking to a woman just as blindingly yellow-haired—his wife? another parent?—who was sitting in a red-and-blue lawn chair. No doubt the guy was reenacting Adam's unforgivable failure.

The team was called the Blue Hornets, Matthew's mother had said, and the man with the curly brown hair who the blond guy had yelled at after Adam's screw-up was the team coach—the one who must have put Adam in the goalie spot—and the only good news was that it was the half-time break, so when they went back to playing the second half, Adam wouldn't be goalie any more. Five or six Hornets swarmed around the coach, boys jumping in front of him, boys shouting, boys wanting to be forwards, boys wanting to be goalie, and he smiled at all of them and soft-punched a few shoulders, slapped a few high-fives. He had a nice, big smile that lit up his whole face. Even if he was a complete jerk for making Adam the goalie. Which Eleanor would have to discuss with him.

Adam wasn't one of the boys crowded around the coach. Nor was he with the group grabbing granola bars and juice boxes from a set of big plastic bags. He was standing by himself at the chain-link fence that bordered the soccer grounds, as far away as possible from the field. The only person within four yards of him was a boy who was bigger than the players, who was not wearing the team's white shorts and blue socks, and who was fiddling with some kind of electronic cube. Probably an older brother of one of the Hornets, dragged to the game. Like Adam.

If only she could go to Adam. Give him a hug…. No, of course not. In front of his team? That would be worse than flubbing the goal.

Matthew's mother—Betsy?—frowned in the direction where Eleanor was pointing, toward the blond guy. "That man's son is our star player," she replied firmly. Her own arm pointed at a skinny blond kid in white and blue who was turning cartwheels by himself off in a far spot on the side grass. "Last week he scored four goals."

"But can't they keep the father away from games? Is that allowed?"

"Why should they?"

Matthew was suddenly in front of them; his mother dug into her big canvas pocketbook to hand him a water bottle, and he sprinted a few steps away, toward the rest of the team, then plopped onto the grass.

"Good sportsmanship?" Eleanor continued. "Isn't that something they're supposed to teach?"

A whistle blew nearby, long and urgent; the game was going to resume. Adam was still kicking the grass by the fence.

"I don't know, Eleanor. He's just a team-spirited father."

"But he yelled at Adam!"

"No he didn't. Really."

The curly-haired coach was gesturing and laughing, toward one boy after another, and each time he gestured, the designated boy ran off to take his position. Three in the front, near the center line. Three lined up behind them. The skinny blond star player nearly bumped into Eleanor as he raced toward the field.

Very slowly, Adam trailed vaguely toward the coach.

Along with most of the parents, like a gentle roll of the tide, Betsy was moving closer to the field. "Ask Ben's dad, he knows everyone," she said over her shoulder, inclining her head slightly back and toward the right, where a man in a red-striped shirt was orating to a couple of other lingering parents.

Ben's dad. Another person to remember. Okay, but the coach first, before the whistle blew again and the next half started and he would be too busy to listen to her. Eleanor strode over to him, managing to smile. She held out her right hand. "Hi. I'm Adam Phillips's mother. You know, the goalie who screwed up last quarter?"

"Hey, none of that. No one screws up in fourth-grade soccer." The coach beamed his broad smile at Eleanor, bending his head down a little, toward hers. He gave her hand a strong squeeze. "Mark Hirsh."

"Look, is there something you can— "

"Adam will be fine after another quarter."

"But what about that father? The blond one who yells?"

The coach frowned.

"Can't you ban him or something?"

The frown burst into a laugh. "I can only coach the kids, not the parents." Then Mark Hirsh leaned even closer, and his lips brushed Eleanor's ear as he whispered, "I've paired Adam with two strong defense players. They'll take care of all the blocking, and he'll feel good."

And by then it was too late to move her ear away.

* * *

Actually, there might have been one time before today that Rose had spoken Polish. One other time, in all of Eleanor's nearly forty-two years.

It was when Rose and Izzy first met Nick. Eleanor had been eight months away from graduating from NYU, bringing her "serious boy-friend" home to meet her parents.

Nick did almost everything right that evening. He dressed just for-mally enough, without being a nerd, for a college student meeting his girlfriend's parents for a Saturday night dinner: a blazer, an Oxford shirt, and his best pair of jeans. He could have brought flowers, but that would have been way too boring and predictable. So Nick did much better, wooing the parents by arriving with a homemade salmon mousse and stuffed mushrooms, which was not too gourmet, nor weirdly Zen-vege-tarian, and in fact almost Jewish-style.

Rose raised her eyebrows. "You found a boy who cooks?".

"How do you know I didn't make this food myself?"

Rose just shook her head.

The only slip-up came at the crucial moment of first helloes on the front porch, when Nick shook hands with Izzy and leaned down to kiss Rose's cheek. Even that was probably Eleanor's fault more than Nick's, because she should have warned him. Rose didn't do social kissing. Nor much kissing of any sort.

Rose subtly took a step back and glanced at Eleanor.

That moment could have tilted things wrong. Except that as soon as they were inside and had laid their food offerings on the kitchen counter, Nick went straight to the framed displays of Izzy's best stamps on the hallway wall. He pointed to one of them, asked Izzy something, and Izzy immediately pulled out all of his albums from the bottom drawer of the old mahogany étagère in the living room and spread them out on the cof-fee table. For half an hour, they huddled over the wide pages, their two sets of voices rising, eager, question and long answer, sometimes laugh-ing. Nick was still talking about the collection when they all sat down to Rose's dry brisket. "Did you know that your father would ask friends to write to him when they went on vacation to other countries, so he could have the stamps?" he said to Eleanor.

"I told them they didn't even have to write anything," Izzy interject-ed. "Just send me an empty envelope."

"We have the biggest collection of empty envelopes in New Jersey," Rose added. She might have been starting to smile.

The stamp albums naturally led to the photo albums, and the framed and mounted stamps led to the framed family photos. Eleanor pretended to grab away the album that had the snapshots from when she was eleven and twelve, to prevent Nick from seeing how chubby and ugly she'd been then, with her braces and dark, tangled hair. Nick tickled her as they turned the pages of baby pictures. The oldest photo was a formal studio shot of Izzy's mother as a little girl in New York in the early 1900s, standing rigidly with her siblings and her own parents against a painted background of Greek columns, curtains, and a flowered arbor, the girls in black skirts and heavy stockings, the boys in knee-length knickers. After that, Izzy had to bring out his Army discharge papers, for some reason, and then the foreign language award Eleanor had won in junior high school.

Nick didn't ask if there were any photos or mementos of Rose's childhood in Poland.

Nor did Rose ask Nick, at that first dinner, the usual girlfriend's-parent questions about his classes and his career plans and what his father did for a living. Nor about how New York must be different from Cincinnati. Nor about religion; she and Izzy already knew he wasn't Jewish.

She asked him, instead, if he'd read *All the President's Men* and what he did in the Earth Day Club. Had his mother taught him to cook, or was that a hobby he'd developed on his own? Had he ever driven a motorcycle?

When it was time to leave, Nick shook hands with Izzy on the porch again and simply dipped his head at Rose, like an American imitation of a formal Japanese bow. Izzy winked at Eleanor. Rose gave Eleanor her copy of *All the President's Men* for Nick to borrow, with just her usual polite smile and a quick brush of the cheeks, nothing more. And that would have usually been the end.

But Rose said something to Eleanor. Some garbling of M's and W's and Ch's. Eleanor asked her mother to repeat it.

There was a look on Rose's face, briefly — more than discomfort. Close to horror. "Go. You'll miss your bus to Manhattan." She made a pushing gesture, sharply flapping her hands.

"What lang— ?"

"GO!"

Of course, those garbled sounds might not have been Polish. But what else could they have been?

* * *

The Blue Hornets lost two to one.

"It's that goalie who messed up in the second quarter," the big blond father declared loudly to a couple of other men.

Adam was standing only a couple of feet away.

Oh shit, did Adam hear them? How could they—Right in his face? Adam was just staring down at the grass. He must have heard.

"Why does the coach put him on team?" the blond father added, even louder. "We never win with such players." He spoke with an accent, rich rounded O's and rolling R's.

Where was the coach, to stop this? Who was this guy?

But the skinny blond star player was suddenly in front of Adam, and he said to Adam, "That was a really hard goal-kick to block," and then he was gone, racing after his father and the blonde woman from the red-and-blue lawn chair and the kid with the electronic cube as they walked rapidly away from the field.

"Who is that guy?" Eleanor demanded, whirling around.

* * *

"Oh yeah." Ben's dad laughed. "That big blond fellow? His kid—Todd? I think that's his name. Or Ted? He's terrific, isn't he?"

"I don't know. But what about his father? Isn't he kind of—you know—angry?"

"They're new, I think. Last year was their first year in the league. I think the parents are from Poland. Hey, do you ever try your hand in the stock market?" Ben's dad was waving a business card toward her. "There's this great company that researches new drugs— "

Chapter Three

Rose was sleeping, breathing steadily but squirming a little and lying oddly on her back on the hospital bed, mostly covered by a dark-
blue blanket. Natalie dozed, too, without squirming, in a vinyl armchair
nearby.

In the room's other bed, closer to the window, a younger woman
was whispering loudly to the man in her visitor's chair, in peaks and
valleys of background murmuring. A faint whiff of rubbing alcohol
wafted in from the hallway through the open doorway, mixed with a
flash of cologne.

Since there was no empty chair, Eleanor leaned against the wall
nearest to Rose's IV pole. Rose's dark-framed eyeglasses sat, folded, on
the cabinet next to her bed. Her wavy silver hair was flattened on the
right side, deprived of its usual hairspray, and her lipstick must have
smeared off hours ago. Her small body made a series of slight bumps
down the blanket, with her skinny arms splayed on top. It was hard to
believe that any part of Rose Ritter could break.

Would she wake, if Eleanor gave her just a little hug? Would she
mind?

Her left forearm had no numbers burned into it. That was the
only thing the family had ever known for sure about what might have
happened to Rose in Poland, and that one little fact still didn't tell them
much. It only proved that she hadn't been at Auschwitz. She could have
been at one of the other concentration camps, which didn't engrave
their prisoners' arms. Or anywhere else.

Then, in March 1946, a letter arrived from a DP camp in the American sector of Germany, to Chana's house in Brooklyn, and Rose fol-

lowed in person soon afterwards carrying twenty dollars, a pillow, and a small box of clothing. As quickly as she could, she learned English, shed her Polish accent, graduated from night school, changed her name from Ruzia to Rose, and became an American citizen. End of story. Fresh start.

Sure, Chana had lots of stories. The family had lived in an apartment on the second floor in a town near Warsaw—Chana, her parents, her brother Avram, and her little sisters Ruzia and Feiga. Their father was a teacher at the Jewish high school, the *gimnazjum*. They walked to school, and almost everywhere, although for something really important they could hire a coach with horses. Sometimes they took the train to Warsaw, to visit their rich aunt and uncle there, and they would stroll along the grand boulevard. The aunt and uncle had a big chandelier in their dining room. Their mother let Chana and Ruzia play house with her enamel pots, and their father read stories to them from the Brothers Grimm and Jules Verne and Sholem Aleichem, sometimes in Polish, sometimes Yiddish, although he said Yiddish was for the grandmother. The little Polish Catholic boy that Chana had a crush on, when she was seven, called her a dirty Jew and she ran home crying. She never saw a banana until she came to America. Those were some of Chana's stories. But the Polish part and the Ruzia part ended in 1935, four years before the Nazis invaded. Chana came to America with the rich aunt and uncle; Ruzia didn't.

Why didn't Chana ever ask her sister for details about how she survived the war? Never? Well—according to what Chana told Natalie—in those early days, people didn't pressure Holocaust survivors to talk, because they assumed it was too painful. Either the memories of what they went through would open up too many raw wounds, or survivors' guilt would torture them even more. Nor were American Gentiles exactly spreading their arms to welcome what they saw as hordes of unwashed foreigners with weird habits who didn't speak English, who probably had foul diseases, and who wanted to sponge off of FDR's welfare benefits. So Chana didn't pressure Rose. She was just grateful to have her little sister alive.

Eventually, Chana contacted the Holocaust archives at Yad Vashem in Israel, which was how they knew for sure that her and Rose's parents, their grandmother, their brother Avram, the baby Feiga, and all the other relatives they could remember were dead, most of them murdered at Treblinka.

Of course Eleanor and Natalie had tried to pry the big mystery out of Rose when they were little, and Steven also did, although not as much. After all, Rose was still living with Chana in Brooklyn when Natalie was born, so Natalie grew up for the first two years of her life with this exotic young aunt who had escaped the evil Nazi monsters, who played peek-a-boo with her and combed her hair into braids, until Rose married Izzy and moved to her own home in New Jersey.

Natalie and Eleanor invented tales of how Rose might have escaped. She was hidden in a secret room, like Anne Frank! A friendly guard took pity on her at Treblinka! She dug a tunnel under the wall of the Warsaw Ghetto!

Rose, however, pushed all queries away. "Those were bad times. Not stories for children." Or, "That was a long time ago. Forget it." Then Natalie and Eleanor became teenagers who wanted nothing to do with old people like their aunt and mother, so they stopped asking. But as Eleanor was heading to college, her mood swung back: Because of Vietnam and the Civil Rights movement, people were saying that it was important to study history in order to make sure they didn't repeat past mistakes, and if that was true of America in general, wouldn't it also be important for Eleanor to study her family history? These were her grandparents, her aunt and uncle, as well as her mother. What had Rose seen and done that had made her so rigid? Was there any key to reaching her?

Eleanor wasn't a baby any more. She'd read Anne Frank's diary. She could certainly cope with whatever horrors her mother might have endured.

Ma, I was thinking of majoring in history at NYU.

All right.

Specializing in World War Two.

(Frown. Shrug.) Why would you want to study that? What kind of a job would you get, studying World War Two?

(Smile) You could help me with my thesis.

What?

Original documents are very important in history. And testimony from witnesses. You could—

Go do your research in the library. Isn't that what students do?

Don't you think it's important for your memories to be preserved?

No.

If we don't learn from the mistakes of the past, then—

Go learn someone else's mistakes.

Why don't you want us to know?

What does it matter?

It's my history, too!

I am not an encyclopedia for your research.

After all these years, surely the memories couldn't still be too painful for Rose to talk about? Certainly not the childhood memories, with her family, before the war — wouldn't those have been happy?

You know, Ma, Aunt Chana told us about how Grandpa used to read fairy tales to you in Polish and Yiddish?

So?

What did you study in school, when you were a girl?

I don't know. What does it matter?

I was wondering what you—

Enough, Ellie!

Okay, okay. Yes, certainly Eleanor did academic research, in the library and with her professors. By the end of her junior year she was living with Nick in a fourth-floor walk-up apartment on West Twenty-Third Street above something called a Hotel for Transients, and they would sit together on the bare bedroom floor, leafing through her piles of history books. "Did you know that Poland once was actually a powerful kingdom, along with Lithuania?" Nick asked her. "Did you know that Poland fought a separate war with Russia after World War One ended?" But all the research was so damn dry without Rose's personal stories. The Polish-Fascist *Enderja* party gained strength around 1935, even before Hitler invaded. They smashed Jewish market stalls; Jewish boys were pelted with stones on their way to school. Yes, but what did Ruzia see, in person, in her little town? How terrified was she? Eleanor expanded her thesis topic to include Vichy France, for more context, and because she'd studied some French in high school, but what was the point of studying about France, if her own roots were in Poland?

Was Rose really going to go through the rest of her life never talking? Wasn't it supposed to be healthy for people to open up about their traumas, instead of stifling them inside? Maybe if Rose would relax enough to talk a little about her past, she could relax about other things and—and just be easier to get along with. Talk about nice things.

Ma, what were the first signs—you know? How did you know the Nazis had inva—

ELLIE!

"Leave her alone!" Natalie shouted.

"What the hell are you doing?" Nick demanded.

"Don't you care?" Eleanor shouted back. "Don't we have a right to know our own history? It's our grandparents!"

"She has a right not to talk about it."

"But she did talk once to me!"

"When?"

"Maybe."

Fuck it all. Eleanor gave up. She switched her major to French, with a co-concentration in French language and French history, so that she could at least incorporate some of her high school French and her research on World War Two. Also, if she was going to study a foreign language, French was a hell of a lot easier to pronounce than the few words of Polish she'd tried.

Rose continued to shut her mouth and fold her arms, silent about Poland, never speaking Polish. Except, perhaps, for a few words on her front porch one Saturday night after dinner, as Eleanor and her college boyfriend were leaving.

And now there was another generation growing up without a past. What did Steven tell his kids? *Oh, Grandma Rose just appeared in New York by magic one day.* Didn't anyone do family history projects in school? True, Kate and Adam had never asked much about Rose, and Natalie had no kids, but maybe Kate would be more interested in having her bat mitzvah next year if she felt her family connection with Judaism and the Holocaust more personally, from her own grandmother's mouth? Eleanor could use any and all help on that battle.

The last time Rose had surgery and anesthesia, ten years ago, for her chest biopsy, Izzy claimed she had revealed all sorts of secrets, though he wouldn't say what they were. The spot on her chest X-ray had certainly scared her enough to finally quit smoking, which even Chana's death hadn't done. So perhaps she had talked about Poland then, to Izzy, under anesthesia. Perhaps she had mumbled some endearments in Polish. But Chana was long dead from lung cancer, and Izzy was two years dead from his heart attack. And now, all of a sudden, Rose was speaking Polish and telling Natalie about Warsaw?

Had she babbled anything about Poland under the influence of anesthesia that morning? Sworn at the doctor in Polish?

There were fingers on Eleanor's shoulder.

Natalie was pivoting Eleanor toward the hallway outside the room, while her other hand pressed her own lips shut. Nodding, Eleanor began to retreat.

But Natalie didn't join Eleanor immediately. She lingered at the side of the bed, watching Rose breathing for a long set of seconds and smoothing her hair. Eleanor had to wave three times before Natalie finally came out to the corridor.

Rose still hadn't woken, during the whole afternoon while Natalie waited. However, Natalie had been able to speak with the emergency-room surgeon. It was a fairly simple, routine fracture of the left femur—the leg bone, Natalie translated—occurring between the very top, where the femur connected with the pelvis, and a piece a little further down where the femur protruded, called the lower trochanter. The point of the surgery had been to support the bone by putting in a metal screw and plate of some sort. Completely routine, especially for elderly patients. So the surgeon had said.

"So she's okay? Basically?" Eleanor had to lick her lips, to swallow.

"Yes. It's really just a broken bone. Just a bit more serious because of her age."

"Like kids get all the time. Falling off bikes and stuff." Not that Eleanor's kids had ever broken any bones.

Rose was okay.

However, she would have to stay in the hospital for at least a week, followed by weeks or even months of physical therapy in a rehab center.

"I'll start looking for rehab places," Natalie added.

No, no, Eleanor could do that—well, later, she would take care of the rehab stuff later. Natalie could help, sure. At least Rose was going to be okay. Eleanor smiled at Natalie. "Thanks for everything. I'll stay with her now."

"Of course." Natalie reached over to hug Eleanor. "Let's see if we can find another chair."

"Well—no—I meant..."

Natalie seemed to stop midway in letting go of the hug, and she tilted her head slightly as she stared at Eleanor.

"I mean, you must be tired. Being here all day? If you want to go home? I mean, we can both hang out, sure, if you want..."

"I'll get us some coffee."

* * *

"What the hell?" Rose demanded.

Her voice was hoarse and groggy, and she was fidgeting herself up on her elbows, squinting and glancing jerkily around.

Almost as if ordered into position, Natalie and Eleanor were promptly back at the sides of the bed where they had been before, Natalie on the right with the chair, Eleanor on the left with the IV pole. Each took one of Rose's hands, though of course Eleanor got the one that had tubes taped on the arm, which made it hard to stand close.

"Hi Aunt Rose. It's Natalie and Eleanor."

"Hey Ma, how are you feeling?"

"You're in the hospital. Apparently you fell down in your apartment."

Shaking off both Natalie's and Eleanor's grips, Rose pushed her flattened hair off her forehead and rubbed her eyes. "So I'm in the hospital?" Her words were slow and quiet, almost dragged out of her.

"Yes. You're probably still feeling a bit of the anesthesia."

"I fell? Yes." Rose nodded at her own question.

"Do you remember what happened?" Eleanor asked, even as Natalie leaned closer and said in her judge-soothing voice, "Don't strain yourself, Aunt Rose. We can talk later."

And Rose did stop speaking for a moment, letting her breaths flow in and out a few times. "I fell," she repeated. "Did I break my leg?" She turned to Eleanor, then Natalie. "I know that happens all the time to old ladies."

"You're not old, Ma."

"You broke a bone in your hip, but it could have been a lot worse. The doctor says it's a very simple fracture, very treatable."

Rose shuttered her eyes again, as her head slid back onto the pillow. "I'm an idiot. I was trying to reach for a towel, and I was too lazy to get the stool."

Could Eleanor give Rose a hug? Well, that might put too much pressure on her broken bone. Rose was so thin.

In the corridor, a metallic rattle was getting louder, and the roommate over by the window was yelling out, "Where's that supper?" and a nurse was suddenly in the room, edging Natalie and Eleanor aside while she wielded a blood pressure cuff. Rose still hadn't reopened her eyes. "Is someone playing music?" Natalie asked. "Is that you, Eleanor? It sounds like 'Frère Jacques.' "

"Oh. It's that dumb cellphone Nick gave me." Eleanor began pawing inside her shoulder bag. "He thought it would be fun to set the ringer to 'Frère Jacques.' "

It was Kate, of course, at home resentfully babysitting for Adam. Nobody ever called the cellphone except Kate and maybe Nick. But her voice was garbled. Eleanor moved out into the hallway. "Can you repeat it?"

"Dad just called. He's going to be late. Are you going to make dinner?" Then Kate added, "Is Grandma okay?"

"Yeah. She's just tired. Do you want to order in a pizza for yourselves?"

But Kate couldn't hear her, so Eleanor moved further down the hall. "And let Adam choose one of the toppings." Damn, she had to stop giving them so much pizza.

"Can I invite Joanna and Rachel, too?"

"Sure."

"Thank you, thank you, Mommy."

"You know where the emergency money is, in the kitchen drawer? And don't forget Adam."

"He's okay. He's watching his stupid sharks video."

By the time Eleanor returned to the bedside, where Natalie was keeping watch, Rose was apparently sleeping again.

* * *

Nick did get home for dinner on Sunday night. Briefly. He would have to go right back to work. But he'd stop in to see Rose on the way, he offered.

Even while he spoke, Nick leaned over the pot where Eleanor was steaming a cut-up cauliflower; he poked a fork into one chunk, tried a second, frowned, and quickly turned off the burner. Then he yanked open the broiler door, pulled out the pan, and flipped over the four darkened hamburger patties. Kate, without being asked, was folding blue napkins into precise triangles and placing them on the white-topped butcher-block table; her hair tonight was somewhere between red and orange.

"When are we going to eat?" Adam asked.

"I need to be back at work by seven," Nick told Eleanor.

"Well, I don't know if the burgers are ready— "

"You'll get sick from raw meat," Kate interrupted. "E. coli. Diarrhea. Vomiting."

"Mom, Kate's talking about throw-up at dinner."

"It's not dinner yet, stupid."

"Your hair's the color of throw-up."

"Mom— "

"We'll eat in separate courses, to speed things up," Nick declared. Then, bowing, he switched to a phony French accent: "Eez not zat what zee French do, *non, chérie*? Zee long dinners?"

"Do you give your French classes food?" Adam asked. "Like

French fries?"

"French fries aren't French," Kate corrected.

But they all listened, sitting around the white-topped table, as Eleanor updated them about Grandma Rose since the accident yesterday. How broken hips were common with grandmothers. How Grandma was already asking why she couldn't at the very least walk herself to the toilet. Even how Grandma had talked Polish. Although Eleanor edited "Nazi bitch" to "Nazi," Kate grinned anyway.

"Mom, was the lady actually a Nazi?" Adam asked, as he chewed.

"Not at all. It's just—kind of a way of insulting someone."

"You shouldn't call people Nazis for a casual insult," Nick scolded, his mouth also full, like Adam's. He was eating fast, hardly talking.

"Nazi-like," Kate promptly amended.

"Still," Nick said, swallowing his mouthful and nodding at Eleanor, "it's not like your mother to lose her balance and fall. Can you let me know what the doctor says?" Shifting in the chair, he turned abruptly to Adam. "You had soccer yesterday, didn't you? How'd it go?"

Adam laid his fork onto his plate, a piece of hamburger still stuck to the prongs. He looked at the plate, unmoving.

Eleanor opened her mouth.

Adam shrugged. "I messed up."

"No you didn't—" Eleanor began.

"We lost cuz of me."

"What'd you do wrong?" Nick asked.

"He didn't do anything wrong!"

Adam circled the broken-up bits of meat and cauliflower around on his pale-blue plate.

"Hey." Eleanor turned to Nick. "Why don't you go with Adam to his game next Saturday? I don't know what's going to be happening with my mother, and I also need to start taking Kate to Shabbat services at the temple. She's got a lot to prepare for her bat mitzvah."

"You know I can't, Eleanor. I have to work on Saturday."

"Again?"

"Yes. *Again.* And every Saturday. The year 2000 is coming in less than four months, and the computer systems are still at risk."

"Well, I can't be in two places at once. Adam has his game in the morning, and Kate needs to be at the temple at ten."

"I can miss services," Kate said immediately, even as Adam said, "I'll skip the game."

"No!" Eleanor shouted.

"For Chrissake, Eleanor," Nick snapped.

"I might have to go to the hospital— "

"Natalie can help."

"You're the one who wanted him to do soccer."

"Kate can miss one time."

"Easy for you to say. You won't even convert for her."

For a few beats, there was no sound. There was nowhere for Eleanor to look, so she looked at her blue plate, with its disgusting little lump of hamburger. Her family was undoubtedly staring at her. The silence went on too long.

"Well," Nick said. His voice sounded brittle, crisp, as if he was barely holding in a long, angry string of words.

"I never asked Dad to convert. I don't even want a bat mitzvah!"

"I have to go to work," Nick declared, and he kicked his wooden chair away from the table with a loud scrape.

Chapter Four

So, I guess you really care about soccer, she could say. *I hear your son's the star player for the Blue Hornets.*

Near the chain-link fence along the outside of the soccer grounds, the big, yellow-haired Polish father was leaning over his wiry son and lecturing intently. Pointing his index finger into the air, tracing imaginary lines and curves. The kid was doing some dribbling thing with a soccer ball, passing it between his feet while he half-jumped and jiggled his legs. The game before theirs was still screaming and racing on the field.

So she could start out nicely, praising the blond guy's son. And then segue into the topic of how that goddam father had yelled at Adam last week.

You know, we try to teach the kids not to take the games too seriously.

Of course we all want to win.

You know, all kids make mistakes.

Further down the fence line, the coach with the curly hair was maybe practicing something?—a kicking maneuver?—anyway, he was showing something with the ball to a few boys. That was a good idea. Adam ought to be there, getting some extra practice. But Adam was lingering at the farthest end of the fence in the other direction, just like last week, way behind the back goal line. Eleanor waved to him until she caught his glance, then pointed sharply to the group that was hovering and shouting around the coach—what was his name? Mark? Mike? Curly brown hair. Their voices cut high-pitched spikes of sound into the air. Adam didn't move.

The Polish kid was now turning somersaults on the grass.

I understand that you're from Poland. Maybe sports are different there.

Too bad she hadn't studied anything in college about Polish youth soccer, as long as she was learning about the Polish-Lithuanian commonwealth of the sixteenth century and prewar Polish anti-Semitism. Could she ask Rose whether boys played soccer when she was growing up in Poland? Oh yeah, sure.

Well, if Rose was suddenly willing to talk to Natalie about all the fashionable stores in Warsaw, why not soccer?

Of course, if this Polish mother and father were roughly Eleanor's age, they wouldn't even have been born yet, back when Rose and Chana had lived in their little town near Warsaw. The time of the Polish-Fascist *Enderja* party, when people were breaking Jewish-owned store windows. When the little boy called Chana a dirty Jew. When everything happened that Rose wouldn't talk about.

But *their* parents would have been alive then.

Ben's dad was standing barely a foot away from Eleanor, speaking with a couple of other men. "Have you done any more thinking about that stock I told you about? Drugtrials-dot-com? It's already up ten percent." Oh, he was talking about his stupid stock again, not about the Polish father.

"It's a drug company?"

"Drug *trials*. They have a database on the World Wide Web that tracks all the trials that are going on for new drugs."

Farther off, on Eleanor's right, a woman was saying, "Do you think it's safe to buy plane tickets for Christmas? They keep talking about that computer mess-ups and the Year 2000."

Eleanor gestured once more to Adam. He moved a step toward Mark-Mike the curly-haired coach, who had squatted down, more or less to the height of the boys grouped around him, and was demonstrating something.

A whistle shrieked. The Polish kid was racing up and down along the sideline, while the mother was sitting on her red-and-blue lawn chair next to a cooler, two big plastic shopping bags, and another empty chair. Nobody else brought chairs to soccer games. The older brother, the one with the video game, didn't seem to be anywhere.

"You've seen what's happening with stocks lately? With dot-com stocks? You get in early enough, and you can double your investment in just a few weeks."

The teams on the field were in two lines at the center now, doing their mandatory, lopsided hand-shaking. Their game was finished; in a minute, the Hornets would have to play. The Polish father had moved and was planted right up at the sideline. Eleanor should probably drop the whole idea of talking to him about anything. He didn't exactly seem open to chitchat during a soccer game. No one would want to interrupt him and make him miss seeing a goal that his son might score.

What would his parents have told him about World War Two and the Nazis? Would they have been more talkative than Rose? Or even less? Were they as angry and mean as he was? Were they the kind who threw rocks at Jewish boys and Jewish store windows?

What did your parents do to my mother in World War Two?

Shit, no, she couldn't ask that.

Just leave my son alone.

* * *

So Nick was at work, Kate had slept over at Joanna's house, and yes, here was Eleanor at soccer with Adam once again.

But from now on, everyone had agreed, things would be different. They would coordinate and compromise. They had sat down for a family talk on Sunday night, and Eleanor and Nick had apologized to the kids for setting such a bad example, and to each other, and then they had hammered out an agreement based on the soccer schedule, which changed every week. For instance, today soccer and Shabbat services were both in the morning. But next Saturday Adam's game was at two o'clock, so Eleanor could bring Kate to services in the morning (Kate groaned) and also be with Adam at soccer in the afternoon. (Adam just kept leafing through his new book about sharks.) And the week after that, Nick would handle soccer duty. He promised. Yes, even the most indispensable expert on Y2K could take a few hours off on an occasional Saturday, to be with his son at something he considered so important. Father-son bonding. Nick would, in fact, reserve that time-off from work immediately.

Eleanor apologized for being pushy.

Nick apologized for not helping enough.

Eleanor conceded that Kate did not have to go to services every week. Only twenty-five times before her bat mitzvah next fall.

Kate conceded that maybe sometimes it might not be so awful to go. Since her friends Joanna and Rachel needed to do their twenty-five Saturdays, too, she could sit with them.

Everyone wanted Nick to cook dinner more often. Kate pointed out that when he wasn't home, they ate too much pizza, and that wasn't healthy.

And after December 31, everything would be easier. Y2K would be over, and Nick would have all of his Saturdays free again. Or else modern civilization would have been destroyed, making all of these arrangements moot. True, soccer season would be finished by then, but the point was, Nick would be more available.

Thus, today, according to their new schedule, Kate got a pass, and Adam would go to soccer.

Or maybe that decision had been a mistake. Because right now Adam was putting on the special goalie shirt and gloves.

How could that stupid jerk of a coach do this to Adam again? Did he hate the boy? Did he want the team to lose? Eleanor really had to stop this, immediately. She had been too easygoing last week. She had to find that coach.

However, the teams were already facing each other in their formations across the field, the scattered pinpoints of blue-and-white for the Hornets and black-and-orange for the other team — like Halloween? who chose these stupid colors? — the referee's sharp whistle pierced the buzz of conversation, and all of a sudden the blond Polish kid was charging down the field toward the Halloween goal, kicking the ball forward every few pounding steps as if he and the ball were attached by a taut string, never losing it, never stopping. Within two minutes, he'd scored.

The Polish father actually jumped off the ground, pumping both fists into the air, as their side of the field cheered and hooted.

The Hornets gained one more goal during the next ten minutes and barely missed two other attempts—including a kick by the Polish kid that bounced hard off of a goalpost—while the Halloween team never got within half a field-length of Adam's goalie turf. As the field emptied for the first-quarter break, the coach was looking over at Eleanor, grinning in that great way that seemed to make his whole face delighted.

Of course his usual fan club of boys was immediately surrounding him, but shouldn't Eleanor go thank the coach? Or apologize? And make sure he understood that even if it worked out okay this time, Adam should never be goalie again? Really, to be a good mother? Jogging a little, Eleanor stretched out her hand when she was still a few steps away, even as the various boys were drifting off. "I have to admit," she began, panting, "I was going to yell at you for making Adam the goalie again."

"I know." The coach leaned closer. He smelled like peppermint. "And I also knew that the other side isn't a very strong team, so Adam probably wouldn't have to do much work blocking goals. This might help renew his self-confidence."

Indeed. Adam had raced off the field laughing and shouting, just like his teammates, crowding around the mothers with the big bottles of Gatorade and water and the bags of granola bars, chortling, slapping high-fives, talking with his mouth full.

Still panting little, Eleanor looked back at the coach. She smiled. "You have to be a bit of a child psychologist to be a sports coach, don't you?"

"Well, my son isn't the best player himself." The coach pointed to a boy with curly, light-brown hair like his own but surprisingly a bit chubby, gulping down Gatorade from a paper cup that he grasped two-handed. "Sometimes I wonder if I'm pressing him too hard into this, just so I can be his coach and have quality-Dad time. You know, it guarantees that I get to see him every Saturday in soccer season. He lives with his mother. But he likes being on the team." The coach added, "We've been divorced since Josh was three."

So this coach pressed his son to play sports, too? Like Nick.

Except that unlike Nick, he realized what he was doing.

The referee in his bright yellow shirt was already blowing the end-of-break warning whistle. The air was getting grey and heavier, filling up with preparations for rain. During the next quarter, the Polish kid scored twice more, and although the other team did manage to achieve one goal, that wasn't Adam's fault, since he wasn't goalie that time. The Polish father couldn't get mad at him for that.

* * *

They were a few steps away, sitting by themselves on their folding chairs. The father was tipping a can of Coke vertically toward his mouth; the mother's blonde hair was in a perfectly cut Fifties pageboy style with bangs. Any minute now, the next quarter would begin, and the father would jump up to head for the sideline. Or else the rain would start pounding and the game would be canceled.

Really, what was there to say to them? The father hadn't yelled at Adam or about Adam during this game. Maybe he didn't even remember how Adam had messed up last time? Well, no, he didn't seem like the kind who would forget any mistake that occurred in any of his son's soccer matches. Okay, but Eleanor should have said something to him last week, at the time he was saying all his horrible things right in front of Adam. Now it was too late.

But what if Adam messed up again?

The referee would be blowing his whistle any second now.

Just to break the ice. So that if she ever had to confront the father in any awkward way, there might be some reservoir of good will.

"Hi," she said.

Her voice came out as a half-cough, so she finished coughing.

Because she was standing and they weren't, Eleanor was actually looming over the couple in their chairs, and they looked up at her with quizzical expressions.

"Is that your son? Boy, he's a terrific player." Eleanor pointed to the kid, who was racing alongside the field, kicking the ball ahead of himself. She coughed again.

The man and woman both beamed. "Thank you, yes, our son Tadek—Tad, for American nickname," the father replied.

The rolled Rs, the rich E: It was definitely an Eastern European accent.

"I understand you're from Poland?"

"Yes, near to Krakow." The father seemed very proud of that, almost pulling himself taller.

Oh right, there was some longstanding Warsaw-Krakow rivalry—it was in her old college history books; some rivalry about which city was better or more important in Polish history. *Ma, was Warsaw better than Krakow?*

Now the man and woman were holding out their hands, presumably for shaking, so Eleanor held out hers, and they all said their names. Janek Wysocki. Maria Wysocki. Eleanor Ritter. Janek worked at the big drug company Pharmacia. Maria also worked with medicines, at the CVS pharmacy on Edgewood Avenue. Eleanor taught French at Edgewood High School—"That's why I notice accents." "Ah, yes." The father—Janek—had pale blue eyes. Maria wore matching blue eye shadow. Tad was their younger son. Uh oh, what if they asked which Hornet was Eleanor's son? *The goalie who messed up...* But a second later the whistle blew, the game re-started, and the father's attention was gone, zeroed in on the field. "Go, go!" he shouted, quickly heaving himself out of his chair.

When the game was over, the rain was just starting to sprinkle, and the Hornets had blown away the Halloween team, seven to one, with Tad scoring five of the goals. Adam didn't do anything special, neither good nor—thank God—bad. Janek spent most of his time shouting happily.

Ma, I met a family from Poland.

Chapter Five

Rose's scrawny biceps were as tense as a bodybuilder's, straining all her ninety pounds, and her face was dead serious as she gripped the handlebars of the aluminum walker and, slowly, moved one foot forward from her bed toward the door of her hospital room. Five inches. Then the other foot.

"Very nice, dear," the physical therapist said. "Now just two more steps and here's your chair."

Rose glanced at the woman, showing no particular emotion. And proceeded to pull herself forward three more steps.

"Oh my." The therapist reached out.

Another.

"Now don't overdo— "

Rose began Step Number Seven.

"Ma—" Eleanor warned, moving the vinyl armchair toward her mother.

Panting but flashing a grin, Rose pushed her right foot in front of her on the linoleum. And then the walker wobbled.

"Ma!"

The therapist was quick. She grabbed the handlebars with one hand, Rose's arm with the other, and then she slid her arm around Rose's lower back to ease Rose into the chair, which she nudged closer with her own foot. Her black hair was pulled back in a short ponytail that flapped as she moved.

For a long, silent minute, Eleanor and the physical therapist watched Rose, in the chair, staring at her lap, breathing loudly.

"Mrs. Ritter? Now it's just wonderful that you're so eager to make progress, but of course, you don't want to strain yourself, do you?"

"What's— " Rose took a deep breath and after that, her voice came out louder. "What's the next step?" She paused and breathed again. "To get me out of here."

"Well, now, let's not jump ahead— "

Rose glared. "What—comes—next?"

The therapist glanced at Eleanor, who had sat down on the edge of Rose's temporarily abandoned bed. "Ma, if we need to slow things down—"

"We don't."

The therapist looked at Eleanor, then Rose, her ponytail bobbing. No one spoke. The therapist checked Rose's pulse. "I need to talk to the floor nurse," she mumbled.

Mrs. Ritter would continue this program every day, the therapist finally announced, after she returned. A little walking to build up her strength and tone the muscles. The goal was to go 150 feet with only a walker, no human assistance, and also to get in and out of a chair. Once Mrs. Ritter could do all that, she would be transferred to a rehab center for more extensive physical therapy. And then, eventually, home.

And when would all that be?

"Well, we had been aiming for, uh, maybe in the next couple of days to—"

"So, today is Monday," Rose declared. "I'll be out of here on Wednesday."

"No, I don't— "

Rose brushed the air with a weak wave.

She was leaning against the chair back, eyes closed, face expressionless. Panting more heavily. Without her red lipstick, her skin seemed paler, the wrinkles around her mouth carved more clearly.

* * *

"Well, you have a recovery plan now," Eleanor ventured, after the therapist had left.

Rose, lying in her bed, half-propped up against the metal headrest, shrugged.

"Just another few days of this hospital food. Maybe the meals at the rehab center will be better."

Still no reaction from Rose. Eyes still closed.

"You want me to bring you anything to eat?"

"Only if your husband cooks it." Rose opened her eyes and glanced toward Eleanor, lifting her eyebrows.

Well now, that was the normal Rose Ritter.

Of course, Rose was undoubtedly still weak from the surgery. They should stick to safe, unstressful topics of conversation. Food. Uh, Eleanor's job. Nick's job. Well, maybe not Nick's job, that was kind of stressful. Obviously, nothing about Poland. Even if Rose had started talking about Warsaw with Natalie?

What's Polish food like?

No, no. Not yet. The Warsaw conversation with Natalie had been before Rose's accident and surgery. And there was no knowing why she'd said that out of the blue. Maybe it was just a once-in-a-lifetime slipup on Rose's part.

"So, speaking of food. We're starting to plan Kate's bat mitzvah party next year." That should be a safe enough subject, if Eleanor could stop herself from worrying aloud about the cost. Sitting in the vinyl-upholstered chair that Rose had vacated, Eleanor tugged on the guardrail of Rose's bed to scoot closer.

"Don't use that rail! It's not strong."

Eleanor exhaled, let go of the rail, and tried to rub her shoes against the linoleum floor to propel the chair forward. The chair didn't budge.

"Kate decided she wants blue and gold as the color scheme for her party—I have no idea why, but at least she didn't choose black, which apparently is the 'in' color these days. So now we have to get blue-and-gold yarmulkes and blue-and-gold candles, and I suppose blue-and-gold invitations, if you can even find—Ma?"

Rose was breathing in quiet puffs, at long intervals. Sleeping? Her bony chest went up and down just a little bit under the dark blue blanket. From the other side of the room there was the background soundtrack of voices, only semi-muffled by the thin curtain, like someone else's loud car radio coming through the window at a traffic light: The roommate high-pitched and emphatic, and the visitor in a deeper and quieter rumble.

"I'm not sleeping." Rose's voice was somewhere between grumpy and toneless.

"Oh. Okay. Do you want anything?"

Rose turned her head toward Eleanor, pulling herself up a little higher against the pillow. "Blue-and-gold bat mitzvah. Go on. Are you fighting with her over the dress? She wants something too sexy?" Rose straightened out her nightgown where it had bunched underneath her hips.

Was fighting with Kate a safe topic or stressful? "Hmm, we haven't gotten to discussing the dress yet."

"And she'll have blue-and-gold hair?"

Eleanor laughed. "I don't know. I guess she'll try."

"She still wants to put rings in her nose?"

"Well, you know."

"She'll look beautiful, you know that."

"I know."

"Even with rings."

"Let's hope it doesn't get to that point."

"She's studying Hebrew?"

"Uh. Yeah."

"You fight over that, too?"

"Well. You know Kate."

"So you fight."

"Not that much."

"And Nick? He's going to participate?"

No, the bat mitzvah was not a safe topic. A new topic. Fast.

"What did people do for bar mitzvahs in Poland?"

Holy shit, how did that slip out?

Eleanor sucked in a breath. Then she glanced at Rose.

Shit, now Rose would snap at her, *Stop asking me about Poland!* Or, *They killed all the Jews so there were no bar mitzvahs.*

But Rose merely shifted her shoulders so that her head faced slightly away from Eleanor and stared down at the blanket. "A boy went to synagogue with his father one day and read Torah," she said.

She was still looking at the blanket. The thumb and first two fingers of her right hand were rubbing her left index finger, up and down.

Rose wasn't shouting. She wasn't saying: *Stop asking me about Poland.* She was—answering a question about Poland?

Very, very slowly, Eleanor began to let her breath fizzle out of her mouth.

"We didn't make a big fuss about it the way you do," Rose continued. "All the *mishpokhe* came to our house for dinner." She was silent for a few beats; ten seconds, perhaps. "My brother Avram had a new suit, and our grandmother insisted he had to put a clove of garlic in his pocket to ward off the Evil Eye. He smelled of garlic the whole dinner."

She stopped again. For a longer time. She breathed in and out, peacefully, normally.

Was Rose simply too tired to argue?

Would she answer more questions?

Would she get angry if Eleanor asked?

"What did"—Eleanor whispered—"what did you eat at the dinner?"

Rose responded, quietly, right away. "My mother was a wonderful cook. I don't remember what exactly she made for that dinner, for Avram, but for our birthdays she always baked *sernik*. Cheesecake. It was magnificent. It melted in your mouth. One year, *oy*, Feiga punched her whole fist into the cake, and then she smeared it all over her dress, and then to make matters worse, she ran around the house bumping into the furniture with that dress with the cake all over it. *Oy*! She was a little tornado."

Now Rose leaned her head back on the pillow, although her eyes were still wide open, and she glanced in turn at the curtain, the wall, the lamp. Her lips curved up, just slightly. Her silver hair was bunched a little near her right ear. If Eleanor tried to smooth it ....?

"Everyone knew my mother's cooking. My friends at school always asked me if she had given me any desserts that I could share. *Babka*. *Sernik* with raisons." Rose's voice trickled away. Of course, she was exhausted. She'd had enough. She would get mad if Eleanor asked anything more.

But she might never again talk this much.

What else did your mother cook?

Tell me about your friends.

How did you manage to survive the Nazis?

Eleanor stretched her hand—just her fingertips — the gentlest touch, on Rose's arm. "Tell me about your friends," she whispered.

Rose looked at Eleanor's fingers.

"We were modern girls," she answered, more slowly now. "Our mothers kept kosher, but they didn't wear wigs, you know, like our grandmothers did. Certainly not. A few of the families were Zionists. My best friend Salka, her father was some kind of big *makher* with the Socialists."

"Your friends were all Jewish? But you didn't live in a ghetto, did you?"

The pause, this time, was longer. Under the dark blue blanket, Rose shifted her weight from one side to the other, wincing briefly. She drew in her bottom lip while taking a long breath. "There was also Krystyna."

All the muscles in Eleanor's left leg tingled, screaming for her to switch position and shift that knee over the right one. Her lungs wanted more oxygen. Her back ached from leaning forward. She didn't dare move. The chair might creak. The air might rustle.

Krystyna. Salka. Cheesecake.

Beyond the curtain, the roommate laughed, and the visitor replied with some loud and sharp words. Something heavy dropped on the floor. More loud words.

If they would just shut up and let Rose talk.

Rose patted the mussed hair by her ear. "My father taught mathematics in the Jewish *gimnazjum*, the high school. I think you knew that already. He was also a volunteer in the fire brigade. So he became friendly with another mathematics teacher in the brigade, who was Catholic, who taught in the grammar school where my sister Chana and I went—yes, Polish and Jewish girls together went to that school. And that Polish teacher had a daughter who was a year older than I was, and so sometimes she and I played together. Dolls. Her mother sewed the most beautiful clothes for her dolls. I still remember there was one green ball gown made out of a shiny material that I thought was silk. Maybe it was, maybe it wasn't. Oh, I envied those dresses. And Krystyna had long braids, and I envied those, too. My hair was a dark blonde, but it was too wild and curly for braids."

She halted again. Squirmed for a moment, as she tugged another time at her hospital gown underneath her hips.

"What kind of games did you play with the dolls?".

Abruptly, Rose slapped her blanket. "That's enough. Stop asking me about Poland." She brushed the blanket away, then yanked it back up. Her voice had become a little hoarse, the way it rarely got since she'd quit smoking.

"Did you play house—"

"Please call the nurse. I want a sleeping pill tonight."

The hallway was blindingly bright after the dimness of Rose's room. The moment Eleanor stepped out of the room, she fell back against the nearest wall, and she remained there for a few seconds before turning her head to look up the hall, then down.

Once upon a time in a town in Poland there was a little girl named Ruzia who had wild, dark-blonde hair. And she had a friend with long blonde braids named Krystyna. Whose mother sewed beautiful ball gowns for dolls. And her brother Avram had a bar mitzvah. And they lived in an apartment on the second floor, and they played with their mother's enamel pots, and once they went to Warsaw and rode on an electric trolley. Those were Chana's stories. And now they were also Ruzia's stories.

* * *

Eleanor stayed another forty-five minutes, until Rose got her evening meds and her dinner. Rose made a face as she poked a fork in the meat, two brown lumps of something next to a small mound of canned peas, on a metal tray positioned across her lap. "They want to poison us so then we'll have to pay them to pump our stomachs," she muttered.

"I'll ask Nick to cook you a care package."

Rose nodded. "How about the book I got Adam? Did he like it? It was about those fish, like you said."

Did Rose have to dredge up every problem with Eleanor's family? Nick didn't want anything to do with Kate's bat mitzvah. Nor did Kate. Kate wanted to pierce her nose. Adam was slow in reading. Why not ask how they could afford to pay for the big blue-and-gold bat mitzvah party, while she was at it?

"Sharks. Sure. You know, when it's a topic he wants to read about, like sharks, he'll read a million books," Eleanor replied quickly.

Rose was peering closely at the meat. "Hmm," she said, not looking at Eleanor, "how about broadening his horizon a little? Try a book about oceans."

That wasn't a bad idea, actually.

Ma, what did you like to read in Poland?

How did you manage to survive?

"I don't mean to be so harsh on the poor boy, Ellie. You know I love him. I'm his grandmother." Finally, Rose had found a piece of meat worthy of her fork, and she speared it. "Avram will find his way."

Avram?

* * *

Eleanor couldn't even punch the keys for Natalie's number on her cellphone. Twice, shaking, she had to start over. Then she lost the signal anyway.

She moved to a spot on the sidewalk right outside the hospital. This time she finally got a connection, but Natalie's secretary answered. Natalie was in court.

Why, why, why had she ever quit asking Rose for stories? Why had she let Natalie and Nick persuade her to stop? She had to talk to some-one, now, right away. This was much, much bigger than Natalie's lit-tle anecdote about Rose's trip to Warsaw. Certainly bigger than Rose's garbled maybe-Polish words when she and Izzy had first met Nick. Would Susan be interested? She was a history teacher, after all. And she could be a good listener when Eleanor needed someone. But this wasn't the kind of thing Susan and Eleanor usually talked about; they vented more about the bureaucracy at school and Susan's dating woes.

How about Steven? No, he wouldn't care; he'd never cared about Rose's stories when he and Eleanor were growing up. Or Nick? He'd like the *sernik* recipe. But he was probably too busy at work.

Would Maria Wysocki's mother in Krakow have taught her how to make *sernik*?

That was a stupid question.

Natalie was still in court.

Chapter Six

The curly-haired man, who should have just paid for his purchases and promptly left the art-supply store, was instead leaning onto the check-out counter, talking intently with the cashier. Who was pretty and had a flower tattooed on her very bare shoulder.

And what about the ten other people waiting in line to pay? Including Eleanor, midway down the queue, lugging a shopping basket heaped with a mass of crayons, markers, water colors, paint brushes, glue, tissue paper, sheets of multicolored construction paper, and whatever-all else for Adam's big science project on sharks. With all of these ingredients—if she ever got to the cash register to buy them—Adam was going to explain about sharks and the environment, their life cycle, their predators, their food sources, and anything he chose, artistically displayed on a giant poster board.

Finally. The guy at the counter had finished chit-chatting with the tattooed cashier. The line moved up by one spot, as he turned around to face the people he had delayed.

It was Adam's soccer coach.

"Hey! You're Adam's mother, right? From the Blue Hornets?"

He stopped right beside her and gave her that smile that beamed across his face.

How come she'd never noticed that he had blue eyes? Amazing, almost royal-blue eyes. A perfect color for the sea in Adam's poster.

She shook the hand he held out.

Smooth skin. But no flab.

He let go.

Why was a soccer coach buying paint and crayons?

"How is Adam?" he was asking, or something like that.

She began formulating words and a smile in return. "Yes, hi. Hello. You're Adam's soccer coach? Mark? Hi. I'm Eleanor Ritter. Yes. Yes, I want to thank you about last week, you were absolutely right to put him in as goalie. He's actually eager to play this Saturday."

"That's great." His smile got even wider. "I always keep track of the opposing teams' records—that's part of the job of being coach. So if we're facing a tough team on any week, don't worry, I won't make Adam the goalie."

"I mean, it's not like I'm asking you to baby him or anything."

"I understand. Hey, I want the Hornets to win, too." He leaned closer. He had just the slightest bit of stubble around his chin and jawline. "We're not supposed to make a big deal about winning and losing. That's another rule of the coaching job. But you can't fool the kids. Even the littlest ones, the four-year-olds, they know." Stepping away, he gestured at the gear in Eleanor's shopping basket. "You're buying a lot of art supplies. Are you an artist?"

"Oh, no, this is for Adam's science project. Don't ask why a nine-year-old has to be Picasso to do a project for his science class."

Mark grinned.

"I wish I was an artist," Eleanor went on, giggling, "then I could help him. Not that he needs help. He's actually very good at art."

"That's great."

"I'm just a French teacher."

"Really? *Vraiment?*"

He spoke French?

The woman behind Eleanor coughed and pointed to the space that had opened in front of Eleanor. Eleanor moved forward into the space, followed immediately by the woman. Just two more customers, and it would be her turn at the cash register. Already.

"Are you good at languages? Do you speak any others?" Mark was asking.

She giggled again. "Not Polish, unfortunately."

Of course he looked puzzled at her answer. It made no sense for her to mention Polish out of the blue. It was interesting that his eyes didn't seem to get smaller, the way most people's did, as his eyebrows moved down and closer together in a frown.

"I said that, because my mother is suddenly starting to speak Polish, which she has refused to speak for more than fifty years, ever since she came to America," Eleanor said cheerfully, casually, "and my cousin and I can't understand a word she's saying. I suppose a Freudian would say

I became a French teacher to have my own secret language, because my mother wouldn't teach me hers. Maybe it's partly true."

Now his frown melted into a big, easy laugh. "I think the French would enjoy the idea that they have a secret language that no one else in the world speaks properly. Especially Americans."

She had to laugh, too.

The little wrinkles around his eyes got deeper when he laughed.

And abruptly, she was at the counter.

He stayed with her, as she transferred her stockpile from the shopping basket to the counter, and as the cashier — the pretty, tattooed cashier—piled the loot into three plastic bags. He smiled at the cashier.

He stayed even while Eleanor proffered her credit card, and signed the slip, and gathered the bags, and turned to head back through the store, past the same line of customers, past the woman who'd coughed, toward the exit.

"I know you said Adam is good at art," he added, "but if he's having any trouble with his project, I'd be glad to help."

"Are you—an artist?"

People weren't really artists, were they? Earning a living painting portraits and bowls of fruit? In New Jersey?

He gave her a wry version of his beaming smile, his lips closed and tilting up to the left. "Hey, you don't think being a Saturday soccer coach is a full-time job? Yes, I'm a painter. I got my MFA from the Art Institute of Chicago, and my specialty is a socio-cultural reinterpretation of the still-life. Mostly oils. I'm not exactly Picasso, but I'm trying."

Eleanor squinted. Did still-lifes have socio-cultural meaning? Well, it was probably artist-talk that she didn't understand. Maybe she could ask an easier question. "Do you—I mean—do people hire you to paint their portraits? How does it work?"

His smile widened into another full-faced laugh. "You mean like in medieval Italy? Wouldn't it be great to have a rich patron like Lorenzo de' Medici and dine at his table every night? Unfortunately, I haven't found one yet. So I teach art history at North Jersey Community, plus a class at the library."

He was also a teacher?

"And of course I have occasional shows," he was saying.

And then, of all times, she actually heard her stupid cellphone start its song.

So she had to stop, move into a narrow side aisle, put down the plastic bags—smoothly, Mark took them from her—and dig into her pocketbook while "Frère Jacques" kept tinkling away.

"I'm over at Joanna's house," Kate began immediately, "and we're doing homework, okay, don't worry. And her mom invited me for dinner, so can you pick me up, like, at eight o'clock?"

"What homework are you doing?"

"What difference does it make?"

"My twelve-year-old daughter," Eleanor said to Mark, as she pressed the End Call button. "I think her Terrible Twos were easier."

His smile was sympathetic now, even as he pointed to the phone. "Do you like that thing? I've been thinking about getting one, so my son could call me more easily when I'm not home."

"That makes sense."

"Why did you get yours?"

"Um," Eleanor said. "I don't really know. I never even hear it ring when people call," she added. She reached for her shopping bags.

"I'll see you this weekend? At the soccer game?"

It was, of course, time for Eleanor to go.

"Yes," she answered, "the game is in the afternoon, right? That's good, so I can take my daughter to services in the morning and still get Adam to soccer—she just turned twelve, so I already have to start with the bat mitzvah preparation, and so she has to go to Saturday morning services. Twenty-five times. Till next fall. So sometimes I have to miss soccer to go with her instead."

"Oh boy. I guess I'll have to go through that in a couple of years, with Josh. My son."

And he was Jewish?

"Do you and your daughter have fights about her bat mitzvah?" he was asking.

"Fights? World War Three is more like it." Or did that make her sound like some horrible shrill mother? "I mean, it's not that bad. It's just, you know, girls that age don't—they just want to hang out with their friends. Go shopping. Get their noses pierced." Why did she say that?

How long had they been standing there, talking?

Flirting.

No, they weren't flirting! She was a married woman. Mark was just a little too friendly. Smiling all the time. Look at the way he'd talked with the cashier. The pretty cashier. He was a friendly, chatty guy. Hadn't he said he was divorced?

Were the other customers watching? How about the woman who'd coughed? Did anyone in the store recognize Eleanor?

"You know, I really need to get going," she said quickly, and before

Mark even answered she turned away and strode toward the exit door, bumping into a tall bin of crayons.

At the car, Eleanor tossed the shopping bags toward the passenger seat and slammed the door. Two of the bags hit the edge of the seat and slid down to the floor mat, dribbling out a cascade of markers, paint brushes, and water colors. So she had to go back, tug open the door, lean over, and try to feel around for the spilled stuff, probably missing some vital paintbrush or crayon. Cramming what she could into the bags, Eleanor re-slammed the door, jumped into the driver's seat, and hit the gas pedal to just get out of the parking lot.

She'd stayed way too long at the stupid art-supply store, talking with Mark. She had family responsibilities. She had to cook dinner. For her family.

Well, actually, just for Adam. Kate wouldn't be home for dinner; she had called on the cellphone while Eleanor was talking with Mark. Mark might get a cellphone. That was a smart idea for a divorced dad.

He was just very outgoing. That was why they had talked for so long. After all, as an artist, he had to be out there marketing his paintings, marketing himself, all the time.

Speaking of markets: She was going to the market. The supermarket. She would buy some cauliflower, Adam liked that. A good healthy dinner for her son, cauliflower with pasta.

Eleanor heard the bang and the sharp crunch, even as her body jerked forward. Then back.

There was no need to jam on the brake, because her car stopped by itself. Or rather, it was stopped by the car in front. Which she had just hit.

The shopping bags slid forward on the passenger seat and spilled their guts all over again.

A grey-haired woman in a green pantsuit was opening the driver's-side door of the car Eleanor had hit and walking back toward Eleanor. Eleanor unhooked her seat belt, opened her car door, and headed toward the woman. "I'm sorry. I didn't see— "

No! No, she wasn't supposed to admit anything!

Together, they knelt, stood, walked around. Looked at bumpers, fenders, side panels. Part of the left rear fender of the other car was mashed in like a bowl of half-eaten porridge. The tail light was broken. Eleanor's car had a matching horizontal dent on its left front. The other driver produced a driver's license, car registration, and insurance card. A 1997 Chevy Malibu. That driver turned on the ignition, moved forward a few inches, turned it off, opened her door partway. "It seems to drive normally," she commented, not shouting. Eleanor tried to walk to her car to retrieve her own papers, but her legs shook so much that she had to grab hold of the hood. "I'm sorry. I'm sorry."

It was just a fender-bender. No one was hurt. Unless the other driver decided to claim whiplash or some injury in a few days. But Eleanor had only been going thirty miles an hour. Okay, maybe thirty-five. A little side street. Minor damage. No passengers. No smoke curling up from anyone's engine. No need to wait for police. No summons to Natalie's courtroom—Good Lord! Municipal court judges didn't hear trivial cases like this, did they? The other driver seemed calm. With a black-and-gold pen and a matching leather notebook, she copied copious notes from Eleanor's insurance card, license, and registration. Her insurance company would be in touch, she said.

Eleanor would have to inform her own insurance company, naturally. Nick would be furious; their rates would undoubtedly go up, since the accident was technically her fault.

Nick.

She shouldn't have talked so long to Mark in the art-supply store.

Maybe there was no need to tell Nick. He never looked much at her car even in normal times, and he was so busy now that he certainly wouldn't see that one little new dent before she had a chance to fix it. In six months, when the insurance premium came due, who would notice a rate increase, combined with all the other changes that came with every renewal? And combined with the cost of Kate's bat mitzvah.

Chapter Seven

"I've studied enough for my history test." Kate tugged open the refrigerator door. "When's dinner? When will Dad be home?"

Eleanor looked up from her own set of test papers on the kitchen table. *À quelle heure vàs-tu a l'école?* "Do you want to talk about your bat mitzvah party?"

"Really?"

The refrigerator door thudded shut, and in less than a minute Kate was sitting in a chair next to Eleanor, dumping an armful of brightly colored, photo-filled brochures across the smooth white table-top and brushing aside Eleanor's French tests. "So," she began briskly, "there are really only three choices. Now, I've been to two parties at Bergen Manor, which a lot of girls pick because it's like a castle-medieval theme." She splayed out the brochures and pointed to two of them. The main problem with Bergen Manor was that it was so popular, and her bat mitzvah would be so late in the year, in October, that by the time of her party everyone might be sick of that restaurant. The Country Club was much more sophisticated—of course it wasn't actually a country club, that was only the name; however, it was also the most expensive. But the third place, The Dance Floor, might be too small.

"Mmm," Eleanor murmured. "So which one do you like best? Do you feel like being a princess in a castle?"

Kate giggled. "Well, when you put it that way, no. That makes me sound three years old."

"Cinderella. Snow White."

"Ugh!"

"In a yellow gown."

"Honestly, Mom. Cinderella has a *blue* gown. It's Belle in *Beauty and the Beast* who wears yellow."

"Sorry. I'm glad you know your Disney princesses so well."

Kate briefly pouted, but then laughed. "I could write a list of everyone I want to invite, and you could see if we could fit into the Dance Floor. You can even give me a limit. But it also depends on how many relatives you want."

"Point taken."

"Uncle Steven and Aunt Leah and the cousins, right? Grandma and Grandpa from Cincinnati."

"Well, I'll place a limit on my list, too, okay?"

"Tell you what." Kate got one of her dangerous grins. "I'll keep my list short, if you let me get my nose pierced."

"Do you really need me to answer that?"

"Why are you and Dad so uptight about it?"

"Because it would make you look ugly."

Kate's mouth opened.

"And it's not safe," Eleanor added quickly.

"I don't think it's ugly. My friends don't think so."

"I don't mean ugly, exactly. I'm sorry. But why do you want to hide your beautiful nostrils?"

Laughing again, Kate turned another page on one of the brochures, and the two of them leafed slowly through the thick, glossy sheets of paper. Silver platters of three-layer chocolate cake, chocolate mousse, fruit tarts, and cookies shaped like green and pink flowers. Waiters in pure-white jackets pouring thick, orange streams of cheese fondue. Flower-filled lawns rolling down hillsides. They looked like wedding receptions. Any of the venues had to cost at least fifty dollars per person.

"So how's it going with learning the Hebrew?"

"I thought we were talking about the party."

"Okay. Okay. I'll think about a guest list. Are there any other—you know — less expensive places you could— "

"Mom!" Kate stared at Eleanor and shook her head before going back to her room.

Her hair color this week was a psychedelic pink that began halfway between the roots and the ends.

* * *

In Nick's wiry fingers, the knife glided up and down the zucchini. Delicate filets of zucchini, carrots, celery, peppers, onion, and mushrooms slid onto the cutting board while he muttered instructions to Eleanor. A little more chili flakes. Check the rice.

Wednesday evening: So, according to their new schedule, Nick was home to eat dinner with the family before returning to his Y2 world for a few more hours of work. Tomorrow, he would work straight through until maybe eleven. Friday, a dinner break again. And on really good nights, Nick would do the cooking, too.

Even in college, he had actually cooked. When he offered to fix dinner for Eleanor back then, it was not the usual undergrad spaghetti. It was chicken in wine sauce with almonds and currants. Rice pilaf with vegetables she'd never heard of. He told her that she wasn't eating right, the way she grabbed pizza and Granny Smith apples, which of course was true. For her birthday only a few months after they'd started dating, Nick had baked a chocolate cake that flirted with her taste buds like rich cream. Any girl would fall in love with a guy like that.

Now Nick tilted the bottle of peanut oil for a calculated second over the cast-iron skillet, then jerked it away and whipped the pan around in a quick circle. The oil sizzled, and he slid the sliced vegetables in to join it. "So is it safe to ask Adam about soccer tonight?"

"*What?*" Eleanor clutched the dirty cutting board.

"Soccer. The last time I asked, everyone got all frizzed out because Adam messed up some way and I wasn't supposed to have asked."

"Oh. Right." She put the cutting board back down on the counter. "He, uh, he didn't, um, actually do much in the last game, good or bad. But yeah, the team won, so he feels good. The coach was very smart, he put Adam in as goalie again because it didn't matter this time. Because the other team was so lousy, you see?"

Nick nodded as he alternately focused on the vegetables and the chunks of chicken breast marinating in another pan.

If Eleanor could talk so easily and casually about Mark to Nick, then obviously she hadn't been flirting with Mark at the art-supply store.

"Stir-fry chicken à la Dad," Nick pronounced. "Hey, Kate? Adam?"

"I'm studying!" Kate shouted from her room.

"Mom, you didn't get me any red paint," Adam complained. "Can you go back to the art store?"

* * *

Eleanor followed Nick into the bathroom after dinner and perched on the closed toilet seat, while he brushed his teeth.

"The chicken was delicious," she began.

He half-smiled, shrugging, toothbrush in mouth.

"So, you know," she continued, "you asked about Adam's soccer team? Before dinner? Well, I was talking with one of the dads at the first game."

Nick's eyebrows furrowed into brief questions as he glanced at her via the mirror and reached for the water cup.

"He mentioned this company that sounds really interesting. It tells people about new drugs."

Nick sloshed the water around his mouth. "What do we need a drug for?"

"It's not a drug for us to use. It's a company."

"Is it for your mother?"

"No, it's not a drug!"

Nick was already wiping the toothbrush; she had to get her point out fast. "Like it could make a lot of money. The guy at the soccer game, I guess he's a stockbroker, he says people are doubling their money. Drugs-something-dot-com."

"What are you talking about?"

"Everybody is making money in the stock market. The World Wide Web."

"Everybody is going to lose money."

"What do you mean? The stocks keep going up."

"It's phony. Anything with the word 'dotcom' or 'Web.' I work with these every day, I know them."

"No you don't. You work with computer wiring."

"Eleanor, I have to go— "

"Do you know how expensive Kate's bat mitzvah is going to be?"

Nick turned around from the sink and looked Eleanor straight in the face.

* * *

"Hey, Mom." Adam was suddenly standing at the kitchen table, next to Eleanor's chair. "I made a get-well card for Grandma. Want to see it?"

The card truly was beautiful. There was a cluster of quite realistic-looking fish of various shapes and colors, swimming in a pale blue sea that was almost shimmering—how had he done that? Balanced on top of all their heads was a lifeboat carrying a gray-haired lady. The wording read: *I hope this card carries you to safety. Love, Your Grandson, Adam.* Even Kate said, as she dried the skillet and the big saucepan, "That's cool, Adam."

Eleanor rubbed Adam's smooth brown hair. She rested her palms on her stack of class papers. "Grandma's been talking about her childhood in Poland a little bit."

Adam and Kate moved to the wooden chairs and sat down.

And Eleanor told them about the cheesecake and Feiga and the grandmother's garlic and Krystyna's dolls. About Salka's father the Socialist and the Catholic math teacher and the fire brigade.

"Did they still eat the cake, after Feiga put her fingers in it?" Adam asked.

"Don't you dare do that at my bat mitzvah."

"There's a boy in my class who's from Poland. We might do our science project together."

No. There were too many Polish coincidences happening all at once.

"And he's on the soccer team," Adam added. "He's really good."

* * *

With Kate's permission, Eleanor phoned Joanna's mother, who had already booked the Bergen Manor for Joanna's party. For about one hundred guests, and selecting the medium-price buffet dinner with three choices of entrée, the family was figuring on spending five thousand dollars. Adding in printed invitations, Joanna's dress and shoes, party favors, DJ, photographer, embossed yarmulkes, table centerpieces, and the cake, probably another three thousand.

Eight thousand dollars.

DJ. Photographer. Centerpieces. Why did a thirteen-year-old need table centerpieces?

Near the garage door were piled the stacks of newspapers and magazines for recycling. Eleanor found the *New York Times* business sections from the last four days and also Rose's *Newsweek*. The Dow Jones Industrial Average was continuing its strong performance, up about one hundred points from last week. With the aging of the Baby Boomers, health care was one of the biggest growth industries, including for-profit hospital chains, nursing homes, and pharmaceuticals. (Pharmaceuticals! That meant drugs.) This year the Food and Drug Administration had approved Vioxx for pain relief and Xenical for weight loss, which were each expected to earn a billion dollars in sales. (A billion dollars?)

Eight thousand dollars.

For a thirteen-year-old's birthday party?

The Dow Jones was up one hundred points.

People were making double what they paid for a stock, after just a few weeks. That was what Ben's dad said at the soccer game.

Which meant Eleanor and Nick wouldn't actually have to buy that much of Ben's dad's drug stock. If Ben's dad was right, all they really had to buy was four thousand dollars' worth, and wait a few weeks until it doubled, and then sell it. Or, well, maybe five thousand dollars, just to be safe.

And if all the computers crashed on January first and the stock market crashed, the kind of crisis Nick got all worked up about— well then, nobody would be having a party, and they'd really need a God to pray to.

Nick didn't want to invest in the drug-stock company because he just didn't want Kate to have a bat mitzvah, that was the true explanation. After all, he refused to convert. He hated anything connected with being Jewish.

Still, Ben's dad was kind of annoying, always talking about his stock. As though he only signed up Ben for soccer so he could find customers.

Maybe she could ask Susan for advice? Susan had dated a guy from Wall Street once and gotten kind of interested in that financial stuff.

* * *

It couldn't be Nick, when the phone next to Eleanor's bed rang in the darkness at eleven-thirty; Nick never called in the middle of work. Kate and Adam were safely asleep in their rooms. It could only be Rose.

More specifically, it was the night nurse in charge of Rose's floor at the hospital.

"I wouldn't normally bother the family with this sort of thing at night. When a patient is constantly pressing the Call button and shouting, you know. But we're a bit worried that there may be something more serious, and we just don't understand what she's saying. So I was hoping you might be able to help translate."

"Translate?"

"Well, yes. She's been shouting in a foreign language."

Chapter Eight

The hospital wanted to discharge Rose in the morning. Or the next day, at the latest.

"No, not because she shouted in Polish." Over the phone line, Natalie's voice finally sounded a little exhausted. She was home now. Two a.m

"Then what's their rush?" Carrying her phone — the real phone from the house, not the stupid cell one — Eleanor got up from the red leather couch in her den, walked to the bottom of the stairs, and peered into the darkness above her. All the bedrooms upstairs were quiet.

When Natalie had gotten to the hospital, at around midnight, Rose had been sound asleep and not shouting anything in any language, and the shift had changed, so none of the staff knew much about what had happened in the shift before theirs. Nick staggered home an hour after that, and Eleanor could have left him to stay with the kids and joined Natalie at the hospital, but by then what was the point? Natalie was about to leave.

However, Natalie did learn that there was a pending discharge order for Rose.

"Ma still can't walk by herself, can she? So how can they just kick her out?"

"She doesn't have to be able to walk in order to be discharged." Natalie yawned. "Apparently, she's reached the stage where she needs specialized physical therapy, in a rehab center. Hospitals don't like to keep people longer than they have to, because of the risk of infection. Or because their insurance won't pay. Both reasons, actually."

Well, yes, getting Rose to a rehab center had been the goal from Day One, they all knew that; it was what all the exercises with the hospital therapist and going 150 feet using the walker and whatnot were supposed to lead up to. A rehab center where Rose would live for a while and get more intensive physical therapy. Natalie had already found three rehab facilities within twenty miles of the hospital and visited them all and picked out the one she preferred, and she had discussed the whole situation with Rose. Her particular favorite was just ten minutes from Rose's apartment. Natalie especially liked the sitting area on each floor and the open courtyard in the center.

Eleanor hadn't seen any of the places.

"When did you do all this?" Eleanor snapped. "Where was I?"

"Come on, Ellie, it had to get done. Now here's what you need to do in the morning."

Eleanor would have to find Rose's doctor, and also confer with the hospital's social worker. Make sure the rehab center had a bed available. Get Rose's prescriptions and the instructions for follow-up care. Then, of course, a family member must accompany Rose to the rehab center and get her checked in. It might happen today or tomorrow, any time between, maybe, nine in the morning and noon. Or two o'clock. Or four.

"There's a lot you'll still need to find out about the discharge," Natalie went on. "And it would be nice if we could learn more about that shouting, too. I agree. Do you have a pen to write this down with?"

"Oh, now I get to do something?"

"Ellie— "

Damn Natalie—yes, of course everything she'd done made sense. As always. But couldn't Natalie ever, maybe, ask for advice? Pretend to ask? And now, today, why today did it suddenly have to be Eleanor's turn? She'd promised Jessica, Jessie, Meaghan, Sara, and Zoe in Advanced French that she would come in early, before school, to help them with the grammar for their Thanksgiving skit about Marie Antoinette and Pocahontas. And Alex from Beginning French, she'd told him she would give him some extra tutoring during her free period.

"I don't know if I can take today off, Natalie."

"I thought you wanted to do more for your mother."

Shutting her eyes, Eleanor leaned her head onto the hard leather armrest of the couch. It was so dark and quiet, she could have been floating in a vacuum. Or hiding in a cellar in Poland. There was no thump from upstairs of Adam or Kate clunking down their hallway to the bathroom, and Nick would never get up once he collapsed into sleep. The old-fashioned, black-and-white plastic clock on the wall across from Eleanor made annoying ticks as the second hand moved from number to number.

"Ellie?"

Damn. Damn. Yes. Well.

Rose might wake up still wanting to talk Polish, or remembering what she'd shouted during the night. And Eleanor would be there. Rose would need her. Eleanor would be the one getting the instructions from the doctor, guiding Rose in the wheelchair. *How are you feeling, Ma? You've graduated to rehab! Are you tired? I guess you didn't sleep well last night...* It was a long way until Thanksgiving; she could help the girls with their Marie Antoinette skit another day.

* * *

"Do you think," Eleanor asked, lying lengthwise on her couch, in the dark, the telephone propped on the armrest against her ear, "that maybe something happened to Ma's leg or hip during the Holocaust? Like breaking a bone trying to escape? And that's what's making her, you know, kind of confused about whether she's back in time, in Poland. So she starts talking Polish?"

"Hmm." Natalie's voice, through the phone wire, was only a little slower than usual. "I never thought about that sort of thing."

"Maybe she was crouched in a pit under someone's house for years and years, without being able to move her legs? I read about people spending the entire war hiding in pits, when I was still majoring in history."

"People certainly survived the Holocaust in amazing ways."

"Now that she's starting to talk about Poland, we can ask her."

"Ellie—"

"This is the time to do it, Natalie. Now! While she's talking."

"Don't push her, Ellie."

"All the stories she's been telling us! Like the girl with the beautiful doll clothes, I told you about that."

"We have to deal with the discharge and the move to the rehab center right now."

"Okay, but we can't wait too long. Before she clams up again."

"And so what if we don't ask her?"

"What do you mean?"

"The last thing your mother needs right now is stress. Ellie, why are you getting all hung up on this? Again."

"Don't you want to know our family history?"

"It doesn't matter that much."

"It—?" Eleanor sat up.

"Ellie, we have a lot to do just for—"

"You really don't care?"

"Honestly. It's all right with me."

"Well, sure, *your* mother told you all about Poland."

"Hardly anything."

"She baked cookies for you."

"Come on, Ellie."

"Ma doesn't even cook— "

"At least you still have your mother!"

The clock ticked again. A toilet flushed.

Eleanor and Natalie both began "I'm sorry" almost at the same minute.

Chapter Nine

"I can't even get a glass of water here. No one answers the useless call button. Could you refill this?" Rose handed Eleanor a pale-yellow, plastic water pitcher.

And Rose sipped the water that Eleanor brought back, and asked whether Nick was still working so hard, and if Eleanor had gotten Kate's blue-and-gold bat mitzvah dress, as though nothing unusual had happened the previous night.

Eleanor pulled the visitor's chair closer to the bed. "Ma ..." *Why did you shout in Polish last night?*

"So they tell me I'm leaving here today." Rose shrugged. "Or tomorrow. Your cousin Natalie found a place, she showed me pictures. It looks fine. Though I'd rather go home."

"Well, I think they said— "

"I know, I know. I need some *meshugeh* therapy. It could be four weeks. It could be six weeks. It could even, God forbid, be a year. It's okay. Ellie. As long as I don't need a cane."

"What's the matter with a cane? Won't you need some help walking?"

Why did you shout in Polish last night?

Okay, Natalie was right; there was all sorts of bureaucracy to deal with first, before she could ask about last night. Eleanor walked down the hallway to the nurses' station, and the nurse on duty said yes, it was their understanding that Mrs. Ritter would be discharged today or tomorrow, Dr. Davis would let them know when he made his rounds some time this morning. So would the social worker. Did Mrs. Ritter have her Medicare card?

Eleanor sat back down in the chair next to Rose's bed and looked at her mother. "So what happened last night, Ma?"

"They never answered the button, I told you."

"But what else?"

"There's no 'what else.' I pressed and pressed, and you know, Ellie, it's rather embarrassing, and I do not choose to discuss my bodily functions with my daughter. Now would you please stop asking me?"

"Ma, you"—Eleanor wrapped her fingers around each other, bounced them once in her lap, and gave a small smile—"you yelled in Polish."

Rose glared at her. "Polish. And how could you tell whether it's Polish or Hungarian or Chinese?"

"Okay, but it wasn't English."

"Why do you insist on talking about last night, Ellie? I asked you not to. I told you it's embarrassing."

But you—

"I'm sorry, Ma."

Eleanor leaned back in her chair, exhaling.

In a few minutes, she could probably nag the nurses again. Maybe the doctor or social worker would come before then. Maybe Rose would fall asleep. She could call Natalie after eleven. She should have been in Intermediate French class right now, teaching the kids how to say the time. If she took the big noisy clock from her den, she could hold it up in front of the classroom, moving the hour and minute hands to indicate different times of day, while she said a few simple sentences about what people might typically be doing at that particular hour.

"*Quelle heure est-il?*" She would put the hour hand on the twelve, the minute hand on the six, and point to a student.

"*Il est midi et demie.*"

"*Très bien. Le déjeuner.* Lunch time. *Veux-tu manger un croque-monsieur?*" And then she would ask if anyone knew what kind of sandwich a croque-monsieur was. She would hold up photos to match various hours—bacon and eggs, sleeping, and the night sky.

"I'll bet your students don't learn French as fast as I learned English."

"What?"

Rose was grinning, sitting straight up away from the pillow, with her arms crossed over her chest. "Tell me something: You've told me that in some of your classes, you won't speak any English at all, isn't that so? Only French?"

"Um—yes. My Advanced French."

"Well." Rose propped herself a little higher in the bed, plumping up her pillow to brace her back and pulling down the hospital gown. "That's what I did when I came to the United States. I told my sister Chana, 'Don't speak a word of Polish to me. Or Yiddish. Only English.' She thought I was crazy." Rose laughed — not a sarcastic or semi-bitter laugh, but a real one, a happy laugh that pulled her mouth wide open. "She thought it would be too hard for me. She wanted to keep speaking Polish or Yiddish, to baby me, you understand? I had to stop her. I told her, I was making a new life, I was going to be an American. No more Polish." Her smile, directed at Eleanor, was almost triumphant. "All right"—she held up a palm, as though Eleanor had been about to interrupt—"yes, I still use Yiddish sometimes. Even today, yes. There are some wonderful words in Yiddish, okay? But ninety percent, I made myself speak English from the moment I came here to New York, from the start, and I'm lucky, I learned fast. Maybe you inherited some language ability from me, hmm? Tell me: Could your best students pass a mathematics class that was taught completely in French?"

Eleanor shook her head, risking a little smile of her own.

"I did. I studied just one year in an English class for new immigrants in night school, that's all I needed. A year later, I was getting straight-A's at Hunter College. You knew that, right? Everything in English, of course."

"How did you do it?"

"You have to work at it, Ellie. You can't coddle yourself. Concentrate. Listen to the people around you. Read everything you can find. Subway signs, street signs, store signs. Newspapers. And think in the new language. Every time you find yourself thinking in the old language, you stop yourself. Concentrate, concentrate, concentrate."

"So." Eleanor leaned forward. "How much Polish do you remember? Like last night— "

"Why would I?" Rose barked the words, and her palm slapped the blue blanket. "They hated us. Why would I want to speak that language?" Frowning, she stared at the bed while she readjusted the blanket over her legs.

Slowly and quietly, Eleanor exhaled. No; it was a dead end, trying to ask about last night. But not to completely drop this topic of speaking Polish and English and Yiddish, not if Rose herself had started it! She made her voice extra-cheerful. "You're quite a role model for learning a language. Why don't you come to one of my classes and give a guest lecture? My Advanced French girls would love you."

"How could I give a guest lecture? I don't speak French." Rose made a small grunt. But her face was a little flushed.

Embarrassed?

When had Rose Ritter ever been embarrassed?

* * *

At eleven-forty-five, Dr. Davis finally materialized, and suddenly everything was in a hurry. Was the family ready ? They would be discharging Mrs. Ritter today.

"But I have a whole list of questions— "

Eleanor pulled out Natalie's list: How could Rose be ready to leave if she could barely walk six steps? What if she fell again? Would she ever be able to walk normally? How long would that take? How long would she need to stay at the rehab center? What if a room wasn't available?

"So let's do it," Rose announced. "Ellie, please go to my apartment and get my navy slacks and my beige blouse with the round collar. And my cosmetics bag."

Eleanor tagged after the doctor, into the hallway almost as far as the next room. "What about the other part?" she whispered. "Speaking in Polish?"

"Your mother speaks Polish? Really? She seems to understand English so well."

"That's the point. She hasn't spoken Polish in fifty years, and suddenly she's blurting out all these Polish words."

Dr. Davis tapped the folder with Rose's chart against a set of other folders resting on his forearm. "A person's mind plays tricks as they age. Something like a serious injury can remind you of your own mortality. And when you think about your mortality, you also start thinking back in time, to your childhood."

"She's only seventy-two."

Flipping open Rose's folder, Dr. Davis scanned the chart. "Yes, that's true. But these days, with the Year 2000 coming, even a lot of people who aren't very old are doing that kind of end-of-life thinking. Wondering if life as we know it is about to change." He shut the folder again. "You might ask the staff there at the rehab center to keep an eye out and tell you if she keeps speaking Polish." Then he reached his hand out to shake Eleanor's. "You can look at it as an opportunity to learn Polish yourself," he laughed.

* * *

Oddly, when Eleanor returned to Rose's room, her mother reached up to pat her cheek. "I know it's hard for the two of you. You and Natalie. You're both so busy, with your lives."

Rose never patted people's cheeks.

"That's okay."

"But maybe, next time, when you come to the new facility, can you bring a few things? Some more clothing? I'll make a list."

"Of course."

"And maybe some of my pictures? Maybe my wedding picture? If I have to stay there for a month."

If Eleanor moved her fingertips just a couple of inches, she could pat Rose's arm in return.

Chapter Ten

"Hi!" Ben's dad was abruptly next to her on the grass by the soccer field. "I remember you from the second game. You wanted to know about that Polish kid Ted."

"Yes. Tad."

Adam was somewhere in the middle of the field but not playing goalie. So Mark had kept his promise; Adam was as safe as he could be, for now. The other team's uniforms were gray and dark blue, which was way too similar to the Hornets' white and royal blue. How would the players tell each other apart? That would be an interesting question to ask a coach. Especially a coach who was also an artist, who understood colors.

"Remember that stock I told you about?—and now Ben's dad slapped his palms together—"Drugtrials-dot-com. It's the company that runs a database that tracks all the trials for new drugs in the U.S. It closed yesterday at twenty-six and one-eighth. That's more than a dollar above when we talked."

"Oh. Is that good, a dollar?"

"Good? It's great! If you'd bought fifty shares, you'd have made more than fifty bucks. You can check for yourself. Do you know how to find the stock listings in the newspaper? Or on the Web?"

Eleanor simply needed this drug company's particular abbreviation, which was DRTR. And then, any time she wanted, she could show DRTR's latest ever-rising number in *The New York Times* to Nick and say triumphantly: "Remember that stock you didn't want to buy?"

She could have had fifty more dollars to go toward paying for Kate's bat mitzvah.

She and Nick were such fuddy-duddies when it came to money, putting it all in bank CDs.

Of course, that was one of the qualities she'd always loved about Nick, starting back in college. That she could count on him. That he didn't go to frat parties and get drunk and throw up like all the other guys. Or get stoned in his dorm room every day, or rave about his collection of Led Zeppelin albums. And when she got the flu in the middle of sophomore year, he stayed with her between classes every day and made real chicken soup, with big hunks of veggies and potatoes. His current boss probably valued that in him, too: If Nick said he would work night and day until all the computers were ready for Y2K, then he absolutely would. And yes, that was a valuable quality in a person. To be steady and reliable.

Nevertheless, there was a time in life for trying new things, too. Ben's dad was right.

* * *

Janek Wysocki was planted at the sideline, legs solidly apart, arms across his chest. Not yelling at anyone, for the moment. On the field, boys were milling around as the ref conferred with the two coaches. Mark was wearing a bright blue cotton golf shirt again, the same color as the Hornets' shirts, fitting loosely over his taut shoulders and chest.

Matthew's mother Betsy, talking with a small cluster of moms, waved at Eleanor, and Eleanor waved back.

The whistle blew; the coaches walked away from the field. Mark, glancing toward Eleanor, smiled and waved.

Well, of course she waved at him, too, just like at Betsy. It would be rude to ignore him.

Away from most of the parents, Maria Wysocki sat alone, in her chair, wearing bright red Spandex slacks and red, spike-heeled half-boots plus a little red bow pinned atop her perfect bangs. With Janek and Tad ensconced at the field, only the tall blond boy who'd been at the first game—Tad's older brother?—was nearby, sitting cross-legged on the grass, focused on his electronic game. Maria seemed to be looking at his game-thing over his shoulder for a while—he ignored her—and then she reached into her cooler and took out a can of Coke.

Janek and Maria were probably around Nick's age. Forty-five, forty-six. Janek looked older, but maybe it was his bulk and his shouting that made him seem not-young. So Janek and Maria would have been born in 1956 or '55 or even, at the earliest, 1950? And then their parents could have been, oh, twenty-five or even thirty when Janek and Maria were born .... In other words, those parents would have been kids when Hitler invaded Poland. Maybe Kate's age.

Old enough to know what was happening? Even at her age, Kate would have understood a lot.

Old enough to have Jewish friends, like Rose with Krystyna? Definitely.

Old enough to throw rocks at store windows.

But maybe only because someone else told them to?

The grandparents could have told Maria's and Janek's parents to throw rocks at Jews, or not throw rocks. And what did Maria's and Janek's parents tell Maria and Janek about the war? And then what did Maria and Janek tell Tadek and his brother .... ? It was a damn spiral.

Well, if Adam and Tadek were doing their big shark project together, it was really the right thing for Eleanor to do, to walk over and say hello to Maria. And to continue seeding good will, in case Janek ever felt like screaming at Adam again. And, well, perhaps, to understand a little bit of Maria's and Janek's family histories in Poland? How their Catholic families viewed Jews? A little? It couldn't hurt. To fill in a more complete picture, a context, for the stories Rose was telling.

Hey, Maria, how did you learn English? My mother learned it in less than a year.

Because she never wanted to speak Polish again.

"Hi. I'm Eleanor, if you remember from last time? It seems that our sons are working on a science project together? About sharks?"

Maria stood up immediately, her face glowing with a wide smile as she reached out to grasp Eleanor's right hand with both of hers, her Spandex slacks pulled dangerously tight across her thighs, wobbling slightly as her heels sank a quarter-inch into the grass. "Yes, yes, the boy who likes sharks. Yes, Tadek talks much about him. He is good artist, your son." Her accent was rich with deep vowels but not quite as heavy as Janek's; her grammar, like his, was almost correct.

"Yeah. I don't know why my son is so fascinated with sharks."

"There was movie about sharks? I think maybe that is it."

"I suppose it's all those sharp teeth. It's the image of danger." How much could a person say about sharks?

Are there sharks where you come from in Poland?

Did your mother ever make Polish cheesecake?

Did your father throw stones at Jewish stores?

"So I think you said you work in the medical field?" Eleanor asked.

Sort of. Maria was a pharmacy technician at the Edgewood CVS. She took the prescription orders and checked customers' insurance coverage, although she didn't mix the prescriptions herself. Janek was an assistant in the drug company's research labs. "Because we want to help people," Maria said. Also, Maria's father and grandfather had both been pharmacists back in Poland.

Did your grandfather have Jewish customers?

"It's crazy." Maria shook her head. "In Poland the grandmothers are using cabbage leaves, and in America you want always pills. For heart disease, pills. For cholesterol, pills. For sex, pills."

"Yes. Pills. Well." Enough about pills and sex. "Maybe the boys can get together to work on the shark project."

A whistle had blown out on the field — was that good or bad? — oh shit, Janek was striding toward them, shaking his head rapidly, his churning arms propelling him. Oh no. What had Adam done now?

This was the time to say something to Janek!

But Maria had grabbed Eleanor's suggestion as if she were shaking hands on a million-dollar sale, her grammar suddenly jumbled. "Yes, yes, Tadek would like very much. They come to my house, yes? I am finished at the CVS at three o'clock. What day you would like?"

And there was a plan, and a date, and a time, and Adam was going to Tad Wysocki's house next Friday after school, and Janek had pivoted, heading back to the field without injecting a word in their conversation.

Chapter Eleven

"Did boys play a lot of soccer in Poland?"

"Yes," Rose answered, looking straight at Eleanor. "And also basketball."

Did she really say that?

* * *

Rose was sitting on the edge of an armchair in her room at the rehab center, reading a paperback book, probably one of the detective stories Natalie had brought. The room was small and too dark, but at least she wouldn't have to share it with anyone for the month—or more—that she would be staying there. It had a bed with a brown blanket stretched tight and smooth, a beige night-stand, a short dresser made of some sort of thin composite wood that didn't match the nightstand, a TV mounted on the wall across from the bed, a narrow closet, and two Kelly-green armchairs with a small square table between them. Plus, staring directly at the bed, unavoidable, a big bulky wheelchair and a walker. Adam's get-well card was propped on the nightstand, next to Rose and Izzy's wedding photo.

"Do you want to go for a walk?"

"Where?" Rose swerved away from Eleanor. "Where do you think I'm going to walk, with a broken leg? Hip."

"The nurses said you can go anywhere in the wheel—" Oops; what was the point of even bringing up that subject? Why expect that Rose would suddenly be willing to use the wheelchair?

"Fine," Rose declared. "We'll take the walker."

"You're not supposed to use it more than a few steps without an aide."

"Bring it over. I'll show you."

"Ma, they said not to."

Rose glared. "So I just sit here?"

"I can take you in the wheelchair."

"Do you know how boring it is to be sitting here? Well of course you don't."

She should have brought something to keep Rose occupied. She would bring something next time. What? More books? *Newsweek?*

Eleanor sat in the second armchair, and Rose picked up her book again—which she'd nearly finished, to judge by the laminated book-mark—and then Eleanor went into the hall to find a nurse—or an aide—or anyone. However, the weekend staff was minimal, no one was available, no one knew details about Rose's situation, and any-way, after just three days, it was too soon to have much of a progress report. When Eleanor returned, Rose was still reading. Eleanor sat down.

Rose peeked up, then back at her book.

"How's the book?"

Rose looked over at Eleanor again. "If you're bored, you don't have to stay."

"No! Um. So. How do you like Adam's get-well card?"

Then Rose's mouth danced into a quick smile. "Yes, it's very nice. He's a very creative boy."

"Yes, he is."

"If only he would read more."

"You know, he's really gotten absorbed with this science-art project he's doing at school about sharks."

"That's good."

"Yeah, he's working with a kid on his soccer team, from Poland." And?

Rose was carefully sliding her bookmark between two pages and closing her book.

If Rose was going to snap at her—*Why do you keep bringing up Poland?*—okay, then let it happen. But Rose was sure not going to talk unless Eleanor prodded her. Maybe Rose would open up again. Maybe she would have a nice memory that would make her laugh. Even a little. Maybe Eleanor could ask if Poles were obsessed with soccer, which would help explain Janek Wysocki. "Did boys play a lot of soccer in Poland?"

"Yes," Rose answered, looking straight at Eleanor. "And also basketball."

* * *

The book was resting primly shut in Rose's lap. The seat of Eleanor's armchair was too soft; it would be tough to pull herself up eventually. Outside the room, through the open door, the Sunday-afternoon hallway was silent. No one else, apparently, was attempting a stroll with their walker or wheelchair.

"There was a field near the school. The boys had a club. The Maccabee Club." Rose tapped the book cover, in a slow sequence. Third finger, middle finger, second finger, thumb, then back.

"Did Uncle Avram play?" Eleanor finally prompted. "Was he good at it?"

Rose smiled for a moment. "Well, I don't know, but to me, as a little girl, he was good at everything he did. He was my big brother, you understand that?" Eleanor nodded. "I didn't know what they were doing, all those boys running and shouting, with such powerful kicks that you could see the ball flying through the air, but it looked wonderful to me. He hated when I followed him around, of course, so I hid behind a tree to watch him, or behind the school building. The field was near the *gimnazjum*, so if Avram saw me, I could always pretend that I had come to visit our father, you see?"

Eleanor swallowed, still nodding.

"Like you and Steven."

"What do you mean?"

Rose placed her book on the little round table, took off her eyeglasses, and folded them inside the leather eyeglass case that was also on the table. "You don't remember following your brother around?"

"He didn't play soccer."

"You don't remember how you always wanted to see his baseball games? And when his friends came over to watch television, how he asked us to keep you out of the room?"

"Was I that bad?"

"Oh, I think his friends mostly ignored you."

"Did Uncle Avram ever catch you watching him? When you were little?"

"Later, you know, Steven was the one who was jealous of you."

"*What?* When?"

Eleanor leaned forward, resting her crossed arms on the merest edge of the table, leaning into Rose until their faces were almost close enough to kiss each other.

"He admired you, and he was also jealous. All of those French scholarships that you won. The way you went hiking around France after college. We were all very proud of you."

"But—you always told me I was crazy to go camping in France with just a girlfriend. Like I should've stayed in four-star hotels."

"Well. Yes, we worried about you, about the camping. I guess it was Steven who admired that part of your life, more than your father and I did. He felt a bit ordinary, I think, staying on in graduate school while you had such grand adventures. But we all were very proud of your scholarships."

"But Ma, wait a minute—" Dammit, how had Rose managed to move the conversation away from Poland? And therefore away from Janek, too. "Was the Maccabee Club only Jewish boys? Did they have any Catholics?"

Rose shook her head. She tugged slightly at the stretchy fabric of her blue slacks, first the left thigh, then equally the right. "It wasn't like that, Ellie." Licking her lower lip, Rose lifted her head so that she was looking leftwards toward the blank TV screen, not at Eleanor. "Even before Hitler. I told you, Jews and Poles, we mostly kept apart."

Although the TV remote control was on the table next to her, Rose kept staring at the blank screen.

"There was a Polish girl named Agata. Who was very pretty."

Eleanor slid back into her chair.

Pretty Agata. Krystyna with her beautiful dolls. Avram playing soccer. The fancy shops in Warsaw. Once Rose got going, there was a whole — a whole continent full of stories. She simply needed some prompting. If they could talk to her enough, Eleanor and Natalie could recreate Rose's vanished world.

"Agata never played with any of the Jewish girls, of course. But one year, we were nine years old, she invited my friend Salka to her birthday party."

"That was nice of— "

"And then she ignored Salka for the entire party, and all the other little Catholic girls also ignored her. Or else they shoved her this way, that way. They called her a dirty Jew." Rose smoothed the fabric of her slacks again, across her thighs. "After the party was over, Agata told Salka that her parents—Agata's parents—had forced her to invite Salka, only because Salka's parents had done them some sort of favor. I think they helped them read a contract. Maybe because Salka's father was on the town council. And of course everyone knew that Jews were smart."

Now, suddenly, there was noise in the hallway. A voice; the click of heels.

"Well, is that finally one of the nonexistent aides?" Rose sat up straighter to crane her neck. "Ellie, please go see. If I really must have one of them to accompany me."

* * *

Once upon a time a boy named Avram ran and shouted and kicked a soccer ball, and a girl named Agata shoved a little girl named Salka at a birthday party, and Adam kicked a soccer ball, or really he never managed to kick the ball, and a boy named Tad kicked the soccer ball down the field and scored a goal. And another goal. And another. Once upon a time, a little girl named Maria and a little boy named Janek grew up in Krakow, Poland.

Chapter Twelve

The Wysockis' house was on a short, treeless street on the east side of Edgewood, maybe three miles from Eleanor's house and a block away from a strip mall and a line of auto repair shops. Someone had planted two rows of purple and orange impatiens along the brief concrete walkway to the front door, although the flowers were drooping and the concrete was cracked on almost every slab.

At the dining room table, Adam was tracing letters on big sheets of blue construction paper, while Tad bounced up and down on a yellow-cushioned chair next to him. Squeezed into the rest of the room and the adjacent small living room were a china cabinet, a shorter cabinet, a half-sized couch, a torn easy chair, a rocking chair, a TV, and a series of shelves crammed with sports trophies and what looked like wooden eggs painted in bright-colored wavy lines and swirls. The wall above the short cabinet held a large crucifix and a framed photo of Pope John Paul II.

"Tadek and Adam are working very much!" Maria exclaimed happily. Even after a day of taking prescriptions and chasing after cartwheeling Tad, every strand of her blonde hair was exactly in place.

"Yes. Thank you for inviting Adam. Yes."

"Mom, come look!"

"Wow" burst out of Eleanor's mouth. Adam had truly created miracles on the half-done poster, crinkling blue and green tissue paper into waves that seemed to leap off the cardboard and then cutting the gray construction paper into pieces of shark bodies that hid and darted among the waves. With the markers, he'd drawn teeth and eyes on the bits of sharks.

"Adam's a real artist." Tad jiggled his shoulders as he slapped the table-top. Unlike his parents, he had no noticeable Polish accent.

"Will you like to drink coffee while boys do more work?" Maria asked.

Adam and Tad immediately turned to their mothers. "Please, can we stay more?" Adam begged. "*Mamusiu?*" Tad wheedled, hopping up and down in front of Maria.

Tell me about Poland.

"Thank you," Eleanor said. "I'd love a cup of coffee."

* * *

Maria had come to New Jersey from Poland about twenty years ago, through a program to work as a nanny. She started out taking care of a two-year-old girl, then the family had another baby, and then one more little girl after that. The family had sponsored Maria for her green card. They were a very nice family, very wealthy; once the mother even brought Maria with her on a business trip to Paris to take care of the three little girls! They were very sweet girls. Maria had always wanted a little girl of her own, but God gave her boys.

But she was grateful just to have healthy children, when she thought about how old she was when she got married and pregnant at all. Thirty-five, when she married Janek.

She met Janek in America—he had only just arrived from Poland—his cousin had a friend whose wife sometimes sat with Maria at the playground while she watched the little girls—also Polish, of course—and so Maria and Janek got married soon after the nanny job ended. Then quickly came their older son, Konrad, and two years later, Tadek. That is, Tadeusz, that was his full name. Tadek was the Polish nickname. Yes. Tad was the American nickname.

So, finally, when Tadek started school, Maria was able to go to work, to earn a little more money for the family, and she got her job at the CVS pharmacy and her pharmacy technician certification. Also, Janek got a promotion, so that was a lot of good news for them.

"My family, they have stayed in Poland," she continued. "They are my mother and my father, and my brothers and sisters, and then the husbands and wives and children of them. I write letters two times every week to my mother and father, and we talk on telephone every Sunday. I go back to Poland to see them only one time since Konrad and Tadek are born. It is expensive, you know, to take an airplane to Poland, so many of us. And five years ago, my mother dies."

I have relatives who died in Poland, too.

Maria went into the kitchen and returned to the living room with a red-white-and-blue metal tray holding a nearly-full package of Chips Ahoy cookies, two small glasses of milk, two porcelain coffee cups in a pink-rosebud pattern with gilded edges, and a matching plate with some sort of crispy twisted strips of dough, sprinkled with powdered sugar. She placed the tray on top of the short cabinet right underneath the pope.

"This is *faworki*." With a slight nod, she indicated the powdered dough strips. "We are usually eating it only from Christmas to Lent, but I like it too much"—she spread her hands, laughing—"so I cook it a little too soon. Yes?"

Tad immediately dug into the Chips Ahoy bag, and Adam followed.

Damn, Eleanor should have given Adam some snacks to bring with him. To thank Maria for inviting him.

"Tadek plays also baseball," Maria was going on, and she pointed to the shelves of trophies, as she settled into the easy chair across from Eleanor. "These are—medals? No, that is not right. From baseball and from soccer."

"Trophies," Eleanor said. "That's very impressive."

"And Konrad plays sometimes baseball. But most time he plays video games." Maria laughed again. Tad had already returned for more cookies.

"Well"—Eleanor smiled at Tad, then Maria—"Tad certainly is the star of the soccer team. I don't think I've ever seen anyone run so fast."

Instead of beaming back with maternal pride, however, Maria looked a bit sad. "Is not so good. He has ADHD disease, doctors say. You know it?"

"Of course." Eleanor adjusted her smile into a properly serious look. "So I guess soccer and baseball are a good outlet for him? A way to let out some of that energy?"

"Yes, we hope." Maria picked up a piece of the *faworki*. "You teach French language, you said?"

"Yes, at Edgewood High School."

"Why do you teach French language?"

Because my mother refused to speak Polish to me or even talk about Poland, so I switched majors in college.

Eleanor resumed smiling at Maria. "The best teacher I ever had was my high school French teacher. Monsieur Dubois. He told us that he was from Canada and didn't understand a word of English. All the students knew he had to be joking; how could he have gotten a teaching license in the United States if he didn't speak English? But we could never trip him up."

"Trip him up?" Maria frowned.

"Um—Prove that it was a joke. Trick him into speaking English. He taught every single class entirely in French, without using a word of English. He did it with, you know, pantomimes—pointing—facial expressions. And we learned. And we loved it." Eleanor took a gulp of coffee. "And you know, when I was in college, and I needed to fig-ure out what kind of job I could get with my French-history major, well, I said to myself, I want to have that kind of impact. I want to inspire kids like that." She swallowed another gulp. "Actually, I did catch Monsieur Dubois, once. I overheard him talking with another teacher, and of course he was speaking perfectly fluent English, with no accent whatsoever. He saw me, and his face just dropped. I mean, he looked so sad. Because he realized that I had found out his secret. That he really could speak English. And then he winked at me. And I never told anyone that I'd heard him speak English."

Not only were Maria's eyebrows still pulled together in a frown, but now her eyes were squinting and her forehead was deeply wrin-kled. "This teacher talked English, yes?"

Eleanor sighed. "Just to the other teachers. Never to the students. Well," and she flitted one hand toward Maria, picking up her coffee cup with the other, "that's enough about me. Tell me about your fam-ily. I guess your parents, uh, were born in Poland?"

What year? How old were they when they might have been throwing rocks? Or even saving a Jewish family?

Maria was biting into the powdered dough, hunching over her plate.

"Were they in Poland during World War Two?" With one finger, Eleanor traced the gilded porcelain lip of her cup. And then back in the other direction. "It must have been very hard for them."

Maria nodded as she chewed. "Yes, you know, my father says there was not much food. And many bombs. People are scared. But he says, thank God, they are okay, his family. His father has the pharmacy."

"Really?"

"You know, it is Jews that the Germans are killing. We are not Jews."

Tad had returned for yet more cookies.

"They are teenagers, my parents in the war, you know." Maria giggled. "They are already dating, yes? So, I think they are not paying much attention to Germans."

Eleanor's cup hit the table.

* * *

"Let me help clean — I'm so sorry — No, I don't need another—We've got to go. I'm sorry. Yes, thank you, another time."

Chapter Thirteen

Because it was still relatively early for a Friday night, the restaurant that Natalie had chosen was thankfully quiet, the TV screens at the bar showing silent news.

"There's a lot we need to talk about," Natalie began, the minute Eleanor sat down on the other side of the black-leather booth. Before Eleanor even had a chance to utter the name Maria Wysocki.

For one thing, Natalie announced, Rose seemed to be getting worse, not better. "On Monday, she made it all the way to the common room with her walker, without stopping once. But yesterday, she couldn't even finish an entire therapy session. Even after she rested, she barely got from her bed to the chair."

"I thought she was maybe walking better, the last time I saw her?"

"Was that more recently than yesterday?"

Eleanor just shook her head.

Natalie, too, shook her head while she sipped her pale-gold wine. "She's exhausted, Ellie."

That wasn't a reason to stop asking Rose about Poland! "Maybe she should have stayed in the hospital longer?"

"Oh no, it was the right time for her to move. She needs targeted rehab."

"Should we talk to her doctor? Or something?"

"Yes, I put a call in already."

"To slow down the exercises and therapy?"

"Well, let's see what the doctor says. Perhaps a change in medications. Perhaps she was actually progressing unusually fast to begin with, so now she's simply at a normal pace."

"You know Ma really wants to get home."

"Yes, and we both know she always pushes too hard. Refusing the wheelchair, for instance."

Eleanor fiddled in her bag for her cellphone. "Maybe being exhausted is good for her? To keep her from yelling in Polish at the nurses?"

At that, Natalie let out a wine-fueled guffaw. "We needed these drinks," she declared, holding up her glass. The waiter brought Eleanor's wine—the same as Natalie's, whatever—and a small bowl of peanuts, as she glanced at her phone's dark screen.

"And you say *I'm* over-organized?" Natalie pointed to the phone. Her nail polish was dark orange.

"Well, you know, for an emergency? If the rehab center needs to call? Not that I ever hear it ring, half the time. And the rest of the time I don't get bars anyway."

"Even so. I'm never going to buy one of those contraptions. I could never manage it."

"Never? What if the courts require judges to have them someday?"

"I'll retire. Machines don't like me. You know that. Can you imagine me doing Nick's job?" Natalie raised her glass in a toast. "Airplanes truly would crash on January first if I were in charge. *L'chaim.*"

"Who knows if Nick is really doing anything useful?" Eleanor pushed some clusters of peanuts inside the bowl. "Do you get any Y2K cases? People acting crazy because they think the end of the world is coming?"

"Sure. There was one defendant last week who was building an underground bunker to protect himself against Doomsday. Unfortunately, he was building it partially on his neighbor's property."

"That's a good one. What did you do?"

"I told him he had to confine his construction work to his own property, and then I adjourned the determination of damages until mid-January. That made him very happy, since he figured the courthouse would be destroyed on January first and he would never have to show up in court or pay anything."

Eleanor grinned.

A man and woman in matching black suits were sliding into the booth behind Natalie, both of them slapping rectangular leather briefcases on the seats next to themselves. The man had brown hair slicked back, Wall Street-style; the woman's straight brown hair was held at her neck in a sleek ponytail. The man crooked a finger toward the bar.

"I think I was born in the wrong century." Natalie sighed. "I should be writing my decisions with a quill pen and an ink bottle. I love real ink—have you ever tried it? It turns your writing into artwork."

"Hmm, Adam might like that. But would you honestly want to live way back when? Wearing long dresses with corsets?"

"True, I'm not particularly enamored of the corset. Still, tell me the truth, Ellie: Don't you love the vision of yourself gliding down a ballroom floor in a long, silky gown?"

Nope: It was hopeless to picture Natalie in a silky gown, corset or no. With her pumps clicking fast and rhythmically, and her briefcase swinging? "Judges' robes aren't the same as a ball gown, huh?"

Natalie let out another full laugh. "That's a wonderful idea. I think I'll order my next robe in pale-yellow silk, with an Elizabethan neck ruff."

"And a bustle?"

"Better yet, Cavalier-style. Early seventeenth-century England. They cut the women's necklines right below the bottom of the breast." Natalie demonstrated with a slice of her hand across her tailored beige blouse. "So the whole breast hung out. Nipples and all."

Eleanor, caught in the middle of a swallow, spit out some of her wine onto the table and her phone.

"It was a way of advertising that you were unmarried," Natalie added.

"Easier than trying to see if someone's wearing a wedding ring," Eleanor managed to sputter.

Maybe the man and woman behind Natalie hadn't heard. They were both reading stapled sets of papers.

Natalie's smile slid away as she swallowed a deep sip of her wine. "But we didn't come here to talk about fashion, did we?" She placed her wineglass softly on the table. "I wanted to tell you about my conversation with your mother yesterday."

Eleanor put down the cellphone and the napkin she was wiping it with.

"We were discussing nothing in particular. The awful food at the rehab center. One of my cases. And all of a sudden, she looked me in the eye and she said, 'My parents told me she was coming back.

For years, they lied to me, you know.' " Natalie's orange fingernail began tracing lines on the table. "Of course I was bursting to ask, 'Who? Who was coming back?' Or not coming back. However, being a lawyer is good for a few things in life, and one of them is intuiting when to be silent and let the witness keep talking and hang himself with his own words. So I didn't say anything. And after a few seconds, your mother gave her head a little shake, and looked away from me, and then she started talking nonstop for a good five minutes. Which is a long time to talk without stopping." Natalie herself paused. "It was my mother she was talking about."

The big sister. Aunt Chana. Who had played house in Poland with her little sister Ruzia using their mother's enamel pots and pans. Who had cried when the Polish boy called her a dirty Jew. Who had escaped to America.

In Chana's version of the story—the one Natalie and Eleanor had heard so many times—the rich aunt and uncle from Warsaw came to Chana and Ruzia's house in June 1935, when Chana was almost thirteen, and took Chana along with their own children to America for the aunt's sister's wedding. It was a great adventure. Chana got a new dress, and she slept in a cabin with the cousins and aunt and uncle in a big ocean liner. Supposedly, they would be away only for two months. Chana's brother and sisters were too little to go.

But the adventure stretched on and on, until it was autumn, it was time for school, and then it was Rosh Hashanah and Yom Kippur, and Chana should have been home long ago. Instead, she, the aunt and uncle, and the cousins were all crowded into some relatives' apartment in the Bronx, with six kids sharing a single bedroom. Then Chana was sent to the apartment of some other relatives, also in the Bronx, sleeping on the living room couch and going to their American school. It wasn't an adventure any more. She wanted her own family. She wanted her friends and her own school, where everyone spoke the same language as she did, and her own bedroom that she shared with Ruzia.

That was Chana's story, the amazing stroke of luck that got her out of Poland, four years before Hitler invaded. She stayed in the United States, she learned English, and she made American friends. She wrote home regularly, then less regularly, as she got caught up in the life of an American teenager, and her parents wrote to her constantly. Until their letters stopped. By then, with the Nazis in control, any idea of Chana's returning to Poland was out of the question, of course.

There were a lot of missing pieces that Chana had never been able to fill in for Natalie and Eleanor. Was the journey to New York really just for a wedding that somehow got sidetracked, or had the aunt and uncle seen that Hitler was on the rise and secretly laid plans to emigrate? It was hard to believe that a family during the Great Depression, even a wealthy family, would spend all that money on an ocean voyage halfway across the globe simply for a wedding. So then, if it was an escape, perhaps organized long in advance, how much did Chana's parents participate in the secret planning? Whose idea was it to take Chana? How did they manage to extend their tourist visas in the United States? The uncle owned some sort of export-import business, so he may have been able to get more permanent visas, or maybe the American cousins were able to sponsor the Polish relatives.

Whatever the true answers were, Chana eventually married a U.S. citizen, so her status was secure. The aunt and uncle died a year apart in New York—old age, illness; the cousins drifted away. And one day in 1946, a letter arrived in Brooklyn from the little sister Ruzia, miraculously not killed in the Holocaust after all.

Chana taught her daughter and niece how to say "good morning" and "thank you" in Polish, but apparently she never asked her sister what had happened in Poland to the rest of their family. Then she died of lung cancer thirty years ago, before there was a chance to ask anything more.

And now, Rose was talking. For a few days.

"According to your mother, our grandparents told all the rest of the kids—your mother, Uncle Avram, Aunt Feiga—that Chana was merely going to New York for a visit and would be back in Poland before school started." Natalie was staring at her wineglass. "So your mother would ask her parents, every day, every week: 'Has school started yet? When will Chana be home?' They always had an answer. Big storms on the ocean and therefore the ships couldn't travel. A shortage of ship inspectors in America. Very creative answers, apparently. I guess our grandparents had a vivid imagination." Natalie placed one palm flat over the other on the table top. "Plus, there were letters to the family from Chana in America, describing all the places she had visited. A big movie theater in New York, your mother said."

Shifting, Natalie folded her arms on top of the table and bit her lower lip. "Your mother said that she began wearing the clothing that Chana left behind and sleeping with Chana's pillow. And she would tell all her friends stories about her big sister's princess life in New York. Some of the stories were from the letters, but sometimes she invented ideas out of thin air, about how Chana went to elegant parties and ate ice cream every day. I guess she had a vivid imagination, too." Natalie paused, to draw a hand across her forehead. "Even the Catholic girls at school who usually ignored the Jewish girls, they would come over and listen and ask questions when your mother—I guess we should think of her as Ruzia then?—when she told the stories about America. There were also gifts, she said; expensive, special gifts that her big sister was going to bring back with her. Dolls with fancy ball gowns. Doll furniture, doll dishes. Matching dresses for Ruzia. That was always the key, your mother said. That her sister Chana would be back. Any day."

Natalie seemed to be finished. She lifted her wineglass for another sip.

However, she had a few more words left. "Then your mother said: 'Even after the Nazis came, when we knew it was actually better for Chana to stay safe in America. I still told my friends that she was coming back. And I still promised them that I was going to get a fancy doll.' "

Eleanor and Natalie looked at each other.

"My mother said all that?" Eleanor whispered.

"Yeah." Natalie glanced off toward a corner, then at the empty table next to their booth, and finally back at Eleanor. "The lawyer trick doesn't always work. I waited, but she only said that she was tired and I should go. I even asked her—" Natalie winced "—I asked her, 'Was that in the Warsaw Ghetto?' She looked at me as if I were a moron—you know how she can do that."

"Oh yeah."

"She said to me, very distinctly: 'No one survived the Warsaw Ghetto.' And then she outright told me to leave because it was dinnertime."

A waiter had carried a heavy cut-crystal glass of brown liquid plus a wineglass of purple-red to the booth behind Natalie. The man said a few syllables quietly to him; the woman didn't look up from her papers.

Natalie leaned forward, placing her right hand over Eleanor's on the table. "My head is spinning, too."

Once upon a time there was a little girl in a town in Poland named Ruzia who had curly, wild, dark-blonde hair, and shared a bedroom with her big sister, and dreamed of fancy dolls from America.

"We probably should get something a bit more substantial to eat than peanuts, before we get too drunk." Natalie waved toward the waiter as he strode away from the other booth. "I still don't know if we're doing the right thing, pushing your mother to talk."

"I've been meaning to tell you," Eleanor said quickly, "about this Polish family on Adam's soccer team."

* * *

"And they were kissing while our grandparents were being gassed at Treblinka!"

"What do you expect teenagers to do?"

"*What?*"

Natalie swirled her stick of fried zucchini in the bowl of marinara sauce on their table. "They were teenagers. Teenagers have hormones."

"It doesn't bother you?"

"They weren't the ones running the gas chambers, Ellie."

"But they knew."

"Did they? You're the historian, but I thought people didn't really know what was going on at the time."

"They knew that their Jewish neighbors were being taken away!" Eleanor had moved so far forward against the table that maybe it was only her hands, gripping the edge, that kept her from falling into the marinara sauce herself. "They were throwing stones at Jewish stores, what, 'boys will be boys'? You don't think they realized it was only Jewish stores they were targeting? And that girl Agata and all her little friends were calling Ma's friend Salka a dirty Jew?"

"What are you talking about? Who's Agata?"

"You know, even Adam knows it's wrong to throw stones at people."

"They didn't have the freedom under the Nazis to say No."

"But they do now. It's now that Maria giggled about the Holocaust!"

"She didn't giggle about the Holocaust. At least, not the way you described it. She giggled at the idea of her parents dating."

"Dating *during* the Holocaust. La-de-dah, isn't it funny, the Germans are no big deal, let's go out to the movies, it's just some Jews being killed?"

Natalie didn't seem to have anything to say to that, so Eleanor eased herself away from the marinara sauce, back into her seat. "How can I even look at her at the next soccer game?" she muttered.

Natalie made a kind of hmmmm sound.

"Should I tell her I'm Jewish? Should I bring bagels to the next game?"

"That wouldn't prove anything. Everyone eats bagels nowadays. But why would you tell her?"

"Well—Not to be sneaky?"

The couple in the booth behind Natalie were finally snapping their papers together into neat piles, tucking them into their briefcases, and sliding themselves back out of their seats. Natalie picked up another piece of zucchini and held it in front of her face, studying it.

"But it shouldn't matter, should it?" Eleanor went on. "Maria should be horrified by what the Nazis did whether she's talking to someone who's Jewish or Catholic or anything, right?"

"Well, English isn't her first language, is it?"

"No...."

"And you said she doesn't really seem to talk to anybody at the soccer games?"

Eleanor sighed. "So you're trying to say she didn't mean what it sounded like? Or she didn't realize how it would sound? Maybe she actually was trying to say that she knows her family was lucky, because the Jews had it a lot worse? But instead it came out like, 'No big deal, just a bunch of Jews.'"

Natalie merely smiled at her zucchini. "I try to look at issues from every angle, Ellie. That's my job."

Now it was Eleanor who was fiddling with a zucchini strip. She dropped it back into the sauce. Was this why people started smoking, to avoid aimless playing with food? What did Natalie do all day in court, if she didn't have zucchini strips to fiddle with? Roll a pencil around her big judge-desk while witnesses talked?

Both cousins took a sip of white wine, silently.

"Okay, sure." Eleanor put down her wine. "Maria wasn't even alive during World War Two while her parents were kissing in a back alley or whatever they were doing. But she could have asked them about the war, when she was a teenager herself. Weren't they afraid of the Germans at all? What did they think when all the Jews in Krakow were being taken away? She just seems so—so blasé."

With one hand still on the stem of her wineglass, Natalie tapped the table with the nails of the other. "Let me ask you something." She relaxed back into her chair, holding up her glass. "For the sake of argument, let's say that Maria Wysocki's family was a typical Polish Catholic family in Krakow. They weren't rabid Nazis; just ordinary people, like everyone around them. Maybe they didn't really know any Jews. Maybe they were knee-jerk anti-Semitic. Maybe they even got along with their

Jewish neighbors. What do you honestly expect this family to have done in 1939? If you were a nice Polish Catholic, would you have been brave enough to hide a Jewish child in your attic, for instance?"

"No, I know that. But I hope I wouldn't have called that child a dirty Jew, like the girls at the birthday— 'll tell you about that later."

"Just kept your eyes shut and your mouth shut?"

"Yeah. Well. I wouldn't have taught my kids that killing Jews is something to giggle about."

"And if you were an ordinary, middle-class, white mother in Alabama in the 1960s: Would you have let your children go to a school that black children were trying to integrate?"

"Yes! Well, I hope so."

"And if you knew that mobs were going to be throwing stones?"

"Now you're cheating. You're involving my kids and their possible safety."

"So you wouldn't have had the courage?"

"Not to risk my kids' safety, no."

"Okay, then, let's try an example without kids. If you were the manager of a Woolworth's in Mississippi back then: Would you serve black customers at your lunch counter?"

"I hope so, Natalie. I hope I would have had the decency. I hope my parents would have raised me that way."

Natalie nodded at the plate of zucchini sticks, almost empty now. "Or if your parents had been in a lynch mob, stringing up the civil rights workers who tried to register blacks to vote?" she went on, softly, but unstoppably. "Should those civil rights workers' children hold your parents' action against you?"

"Okay, okay. Enough what-ifs. What do I say to Maria Wysocki?"

Natalie spent a long time staring at the last few zucchini sticks, although she didn't take any.

"Do I have to say anything?"

"Okay," Natalie finally replied. "Here's my verdict, if you will: Most likely your friend Maria's parents and grandparents were no more brave or less anti-Semitic than any other Polish Catholics. They didn't save any Jews, and they didn't turn in any Jews. They shut their eyes and survived, and as Maria was growing up, they made it clear that they didn't want to talk about the war. And she saw no reason to keep asking. Why would she? So in other words," and now Natalie looked full at Eleanor, "there's no reason to say anything at all to her. You can't blame her for anything her family might have done before she was born. And you certainly can't blame her for what happened to our relatives."

"No. You're wrong. I can blame Maria for giggling."

"Ellie—"

"Someone has to take responsibility! At some point, already." Eleanor shoved the plate of zucchini strips, lined with drying yellow grease, toward her cousin. "Don't tell me I can't blame her."

Chapter Fourteen

You were going to take Adam to soccer this week.

That was supposed to be the agreement, mapped out after their fight at dinner three weeks ago. Nick would specifically request today off from work. Eleanor would take Kate to synagogue in the morning for Shabbat services, while Nick went with Adam to the soccer game that he allegedly thought was so important.

But Nick was standing at the kitchen table, wearing his navy-blue windbreaker, holding a cup of black coffee and glancing at the *Times* sports page as he bit off a hunk of a croissant, ready to head out to his computers. While Adam was still sound asleep.

Eleanor could have reminded him.

For what? To start another fight?

"See you tonight," he said, his mouth full, leaning over to give her a quick, croissant-flaky kiss on the cheek. "I'll phone you later." Which he wouldn't.

And he actually called out, "Good luck to Adam at his game."

So Nick remembered that there was a soccer game, huh?

What was the point of arguing? He would still go to work, whatever Eleanor said. Kate obviously wouldn't mind missing services. And if Eleanor took Adam to his game, she would have a chance to see Maria Wysocki. And Ben's dad, and anyone else.

Yep: Maria—wearing bright blue today, including stiletto heels—waved rapidly from her chair, as Eleanor and Adam walked slowly down the concrete path from the parking lot, Adam's arms swinging limply. Janek was already in position at the sideline, and Tad was running circles around Mark, literally. Ben's dad was gesturing to a couple of other men.

Mark, too, turned and waved.

The blue-and-white Hornets moved into their places across the field, and so did seven boys in red and white. Four lines, three boys in each, two goalies. When Mark waved faster, Adam dragged his feet through the grass toward one of the blue-and-white lines.

Eleanor should have said something more at the Wysockis' house yesterday, the minute Maria giggled. Or even earlier, when Maria said it was only the Jews who were getting killed. But it had all been too sudden. Just like when Janek had yelled at Adam at the first soccer game, dammit, Eleanor kept missing her chance. And now that she had waited overnight, she would need a more natural-seeming, casual way to launch a conversation with Maria.

She could compliment Tad, as soon as he scored a goal, which was bound to happen quickly enough. Or she could say how nice it was that the two boys had worked together on the sharks project. Yes—and then she'd thank Maria for the powdered dough, and promise to bring bagels next time, and *voilà!* She'd be letting Maria know she was Jewish, or at least hinting, and with that as an opening, she could move into the topic of giggling and Jew-killing.

Didn't your parents feel bad, you know, that their Jewish neighbors were being dragged off to concentration camps?

Oh, they didn't have Jewish neighbors.

Didn't they, um . . . .

Didn't they have any decency at all?

Flashes of blue and white, and of red and white, were racing up and down the field. Parents and kids and coaches were shouting. Janek was shouting and thrusting his arms into the air.

Suddenly, there was an electric jumble of noises.

Shouts. Whistles. Fierce, intense screams. Clapping, hoots, hollers.

The boys from the other team were dashing up to each other, high-fiving and laughing, while Janek was yelling louder than Eleanor had ever heard, yelling and red-faced and pounding one fist into the other, "IDIOT! AN IDIOT!" and the ref was blowing and blowing his whistle over and over, and some blue-and-white Hornet boys were yelling, and even some of the parents from Adam's team were talking loud and angrily, while over on the opposite side of the field people were laughing vivaciously, and suddenly Adam was charging toward her, past her, tearing past all the grown-ups, straight to the far corner of the fence, with his hands covering his face.

Maria was somehow standing next to Eleanor. "I am sorry, Janek, my husband, he gets too much excited."

Mark was on her other side, his fingers lightly on her upper arm. "I'll go talk with Adam. It's okay."

"But what—?"

Mark sucked in a breath and released it. "Adam just scored a goal for the other team, by accident." He gave Eleanor's arm a quick squeeze. "Look, why don't you bring him a half-hour—"

She pushed Mark away.

"I'll go to Adam. I'm his mother," she snapped.

* * *

Adam was crouched against the chain-link fence, facing the parking lot with his butt to his team, curled into a cramped, blue-and-white C. His head was tucked into his chest, cradled by his crossed arms. He shivered, briefly, when Eleanor crouched beside him.

Anything she said would be the wrong thing.

Hugging him would definitely be too babyish.

"Hey," she said quietly. "Want to go get some pizza?"

"NO! Pizza's not *healthy*."

"Ummm. How about a carrot?"

No response. No movement.

"How about if we sit in the car?" she asked.

He stood up this time, but wordlessly, still staring at the grass. He followed about a yard behind Eleanor as they trudged to the parking lot, taking the long route next to the fence, away from the Hornets' field, and he managed to get into the front passenger seat without ever lifting his gaze above ground level. She took the driver's seat, also looking down, not at him. She did not turn on the ignition.

They sat, for a minute at least.

"So you feel like you messed up," Eleanor finally said, speaking to the steering wheel.

Adam's breathing was coming out in short, hard thrusts of air. When Eleanor tried to squeeze a glimpse at the passenger side out of the corner of her eyes, he didn't seem to be moving. His neck was craned downward like a gooseneck lamp, his eyes focused on his dirty sneakers.

"We all mess up, you know," she said.

The noises from the far-off fields were only faint wisps, and it was too soon for players to be arriving for the next round of games. For the moment, the car was a cocoon, a spaceship that no one else could touch.

"Next week someone else on the team will do something— "

"Not as bad as I did!"

She nodded.

"Everyone won't laugh at them," Adam went on, spitting out his words.

"Maybe."

"They won't make their team lose."

"Maybe."

"They won't make the stupidest mistake you can make in soccer."

Without the heater turned on, a chilly edge was beginning to seep into the car.

"Maybe we can talk to the coach," Eleanor began.

"No! I don't want to talk to anyone."

Adam's voice halted abruptly. A few spots away, a car was pulling into the parking lot. Late for their current game? Early for the next one? Faintly, through the closed window, there was a whistle from the daily Amtrak run, heading north from Philadelphia.

Silence was bad. It would expand until it smothered. The conversation needed to keep going—not about Adam's dreadful mistake during this game, of course, nor about future Hornets games, but about almost any other topic. To maintain connection. Like with Rose. Keep talking.

"You know, I just learned that your uncle played soccer in Poland."

Adam inched his glance partway toward Eleanor. "Uncle Steven?"

"Oh—no, I mean, *my* uncle. Your Great-Uncle Avram."

Adam's attention returned to the floor.

"You're named for him."

"How come I never met this uncle?"

"Um. Well. He died in World War Two."

Adam let out a sharp exhale.

Oops, that maybe wasn't the best way to inspire Adam: Uncle plays soccer and dies.

"So how do you like the idea of blue and gold? That's what Kate wants for her bat mitzvah colors."

Adam shrugged.

"Well. So, some of my French students are writing a play about Pocahontas...." No, dammit, Adam had hated the Disney movie. A *girl* movie.

"Remember," Eleanor tried again, "at Kate's piano recital, when I dropped my piece of cake on the piano teacher's shoe?"

Now a little grin began to flirt with the edges of Adam's mouth. However, he kept his eyes focused downward.

"The piano teacher jumped like she'd been bitten. Remember that? I wanted to sink into the carpet."

After enough time to breathe in and out, Adam moved his head the slightest inch, so that, again, he was almost looking at Eleanor. "Was the teacher mad?"

"Well, I think that's partly why Kate quit piano lessons. She was too embarrassed to face the teacher ever again."

"But you didn't want her to quit?"

"Nope."

Another breath.

"But I never took piano lessons," he muttered.

"Well, you really wanted to go to art club instead. And that turned out great, didn't it?"

Adam stared at his lap.

Further down the parking lot, a new car was arriving.

"Can I go home and watch my *Star Wars* video?"

Eleanor had to keep her voice steady and her breathing soft, normal, under control. "Sure." Her hand inched over, hovered, and briefly patted Adam's knee. Then she turned the key in the ignition.

"Do I have to keep playing soccer?"

She looked right and left toward the lanes of the parking lot. She didn't answer.

Chapter Fifteen

It had been too long since college. She needed to refresh her knowledge of Polish history, if she wanted to have a real talk with Maria. But there was no telling where her old textbooks were; she'd probably left them in cartons in her parents' house in Teaneck, which meant Rose would've thrown them out after Izzy died and she sold the house and moved to her apartment. What Eleanor ought to do was get herself to the big New York City research library on Fifth Avenue in Manhattan, but how the hell would she squeeze that in, with teaching and Rose and if she could ever drag Kate to services or Adam back to soccer? The crappy little county library ten minutes away was open on Sunday afternoons. That would have to be a starting point.

Nick could damn well take a few hours off and spend some time with Adam, while Eleanor went to the library. Father-son bonding. Guys' Day Out. Especially after poor Adam's disaster at the game.

("Can you just tell Adam a couple of embarrassing stories about times you flubbed really badly in basketball?" she asked Nick.

He winced. "Actually, uh? I never really flubbed — but that's okay, I'll make something up. Don't worry.")

"Guys' Day tomorrow?" he said to Adam at dinner.

"Can we see *Sixth Sense*?" Adam asked immediately. "None of my friends've seen it 'cause it's PG-13."

"You jerk," Kate told him. "You're not supposed to tell Mom and Dad it's PG-13. Then they'll say No."

But all Nick asked was if the PG-13 was due to sex or violence, and when Kate said violence, he said, okay. And ice cream? Adam asked. Okay again.

Eleanor smiled around the white-topped table at everyone.

"That doesn't mean Mom and I have to do Girls' Day, does it?" Kate demanded.

* * *

For a thousand years before Ruzia and her family, Jews had been living in Poland. In fact, it had probably been the best place in Europe to be Jewish, back in the fourteenth century and also in the sixteenth. King Casimir the Great had invited Jews who were persecuted or expelled anywhere else in Europe, to move to his country—which meant, hey, that Eleanor's great-great-etc-grandparents could originally have been French, and then fled to Poland.

On the other hand, Poland maybe wasn't such a great place for Jews, being so religious, so heavily Catholic, and the priests constantly stirring up pogroms against the "Christ-killers." Pogroms that Maria's and Janek's ancestors joined? Why not?

It probably didn't help, too, that the main career paths available to Jews were as traders or as tax collectors for the nobility. Oh wonderful: Showing up at Maria's great-great-etc. grandparents' little hut, demanding money.

With a book on the history of Poland propped open in front of her on the long, laminated library table, Eleanor scribbled furiously in a marble composition notebook.

Yeah, it was starting to become familiar again, from those couple of years of college classes. Poland as a nation disappeared in 1795, carved up by Prussia, Russia and Austria-Hungary. Then, hurray! World War One gave Poland back its independence and a new Golden Age. Democracy, equal rights, a flowering of arts and culture, Yiddish theater, Socialism, Zionism, yada yada. Jews and Catholics attended public schools and universities together. Ruzia played with her Catholic friend Krystyna while her friend Salka's father joined the Socialists. Altogether, more than three million Jews were living in Poland by the time of World War Two, the largest single Jewish grouping in Europe outside of Russia.

But it was during that supposed Golden Age that Agata and the girls at her birthday party were spitting at Salka.

Jews might have been allowed to enroll in the university along with Catholics, but only up to a quota. The older, ultra-religious Jewish generation, the women with their wigs and the men with their uncut beards and long black coats, seemed alien and creepy to modernized Catholic Poles. A lot of that generation didn't even speak Polish—perhaps like Ruzia's grandmother, who had wanted Avram to carry a clove of garlic at his bar mitzvah.

At any rate, the worldwide Depression pretty much destroyed any pretense of a multiethnic Golden Age and reinforced all the thousand-year-old resentments. The sturdy Polish peasant versus the effete-intellectual Jewish-Socialist shopkeeper. The rich Jews who had gold hidden in the walls of their houses. Starting around 1935, the situation got a lot worse, even before Hitler ever set one jackboot across the border. That was when the Fascist *Enderja* flourished, and thugs threw stones at Jewish schoolboys and pulled old men's beards. Maria's father? Grandfather? Jewish-owned stores were boycotted. There were pogroms in Grodno, Przytyk, Minsk Mazowiecki, Brzesc nad Bugiem, and Czestochowa between 1935 and 1937.

Where the hell were Grodno, Przytyk and all those unpronounceable places? Had she studied them in college? Were they near Warsaw?

It was in 1935 that Chana left. The aunt and uncle must have heard about the pogroms. Or been victims of them?

In all of Chana's stories, had she ever said the name of the town their family came from?

"Christ," Natalie exhaled, when Eleanor called from her cellphone, just outside the library building. "My mother did mention the name of the town a few times, but I don't think I could pronounce it, let alone spell it."

"Did it sound like—" Eleanor looked at her notebook—"Grodno? Or Pruh—um—Pruh-zee-teek? That's spelled P-R-Z-Y-T-Y-K."

"You've got to be kidding."

"Well, it's Polish. All Z's and K's and Y's."

"You're the one who's good at languages."

"French is nothing like Polish. The pronunciation rules are totally different. For instance, Polish has two different Ls— "

"Ellie, I don't know."

Only Czestochowa was a big enough town to be on the map of Poland in the library's atlas—yes, because, it had a famous shrine. The Black Madonna. It was pretty far away from Warsaw, toward the south. Krakow was further south. And—what the—Krakow was less than forty miles from Auschwitz.

Janek's and Maria's families had lived less than forty miles from the ovens at Auschwitz.

How far, practically speaking, was forty miles? Could the stench from burning bodies reach forty miles? If the wind was blowing in the right direction?

But of course Maria's and Janek's families had to know, even without the smell. There were too many people arrested and shipped off to the death camps—Jews and non-Jews—not to notice. Intellectuals, civic leaders, anyone who helped Jews, plus their whole families. Six million Poles, altogether.

Except, apparently, for Maria's family, who had their nice safe pharmacy and spent the war years smooching. *We are not Jews.*

The library was closing in forty-five minutes. Eleanor could check out the Polish history book, and there was also a book on World War Two that she hadn't gotten to yet, but really, she'd drained this place. She needed to get to the Manhattan research library—or better still, she should learn how to do research on the World Wide Web. That was what people were doing nowadays, instead of going to libraries.

Half a shelf away from Poland was France. There was an idea! She could teach her Advanced French students a little about the shameful role of Vichy France, when the French government collaborated with the Nazis. The kids probably thought France had spent the entire war valiantly fighting Hitler. They should have their eyes opened up a little. Eleanor could give a World War Two lesson in very simple sentences, using vocabulary words the class already knew. *Au cours de la deuxième guerre mondiale, malheureusement, les français n'étaient pas courageux.* And there was a better chance she might have saved the French history books somewhere at home. Of course, she probably ought to ask her principal for permission first, since it wasn't in the standard curriculum.

One final quest in her forty-five minutes: Did the library have any books where she could look up information about new drugs and drug trials? The three-hundreds, across the hall, the reference librarian said.

No, the three-hundreds were useless. Books about the U.S. presidency and military history on one shelf. The evils of the drug companies, oil companies, and tobacco in another section. Also unhealthy food. Nothing that could really help a person decide whether to buy stock in a company that did drug trials, to pay for a bat mitzvah for a daughter who didn't want one.

Damn.

The library was firmly closed behind her, and she'd forgotten to get Adam a book on oceans.

* * *

"Ma?"

Rose was snoring softly, lying on her right side. Her room was way too warm, even after Eleanor took off her own windbreaker.

What was the name of your town in Poland?

How did you survive?

Why are you talking now?

As quietly as she could, Eleanor pulled a chair close to the side of the bed where she could see Rose's face. The library book on World War Two was screaming to Eleanor from her shoulder bag, useless though it probably was. Would Rose be annoyed, when she woke up, to see her daughter reading about Poland? With this newly talkative Rose, there was no way to predict. But she was still snoring, so Eleanor opened the book and quietly flipped past the introduction, to Chapter One, keeping it half-covered by her bag. She glanced toward the bed; Rose was still sleeping.

When Eleanor looked up again, Rose was sitting propped against the headboard and staring at the wedding photo on her nightstand. Shoving her bag and library book under her chair, Eleanor leaned over to kiss her mother. "Hi, Ma. Um. How did your therapy go today?"

"I didn't do it today." Still looking at the photo.

"Oh. Why not?"

"He proposed to me," Rose said softly, "the day he was offered his first job. In 1949. A week before he graduated from Columbia. He told me he waited until he was sure he could support me, the right way."

"I know. That was the assistant manager's job at Gimbel's, right?"

"I'm an old lady, I'm allowed to repeat stories. I'm sure I've told you a million times how we met?"

"Aunt Chana's friend's mother set you up. And you were annoyed, because you wanted to be a modern American woman, and you didn't need a matchmaker like back in the *shtetl*."

Rose nodded. "Today is Sunday," she added, finally looking at Eleanor. "The physical therapist doesn't work on Sundays. That's the most exciting news around here, the change in schedule."

"That seems stupid in a place devoted to physical therapy, not to actually have therapy one day every week."

"It's just as well. I'm tired of all these exercises. The same exercises, every day. Slide your heel toward your *tuchas*. Slide it back. Ten times. Slide your whole leg. Point your toes. Slide it back. Ten more times. I can't even remember all of them. And then they come back again, in the morning, in the afternoon. Sometimes three times a day."

"Um."

"What for? I don't notice that I'm walking any faster."

"You're not getting any better?"

"I'm just tired of this nonsense."

"What town did you live in?"

They both stared at each other, wordless, for perhaps a second, perhaps more.

"In Poland," Eleanor added.

"You and Natalie," Rose snapped. "Why are you all of a sudden asking about Poland?"

"You started it!"

Looking down at her blanket, Rose clasped her fingers together, gripping hands with herself. Her engagement ring with its petite diamond was wedged right below her yellow-gold wedding band.

"Were the Jewish and Catholic kids friends? Like you and Krystyna? Did you go to school with them?"

Rose shut her eyes.

She was wearing a light-green blouse with a darker green cardigan; the cardigan had slipped partway off her left shoulder.

"We got along when we had to." She opened her eyes and coughed; her voice was slightly hoarse again. "I went with my mother to the market every week when I was little, and the Polish farmers were all there, at the stalls. Where we bought the food." Briefly, she smiled. "You brought your own can for the milk, and they poured it from their big metal cans into yours. But Ellie, you understand, with Krystyna, that was very unusual." She rubbed a palm against her neck, from the back almost to the front. "Maybe it was better in the big cities like Warsaw, with more educated people."

Another silence. Was that all? Milk cans?

"One birthday, I think I was six years old. Maybe seven. Chana was still living with us. I had a new dress." Rose ran her hands down her blanket, almost as if she were straightening the skirt of her new birthday dress. "A pink dress that tied with a big bow in the back. I remember this. We weren't poor, but I didn't get a new dress very often, not even for a birthday—you know, I wore Chana's old dresses—so this was very special, my new pink dress. And of course it was pink for my name, Ruzia. Ruzia means a rose." She glanced at Eleanor. "There. I just taught you a new vocabulary word in a foreign language. So, I didn't want to take it off. I even slept in it that night, and then I insisted to wear it the next day."

A stubborn little girl with dark-blonde curls. A little girl who adored her big sister but was maybe tired of her sister's hand-me-downs.

"Someone was sick that morning, I suppose my brother or one of my sisters. My mother sent me to the pharmacy for some medicine. And the pharmacist—" Rose halted. She sucked in her top lip, then released it. "He was very tall, and he stood behind his counter, and he stared down at me, and I was still wearing my special brand-new pink dress, and he said in a voice cold as ice, 'Of course a Jew would wear a dirty dress. Go home and come back when you're clean.'" This time, Rose sucked in her cheeks. "I would not go back. My mother had to go."

It took too long for Eleanor to move her arm, to try and reach for Rose's hand, and then Rose's hand was too far away, and Eleanor had to stand up and walk closer.

"He was a Nazi, that pharmacist. After the Germans took over—" Rose pulled her hand away from Eleanor. "I don't want to talk about him. What time is it? It's probably close to dinner time."

With her freed-up hand, Eleanor rubbed her nose, then let her fingers slide down so that they cupped her mouth. She exhaled into her palm, twice. "What is it with pharmacists and Poland?" She almost managed to keep her tone light-hearted. "Is everybody in Poland a pharmacist? Like Koreans coming to New York and opening fruit stands?"

"What do you mean?"

"It's just that there's this family from Poland on Adam's soccer team, I think I told you, and the mother works in a pharmacy, and her father was a pharmacist, too, back in Poland. But they're from Krakow," Eleanor added quickly.

"I don't know. We had two or three pharmacies in our town, but the Nazi was the closest to our apartment. It wasn't like the drugstores in the United States today, you know." Shaking her head, Rose tugged more forcefully at the blanket. "You didn't buy a prescription ready-made in a bottle. They mixed it right there, in the shop. Oh, the grandparents, the superstitious old people, they still used the *feldshers*. The—what would you call them? Barbers, I think they were. Or they would do—oh it was nonsense, with cabbage leaves, and then the glass cups on your back to get rid of fever. Stupid old superstitions." Rose gave an abrupt wave. "But my parents were modern, so we went to the pharmacy."

A Nazi pharmacist. A brand-new pink dress. Rose refused to speak Polish when she came to America, but she chose an American name identical to her Polish name. It was as though she was begging to talk— but then she always stopped. She pushed away the hands, the squeezes, the hugs. What was the magic question that would keep prying open her lips and let her accept a hug, before she came up with another excuse to stop? Or got angry? Or, maybe, grew too sick to talk?

"So when this pharmacist got nasty, was there another—?" Eleanor began.

This time, it wasn't Rose who shut off the questioning. There was a timid knock on the open door, and Rose's friend Anna was hovering in the doorway holding a huge bouquet of some sort of white and pink and purple flowers.

* * *

"Adam? We need an adjective," Nick commanded.

"Smelly!"

"You always say 'smelly,' " Kate protested. "Didn't he use that already, Dad?"

"Okay—stinky!"

Kate rolled her eyes.

"Stinky," Nick repeated, writing it down on the Mad Libs page. "Kate, your turn now. A noun."

"Earrings."

"Hey Mom!" Adam called out. "The movie was really good, and I figured it out and Dad didn't."

A nearly empty bowl of popcorn rested, slightly tilted, on the scuffed wooden coffee table in the den. Nick was sitting behind it, on the leather couch, while Kate—with blue hair today—curled up a few feet further down the couch, and Adam sat cross-legged on the carpet, leaning against his father's legs. All three sets of hands took turns dipping into the popcorn.

"I knew there was something fishy about the movie," Adam was saying, while he chewed, " 'cause at the beginning he gets shot right in the stomach and he bleeds so much, right? And then in the next scene, he's not even limping or anything? Like he wasn't even hurt."

Nick shook his head. "I was completely fooled. I confess. Thank you, Adam, for not giving away the secret before the end."

"And I drew Grandma another get-well card," Adam added.

It wasn't that long ago, was it, that the four of them used to do things like this every Saturday night? Family Night at the Movies: They all went to the video store to choose the movie together. Some weeks the kids picked the newest Disney cartoon—*The Lion King*,

Toy Story, Hunchback of Notre Dame—but some weeks she and Nick introduced them to older classics, like the *Marx Brothers* and *ET*. Of course, there were also weeks when the kids fought and couldn't agree on any movie. But Nick always made popcorn and lemonade, with Kate and Adam cuddling on the couch between their parents.

And in Poland, in 1939, in whatever the name of their town was, it would have been Grandpa the schoolteacher on the couch, with Ruzia, Feiga, and Avram—Chana would have been safely off in America by then—and they might have been snacking from a bowl of—what? Fruit? What kind of fruit did they have in Poland? They didn't have bananas, Chana said. Maybe that special cheesecake that Grandma made for birthdays? And maybe Grandma would come in then, to say that she'd just heard the news on the radio: Germany had invaded.

Chapter Sixteen

Eleanor waited in her car, in the driveway.

Of course Kate would take her sweet time changing her clothes and coming back downstairs. She would be delighted to create any excuse to be late for Shabbat services. Well, Eleanor was not delighted, but Kate was not going to the synagogue dressed like a—a—junkie. No, she didn't need a pink birthday dress with a big bow like her grandmother had in Poland, but she would not be allowed to wear torn jeans and a so-called shirt that looked like a bra. Not to mention hair the color of a honeydew melon, but there was nothing Eleanor could do about that right now.

It was ten full minutes since Eleanor had sent Kate to change her clothing. And if that girl didn't show up at the car in two more, Eleanor would march right into their house and dress Kate herself, twelve years old or not. Dammit.

This was not going to make the prospect of a bat mitzvah any more appealing to Kate.

Why did everything have to be so damn hard?

And Nick was sitting in the den counting the seconds on the clock, no doubt.

Making such a big deal about how he was taking time away from his precious work of saving the world, first by seeing the movie with Adam last Sunday, and now staying home for two hours with Adam while Eleanor and Kate went to services. A whole two hours.

Where was the Nick who had talked about wanting to be a dad way back in college? That was another quality that made him so different from all the beer-drinking, junk-food-eating, partying guys at NYU. When Nick and Eleanor finally decided, a few years after grad school, that it was time to think seriously about having a baby, he was as excited as a kid whose own birthday was coming. Right away, he grabbed two pairs of scissors, one for each of them, to cut up her diaphragm. And that first year, month after month, every time she walked out of the bathroom holding her package of tampons and slowly shaking her head, he was there. He didn't say much; he hugged her and baked chocolate chip cookies for her. And the next month. And the next. Until, finally, Eleanor showed him the little blue "plus" sign on the home pregnancy test. And his smile had grown, slowly at first, like he couldn't believe it, then faster, wider and wider, and he'd grabbed her and kissed her so hard —"You want to make a twin for the baby now?" and she'd cracked up.

Nick read all the baby books along with Eleanor, and he helped her write the list for the suitcase for the hospital: toothbrush, extra socks, nursing bra, camera, soothing picture of a forest to tape on the delivery-room wall. He gripped her hand so tight that it almost hurt more than some of the contractions—well, the early contractions—and his voice was hoarse. He kept giving the midwife instructions: "You're hurting her! Slow down! Hurry up!"

He was the first one to diaper Kate.

He pureed fresh fruits and vegetables. No canned Gerber's for Nick Phillips's daughter.

And then, when Kate was almost one year old, Nick took her to the bagel shop and put her, in her car seat, on top of a table while he went to get napkins and cream for his coffee. Somehow she rocked, or she rolled, and he hadn't belted her in right, and she fell off the table, out of the car seat and right onto the floor. Hard. She screamed. Terrified, his heart galloping, his lungs jammed, he knelt down on the floor and stared at her eyes to see if they were rolling back in her head. Or if one pupil looked bigger than the other, or if blood was pooling up. He felt all around her thick, dark-blonde hair searching for cuts, bumps, blood, anything horrible that he didn't want to find, while she screamed and cried more, and he hardly dared to move her.

The thing was, Nick could have kept the incident a secret. Eleanor hadn't been at the bagel shop. Kate had no obvious injuries. She stopped screaming after Nick cuddled her for a couple of minutes, and she was certainly far too young to blab out the story herself. Nick could have come home, la-de-dah, we had a great time, Daddy and daughter shared a bagel. But he had told Eleanor the truth. He was still shaking and shivering so badly when he walked through the front doorway, his face was white, and he practically shoved Kate into Eleanor's arms, as he burst out crying. "Don't trust me with her again. I'm no good. I can't do this right."

So where was that Nick now, eleven years later? Didn't he want to be a father anymore? Okay, it would be an exaggeration to say that he loved his computers more than his kids. Y2K, world coming to an end, very busy, yada yada. Yet what kind of job could he have, that would demand its employees' total devotion seven days a week? Was his work just a pretense? Was he having an affair?

Suddenly the car door was being tugged open. Kate had actually returned without being fetched, wearing a white T-shirt that at least covered most of her stomach.

"Are you satisfied? I thought you were in such a hurry to be Jewish." Kate plopped herself in the shotgun seat and crossed her arms.

"Thank you. Put your seat belt on."

"What if I wore a fancy dress and had my nose pierced? Would that make you happy?"

"Let's just deal with your clothing for now."

* * *

Kate strode immediately to Joanna, Rachel, and her other friends in the farthest-back pew, promptly and ostentatiously becoming the giggly, happy, talkative girl she had studiously not been in the car with her mother.

Never mind; at least she was here.

Apparently, it was someone's bar mitzvah. A short boy in a dark-blue suit was very slowly and carefully chanting the Hebrew of his Torah portion, while three rows of relatives beamed, arrayed in a semicircle of blonde wood and plush blue-velvet cushions facing the Torah ark, and three other rows of thirteen-year-old-looking boys in uncomfortable button-down shirts and blazers poked each other in the ribs.

A year from now, how many people would be sitting in those same blonde-wood seats for Kate's bat mitzvah? Rose and Natalie and Gary. Steven and Leah and their three kids. Nick's parents; his brother and the brother's girlfriend of the moment. Half-a-zillion friends of Kate's. Maybe even a few friends of Nick and Eleanor's, like Susan. It was a cheerful room, with sunlight streaming through two-story-tall stained-glass windows. Not such a terrible prison for Kate, was it?

In their discreet pew, Kate and her friends were leaning together and giggling.

The bar mitzvah parents had walked up to the *bimah* to join their son, and the mother started to read a special blessing that, she said, she'd written herself. She dabbed at her eyes. What kind of blessing could Eleanor write for Kate next year? It had to be positive, loving, praising: "Ever since you were born, you have had an independence of spirit that I admire ..." In other words: "You never listen to me."

Would Nick stand up at the *bimah* with Eleanor and give his daughter a blessing?

For his sermon, the bar mitzvah boy read in a monotone about Abraham and Sarah getting their new names from God, and how his parents selected his name, which was Ethan (little whispers among the relatives), and the meanings of some names ....

Eleanor had chosen Adam's name in honor of his dead Great-Uncle Avram, whether Rose cared or not. Officially, Kate was not named for anyone in particular, and Eleanor and Nick told people it was meant to evoke strong Katherines and Kates of the arts, like Katharine Hepburn and Shakespeare's Katherine in *The Taming of the Shrew*. At that time, Nick didn't even know about the Jewish tradition of naming people for relatives who'd died, though he said it was a nice idea when Eleanor explained it. And the strong-Katherine motivation was true, partly. However, the real truth, at least for Eleanor, was that Kate was half-named for Aunt Chana, because of the matched K and hard-CH sounds, though Eleanor would never say that publicly, since it seemed an insult to Natalie, who ought to have the first right to name a child after her own mother. If she ever had kids. Which was getting less and less likely by the time Kate was born, but nevertheless.

So then why had Rose and Izzy called their children Steven and Eleanor? The names didn't tie in with obvious ancestors like Avram and Feiga. Perhaps they were in honor of the grandparents — Chana and Rose's parents; did Natalie remember their names? Did Chana ever mention them? Or Eleanor and Steven could have been named for dead relatives of Izzy's. Which was, in fact, a more likely explanation, if Rose didn't want to be reminded of Poland and her lost family every time she looked at her own kids.

The bar mitzvah boy had finished his drone-speech, and a woman in a lavender suit made announcements. Then a man made announcements. The choir sang. There were more prayers, in English, in Hebrew. *Shabbat shalom*. The services were over. Yarmulkes rustled. Was there any part of this that Nick would possibly enjoy? For that matter, was there any part that Kate would like?

Shit, it was ten minutes beyond Nick's two-hour deadline, and they still had a twenty-minute drive home.

Kate and her clique were halfway to the exit. "Joanna's mom is taking us to a restaurant for lunch," Kate declared, over her shoulder. "I'm going to have a BLT. Or else a ham sandwich. Whatever's not Jewish."

Eleanor's cellphone, when she remembered to check it, had three missed messages from Nick.

He called again, just before Eleanor reached their street, and he was backing out of the gravel driveway before her car door was open.

Adam wasn't even dressed in his white and blue yet. His game was supposed to begin in half an hour. "My stomach hurts," he claimed, limping into the kitchen. "Maybe I should skip soccer today."

"No!"

Dropping her keys on the wooden chair next to her, Eleanor squatted down to face Adam, wobbled a moment and lightly kneaded his shoulders. "Remember last year? Remember how you would all gather after the game, the whole team, and those special cheers you did?"

He shook his head vehemently.

"And the pizza party at the end of the season?"

"That was last year."

"They'll have another party this year."

"They'll just make fun of me."

"No they won't, honey. They've already forgotten about last week."

"No they haven't."

She took a breath.

She couldn't ask him, "Adam, are you really really really sick?" Because he would answer yes, even though he wouldn't look at her while he said it.

She shouldn't say: "Okay, you can quit soccer." The parenting books would say that a mother shouldn't give in every time her kid hit a rough spot.

She also shouldn't say: "You're going and that's that." Because parents weren't supposed to give orders without explaining them.

And she certainly couldn't say: "You have to go to the game because I want to talk to Tad's mom about Poland and Ben's father about buying stocks." Although she could, reasonably, say she wanted to talk to his coach.

She said: "You owe it to yourself, Adam. To give yourself another chance. You know that. You can't go through life giving up each time you make—What if your paintbrush slipped and you painted the wrong thing on your sharks project? Would you throw the whole poster out?" She squeezed his shoulders lightly and started to rise. "Let's give it a couple more tries."

"I've already tried."

"Adam." She shifted her weight. "You're not going to kick the wrong goal again. That was a fluke. It doesn't happen twice."

"I'll mess up another way."

"Well, each time you get better."

"I don't want to get better."

"You don't?"

"I don't want to do it at all."

"Adam—"

He never held out this long. This was bad.

"Come on." She stood up fully. "Get your soccer gear on, and I'll make you a sandwich to eat while we drive." Adam wouldn't argue back if she directly told him to do something.

Still, Eleanor had to call him four times before he slowly emerged from his room wearing his white shorts and blue shirt, and by then there were only fifteen minutes until game time. Speed limits didn't count when a kid needed to get to soccer. Nor did red lights. *Officer, my son is going to feel like a failure forever unless he can play in this game and score the winning goal.* They pulled into the soccer-field parking lot just as a chorus of whistles was announcing the end of the prior sets of games.

Adam threw her one last, desperate glance as he opened his car door.

"Hey, Adam, great! Can you take defense?" Mark greeted them with a casual version of his smile and a pat on Adam's shoulder that morphed into a gentle shove toward the field.

Thank goodness Mark didn't make a big issue over it. Didn't shout, "HEYYY! High-five, buddy!" or slap Adam's back, "Atta boy. I knew you'd show up." But would the teammates be so forgiving? Or Janek? Hell no, not Janek.

Mark turned his smile to Eleanor next. Now it was the beaming smile that spread across his face and crinkled the skin near his blue eyes. "How's his week been?" he whispered, even while switching his gaze toward the blue-and-white bodies that were gathering at their positions on the field. "Has he talked about what happened?" However, Mark didn't lean close while he whispered.

"Adam didn't want to come to the game today."

"I figured." They watched, together, for a few seconds, as Adam moved one foot after another, slowly, across the grass toward his team. It didn't exactly help that the ref was blowing his whistle and gesturing at Adam in obvious annoyance, trying to get the game started. "When you guys were late," Mark added, "I was worried that you weren't coming."

You guys. Not *him.* Not only Adam.

"Do you remember my offer from last week?" Mark went on, without a pause though with a quick glance at Eleanor before returning his attention to his clipboard, then to the field, then back to the clipboard, his head bobbing up and down. "Josh and I usually get here a half-hour early for some extra practice. So why don't you bring Adam next Saturday, and he can join us?"

"Oh—great. Yes. Maybe."

"We use the little grassy patch at the parking lot."

"I'll try to persuade Adam. That's very nice of you."

"You can tell him that I'm practicing with Josh anyway, so it might seem like a treat, instead of remedial work."

Eleanor giggled. She reached out her right hand. Mark looked at it, but he didn't reach out his own in return.

"I meant—you know—shake? Like, it's a deal?" She pulled her hand away quickly.

* * *

Adam spent the first quarter of the game standing like a little shrub in his corner of the field, but thankfully other Hornets seemed to be taking care of the ball, running back and forth and upfield and down. Janek was in position on the sideline, shouting, of course; probably waiting for Adam to mess up again. And Maria?

Tell me some more about your parents in Poland during the war.

Could Eleanor just walk over to Maria's chair and ask—out of nowhere?

Mark was standing with his legs in a long V, his arms crossed on his chest, the clipboard dangling from his right hand, rocking back and forth on his feet. His head barely moved, staring intently at the field. His muscles filled the sleeves of his blue T-shirt; his forearms were tanned and dark-haired.

"So," Eleanor began.

His head shifted slightly in her direction, even while his eyes stayed focused on the soccer game.

The ball whooshed out of bounds across the field. The ref blew his whistle, Mark pointed, and a Hornet raced to the far sideline and threw the ball back in to his teammates. Colors swirled. Mark jogged alongside the field. Boys ran. More parents shouted. Mark scribbled on the paper on his clipboard. Finally, another whistle ended the quarter.

But of course Mark was still nonstop busy during the mini-break between the first and second quarters. Boys in blue and white jostled around him. Josh was reaching into his shirt pocket, trying to extract a pack of gum, and one of the dads walked over and began whispering urgently.

* * *

"Hey, I haven't seen you for a couple of games. I'm Jack. Ben's dad. Which one's your kid? Did we ever talk about that new drug for pain relief?"

"No, I don't take any drugs—" She shook Jack's hand, which was thrust directly in front of her.

Well. Okay. It couldn't hurt to ask.

"I think there was a stock that just made fifty dollars? Drugs-something-dotcom?"

Jack beamed.

* * *

A dad was talking to Mark, and Josh was tugging at his arm.

"How did Adam do this quarter?"

Mark glanced at her, a quick smile, then back at the dad. She waited. Josh ran off.

"So are we winning?"

"Down by one," the dad answered, without turning toward her.

"Adam's doing fine," Mark said. "We can talk in a minute."

No, he would never have a spare minute. He was the coach, the center of the Hornets' universe. Another father was hovering, and the referee was looking toward him, and Tad ran by shouting "Can I be forward again?" and Adam wanted to know if he could sit out the next quarter.

If Mark were just a parent, sure, he would be milling around the grass like the others, clustered in twos and threes, chatting about nothing, trivia, life, kids, drug-company stocks. Perhaps she and Mark might even be talking about World War Two. It was possible. Didn't he say he taught art history? Maybe he knew about stolen Nazi art.

He was, finally, taking a step toward her. "Sorry," he said. "It gets pretty crazy sometimes."

"Oh, I know. I just wanted to ask if Adam—"

The referee was already blowing his whistle.

* * *

"Maybe we can talk later."

"Didn't you say you were a teacher?" she blurted.

Hugging his clipboard, Mark frowned at her.

Boys were running to him. The whistle blew again.

"I'd love to ask you—"

"Can I call you later?" He waved the clipboard in the air. "I've got your phone number from the team list."

"Um."

A tall, brown-haired Hornet was hitting Mark's forearm.

"Let me give you my cell number. I'll write it on your clipboard. I'm never home."

* * *

Even as Eleanor was turning away from Mark, Janek and Maria were walking straight toward her.

When they were less than two feet away, Janek held out a beefy hand and looked down at his shoes. "My wife says I am too angry on soccer," he mumbled. "I am sorry I call your son idiot last week. I am the idiot."

All three of them shook hands. "No, no, don't worry." "Of course not." "There's nothing to apologize for." Tad ran up to them and then away. They talked about the goal Tad had scored in the first quarter. Of course, with them being so nice, it would be far too rude to ask why Maria giggled or what her parents had told her about living forty miles from Auschwitz.

Chapter Seventeen

"Mrs. Ritter? Ah, she's such a smart lady, isn't she? She always makes sure she gets her newspaper. I'm Raquel." The Sunday manager shook Eleanor's hand across her desk. "However, her progress in her therapy is a tad slower than we'd like to see with that hip." Raquel had tilted her head to the side, her eyebrows slightly furrowed.

"Slower?"

"Yes, well, the weekday staff can explain."

"But how slow is she?"

"The weekday staff will all be here tomorrow. They interact with her every day, and they will have a lot more to tell you, I'm sure."

"But, for instance, what should she be doing, that she's not doing?"

"Really, you're better off talking with the staff tomorrow. I only spend time with her on the weekends."

There had also been an incident the previous night.

When Sondra, the Saturday-night nurse, had gone to her room to give Mrs. Ritter her nine o'clock meds, Mrs. Ritter had started arguing with her. Saying she was tired of eating—well, she'd used some sort of foreign word. *Makove—*? Tired of eating *makove*-something. And asking if the pills were kosher.

"I must say, that certainly surprised Sondra," Raquel added. "You know, people fall into patterns, and then right-dab when we think we know them," she laughed, "they do something totally unexpected, like your mother did. Just to remind us that they're human beings and not diagnoses." Another laugh.

"She asked if the pills were kosher?"

"Yes, that was interesting. She doesn't have an order on file with the kitchen for kosher meals."

"No. No, she wouldn't."

"Well, maybe Sondra woke her and she was a bit confused."

* * *

Rose glanced up from her book when Eleanor pushed open her door, curtly gesturing Eleanor into the room. "Wait until I finish this page." Eleanor sat in the green armchair near her mother, and after a minute or so, Rose placed her bookmark sharply against the inside spine. "This is the last book I have here, and I'm almost finished. Do you think you could get me a few more from the public library? I'll write down some titles." As she folded her eyeglasses properly into their leather case, she added, "Unless I'm back home soon. How much longer will I be locked up here?"

"Locked up? Ma, this isn't—"

"I'm sure the doctors are telling you more than they tell me. They think all old ladies have Alzheimer's disease and don't understand complicated medical terms."

"Actually, I wanted to ask you about something. The nurses were saying—um—last night?"

Since when do you want kosher food?

Damn.

"Oh, please. The nurses don't know anything." Rose's voice was cigarette-hoarse again; her hand was bones and pale skin. "Will I be a cripple for the rest of my life?"

Don't use the word "cripple." That's what Eleanor would have told Adam and Kate, and her students. She spread her hands over her face to brush her hair back on both sides.

"Ellie! How bad is it? What aren't you telling me?"

"No, I'm not—I'm not not-telling anything. There's nothing. I don't know what there is." *Why couldn't Natalie be here, saying the right thing?* "I'll ask," Eleanor mumbled. "'Cripple' is a strong word, Ma. I'm sure you're not—you'll be able to walk."

Rose gave a little sound, between a snort and a cough. "With a cane? Limping like an old lady?"

"I don't know, Ma."

"A wheelchair isn't walking."

"Who said anything about a wheelchair?" What was Eleanor supposed to say? Was Rose's recovery stalled? Or going too slowly?

"Do you remember when your father was in a wheelchair?"

What now?

"Yeah," Eleanor slowly replied. "While I was in grad school, right?"

"After his first heart surgery. He hated it." Rose rotated her wedding and engagement rings, yellow-gold and diamond, one turn to the left, then back. "In those days, before they had the motorized kind, you needed a lot of arm strength to push your own wheelchair around, and Izzy was too weak. So he would be stranded in one place unless he asked me for help. He said he felt like a prisoner. Or an old man."

"Poor Dad."

"He drove me crazy." Rose laughed, as she dropped her hands apart. "That's when I started volunteering on the political campaigns, do you remember that, too? Jimmy Carter, in 1980, when everyone was terrified that Ronald Reagan might have his finger on The Bomb. So I parked your father in the family room, with the picnic cooler and some sandwiches and the TV. And of course his stamp albums. And then I went over to the county Democratic headquarters for a few hours. Oh, I just did silly work. Licking envelopes and what-not. Your father felt abandoned, but he also hated Reagan, so he couldn't kvetch too much."

"I was proud of you for that. I always wondered why you stopped the campaign work."

"Eh, it wasn't really for me. I thought I would like it because I like to read about politics, but it was too much about this neighborhood votes this way and the person at that address is registered that way. Lists. Codes. But I have to tell you, Ellie, as much as you complain about your husband—"

"I do not—"

"You think I can't tell? You're unhappy with him about Kate's bat mitzvah. But I have to tell you, he was wonderful with your father. Wheeling him around endlessly."

Well, yes. Nick would have wheeled Izzy around. And looked at his stamps. The good old days. Patting her mother's shoulder, Eleanor stood up again.

What the hell was she doing? She never patted her mother's shoulder.

"Sorry, I need to stretch my legs." Eleanor headed for the window, across the room. Maybe she could open it a crack. The building was always so overheated, and the hallway smelled of disinfectant. Outside, four stories down, there was a small square courtyard with wrought-iron benches along each side of the square and a tree at each corner, already shedding leaves onto the tightly trimmed, yellow-green grass.

Okay. Too much input; too much to plan. She had to focus. None of the regular staff was on duty today, so tomorrow she would call Rose's doctor. Was Rose keeping up with her therapy schedule? Was she healing too slowly? Natalie had said something about exercises. And Rose wanted more books. And what about that foreign word last night, the *makove*? That must be some kind of Polish food. Would Rose—would she be willing to talk more about Poland? How far could Eleanor push this?

"Tell me about Kate," Rose's voice demanded from a few yards behind Eleanor. "Does she have a boyfriend?"

So much for the view out the window. Eleanor turned toward Rose again. "There's a boy named Will that she talks about, though I can't figure out if she has a crush on him, or he's simply part of her group. But she's a little young for a boyfriend." Well, this could be another conversation-opener: Did Ruzia-Rose have a boyfriend in Poland in 1939? Dating, like Maria Wysocki's parents? She'd been just about Kate's age when the Nazis invaded.

As soon as Eleanor reached Rose's chair, however, Rose was pressing her palms against her armrests. "Okay. Let's take a walk, while you're here."

Rose would not let Eleanor call for help. It would take an aide an hour to answer any call, she argued, and she'd been using the walker for two weeks now. She would tell Eleanor exactly what to do. First, Eleanor brought over the walker and faced it the way Rose instructed, with the two side wings protruding toward the chair. Then Rose shimmied forward to the very edge of the seat, her soft beige sweatpants riding up her bony calves, with Eleanor's hand on her lower back. Glowering, Rose paused to pull the pants legs down properly.

Eleanor's hands hovered, one near Rose's back, the other near her elbow, while Rose gripped the handlebar of the walker and, slowly, half-inch-by-half-inch, pulled herself up.

The walker wobbled; Eleanor grabbed the two aluminum legs to steady it, abandoning Rose's back and elbow.

She returned her hands to their mid-air positions once Rose was finally upright. Together, Eleanor, Rose, and the walker took the first step away from the chair.

"Slow down!" Rose said sharply.

Right foot. Pause. Wince. Left foot. Pause. This was not the way Rose Ritter walked.

After minutes and minutes, they reached the doorway to the hall.

Nevertheless, they made it out the extra-wide, wheelchair-size doorway, and Rose rested against the walker while Eleanor locked the door. Then a few more yards down the disinfectant-smelling hallway, almost to a green vinyl-padded chair that was sitting against the wall, matching the chairs in Rose's room. "Wait here—" Eleanor began.

"Next corner," Rose whispered. "Common room."

Even Rose's meager weight was a lot to ask the walker to support, and for a moment the aluminum frame seemed to buckle as she leaned on it. Then she straightened herself up to a full standing posture and took another step. Yard by yard. At the common room, she clutched the armrest of the closest chair and pulled herself the last inches into its seat, gulping in air.

The common area was about twice the size of Rose's room, with a scattering of tweed and faux-leather armchairs, love seats, and couches in shades of blue and brown. Two chairs and a couch faced a large TV set that was showing a silent football game. A grey-haired woman read a magazine in one of the chairs; neither she nor Rose glanced at each other.

Since there was no chair near Rose's, Eleanor dragged over a blue armchair, which had looked relatively lightweight but was nonetheless pretty damn heavy. Nick would have been useful for this.

Rose was still breathing too rapidly. But she was doing better than when Natalie had visited last week, wasn't she?

"Now I'm my own Pani Helena," Rose said softly.

She was staring at her hands, clenched in her lap, the two rings, the veins jutting through the pale, speckled skin.

"Pani Helena was an old lady who lived out near the *gimnazjum* when I was a little girl. Beyond the field where Avram played soccer. All the children called her a witch. She had long white hair, which she wore in braids that she wrapped around her head, like a peasant girl, and she lived in a—a cottage, I suppose you would say. A little cottage, with one of those thatched roofs. Her husband and baby daughter had died a long time ago, and there was another daughter but no one knew what had happened to her. The witch had put a spell on her, people said.

"And for some reason," Rose went on, still looking at her hands, "she liked me. I don't know why. Maybe I reminded her of her own daughters. Certainly, I'm quite sure I was the only girl who ever visited her. My father sometimes took me there, you see, if we were walking home together after school, and if he might be going to her house to help her with something heavy to lift. At first I hated it—going to see the witch, you know. I was terrified. But I changed. A little bit. I don't know, maybe

I liked all the fuss she made over me? Whenever I came, she gave me a treat. Well, she thought it was a treat." Rose shook her head. She rubbed her right thumb against her left index finger. "A piece of hard, old poppy-seed cake. I could hardly bite into it. But she meant well. So sometimes my mother would bake *pierniki*—Of course you don't know what *pierniki* are. They are cookies, made of very soft gingerbread, filled with fruit like apricots or plums and covered with chocolate. My mother was a wonderful cook, I told you that already. And she made the *pierniki* in fancy shapes. I remember stars and hearts. So, my mother would tell me to bring these cookies to Pani Helena. And that old lady almost cried when I did that. She insisted that I had to stay for tea and share the *pierniki*."

Rose stopped.

Then she continued. "So, Pani Helena walked with a cane. Well, it was actually a thick branch of a tree, and it still had splinters. Probably she'd found it on the ground. So I remember, one day when my father took me to her house—and believe me, he was no woodsman. He was a teacher, as I've told you. But he took a knife, and he smoothed out that branch, he shaved and shaved it with the knife, and he got rid of the splinters. So. But the cane was too short for Pani Helena, and she had to stoop over when she walked with it, which made her look even more like a witch, you see? And I used to walk alongside her, very slowly, while she walked, stooped over that cane." Finally, Rose looked halfway at her daughter. "Exactly like you just did. With me."

"Ma…" Eleanor lifted up her right hand—she looked at Rose—then, slowly, she rested her hand over her mother's clasped hands. "So there were some nice times growing up in Poland."

Rose turned her head more in Eleanor's direction, and she shrugged, although she didn't pull her hands away immediately. "Eh. Depends when and who and what you're talking about." She shifted her feet. "There was a gang that was always in front of the pharmacy, shouting curses at us. The one I told you about. He was the leader. We knew they were the ones who attacked my father." She nodded her chin toward the walker, and then she pulled her hands free from Eleanor. "I'd like to go back now."

Eleanor's grandfather had been beaten up by a pharmacist and a bunch of Polish Nazi thugs?

"Ellie! Are you paying attention? This is the second time today you're not listening." Rose was gesturing at the walker, which rested against a nearby table.

Her grandfather the high school math teacher: Just like Eleanor, he would have faced row after row of kids sitting at their desks, and given them tests, and graded their homework.

If Rose would only keep talking. If they could linger here another minute, without breaking the spell. "Are you sure you're ready to go?"

"Why? Would you rather I sit here for hours?"

"I just—Your father was beaten up by the pharmacist?"

Without waiting, Rose yanked the walker away from the table and began hoisting herself, so Eleanor quickly reached out to support the legs of the walker again. Rose had barely gotten three inches up from the chair before she was leaning on the walker, panting, not moving.

"Ma—"

Rose slid all the way back into the armchair.

That left Eleanor standing over her. Eleanor crouched next to the chair, closer to Rose's seated height. Would Rose be insulted if Eleanor tried to hold her hand again? Rose's breaths were becoming quieter, less deep and gulping. Normal? She was okay now?

"How badly was your father hurt by those guys?"

But Rose's eyes were closed.

"Did it happen more than once?" Or maybe Eleanor should ask something gentler? "So what was that *makove* food?"

"Get me the aide!" Rose forced the words out, barely louder than a sound wave.

* * *

"I'm sure she's fine," the nurse said, steering Rose in the wheelchair. "She's just tired."

* * *

The county library was still open for half an hour more. Enough time to give the European history shelves one more glance and also look for a book about Vichy France for her Advanced French class, in case she hadn't saved her college textbooks. Maybe she should get something on postwar Poland, which would have been when Maria and Janek were growing up? And a book about oceans for Adam, as Rose had suggested—maybe he'd be willing to read it—and a couple more detective novels for Rose. Damn, Rose had never gotten around to writing down a list of the titles she wanted. Well, Eleanor would look for something interesting in the Mysteries section. At least that was something Rose would like. Maybe.

However, the only Poland book that she hadn't already checked out was about the Solidarity union movement, which wouldn't give much insight into Maria's and Janek's lives. No, she really would have to find time to go to the big library in Manhattan.

"The library will be closing in ten minutes," the intercom announced.

Eleanor dashed downstairs from Europe to Mysteries, grabbed two books that might be different from the ones she and Natalie had already brought Rose, ran from there to the children's section on geography, and finally raced to the checkout counter.

In the lobby, some sort of art exhibit had been set up since her visit a week ago. A dozen paintings of various sizes and styles were mounted on the two walls flanking the front door, with maybe ten more propped on easels. There was a series of dark woodland scenes near one corner, right next to some portraits and some pastel, pseudo-Impressionist sailboats and rivers, and across from a set of still-lifes. One or two of the portraits had interesting faces. A guy wearing clown paint and a business suit. The still-lifes, on second glance, were clumsy looking. Jumbles. Instead of the usual bowls of fruit, they were assortments of stuff that wouldn't normally be seen together on a table, things like a ruler, a hairbrush, a pair of scissors, and a head of lettuce. Or was it a misshapen cabbage? One picture showed a Formica kitchen counter with half of a green pepper on a wooden cutting board next to a Barbie doll in a hot-pink bikini and a bottle of ketchup, presumably making a statement about feminism. But the Barbie was such a cliché, and the ketchup bottle didn't look quite like a bottle. The whole scene was actually, well, ugly. A banner stretched across the top of one wall announced: "Art by Local Artists."

Eleanor didn't have to read the labels next to each of the paintings to know: The still-lifes were by Mark Hirsh, Edgewood.

Okay, so he wasn't Picasso.

Chapter Eighteen

"She spoke again in Polish." Eleanor looked from her mug of cold coffee and the pizza crust on her plate, to the pale-yellow walls of her kitchen, to the white refrigerator, to Natalie. "Something about *makove*-food."

"More Polish."

"Did your mother ever make anything called *makove?*"

Natalie smiled while she shook her head. "No, I can't say that I remember anything like that."

"Damn! I wish Ma had talked all these years the way your mother did."

Natalie pushed her own coffee mug lightly against the limp pizza box on the table. Her nail polish was fir-green.

"Yeah, I know, now she's talking. Fits and starts. Today it was something about an old lady with a cane. But I don't know how much more she'll tell us." Eleanor tapped a thumb against the side of her mug. She had the white mug that said "World's Best Mom"; Natalie had the blue-and-grey mug from Paris, with a sketch of the Eiffel Tower. "I wish she baked cookies, too, like your mother. Damn, I wish she'd just—you know?"

"Just what?"

Eleanor blew out a fat breath of air. "Hug?"

For a moment, Natalie stared at the greasy Italian flag on the pizza box. "When my mother was first diagnosed," she said quietly, "I was still at Vassar."

The refrigerator abruptly cranked on. Natalie's glance jerked toward it.

Then over to Eleanor. "My father phoned me, shooting out his sentences like gunfire. You remember what he could be like when he panicked? He thought he was being super-organized, with all of his to-do lists—ven worse than I am—although in reality he was just hyper and hysterical, and he made everyone else around him hyper and hysterical."

Eleanor nodded.

"So he called me to tell me about the lung cancer, and he began reeling off his list to me: Get a second opinion, check the insurance coverage, buy ginger ale, buy throat lozenges—the bottom line of which was that I had to come home immediately. Drop out of Vassar and come home. He all but said, 'If you don't come home this very minute, you'll never see your mother alive again.'

"Naturally, I was terrified. I was twenty-one years old, and my mother had cancer. People didn't use the word 'cancer' then, Ellie. It was as though it was a jinx just to say it. I didn't know what to do.

"And then your mother called." With her elbows propped on the white table top, Natalie rested her chin on her locked fingers and watched Eleanor. "She saved my life, Ellie. When I picked up the phone, I wasn't even able to talk. All I did was cry, and her voice was absolutely calm, but also loving. She said, 'You and I are going to take care of your mother, and each other, and we're going to get through this. Together.' I know that sounds like a cliché, but it was exactly what I needed to hear."

Natalie and the refrigerator paused. In Adam's room, something thudded quietly to the floor, probably a book he was tired of reading for school. The kitchen smelled of ripe mozzarella and coffee and the sweet hunks of watermelon that Adam and Kate had left on the counter, and Adam's Halloween costume was still thrown over his chair, the bright lightning bolts peeking out from the black silky collar.

"Steven and I knew that your mother was very sick," Eleanor said slowly. "But we were just in junior high, so no one told us much about anything. All I remember is Ma talking on the phone a lot in her bedroom with the door shut."

Staring at the open doorway next to the refrigerator, Natalie lowered her hands and rocked them, fingers still locked together, back and forth on top of the table. "It was her own sister. She had to have been hurting as much as Dad and I were. Not to mention that she must have hated herself every time she lit up a cigarette—Do you ever think about that? She was going through her own hell."

Natalie's hands slid into her lap. They were almost as smooth as a thirty-year-old's, no veins sticking out, no extra wrinkles along the knuckles.

She wore Gary's mother's emerald engagement ring on her right hand, in addition to her own diamond on her left. "She took Mom to doctors for second and third and fourth opinions. She went to the chemo sessions with Mom and held her hand, and then she cleaned up the mess when Mom vomited afterwards. Dad was either at work, or useless. Gary tried to help, we talked a lot, but he was away at law school. And she sent me back to school; she relieved my guilt on that score. She pointed out that the semester was almost over and nothing was going to happen that quickly, and also that Vassar was less than two hours away by train and I could come home every weekend. My mother had told me those same things, but I couldn't accept it from her. I needed to hear it from your mother.

"She called me every day, Ellie. She asked about my homework, my health, was I eating, was I making time to have fun, too. She took care of everything."

"You never told me."

Natalie rested one of her palms on top of Eleanor's hands on the table. "My mother claimed that when your mother married your dad and moved out of our house, I screamed for weeks."

"Yeah. I've heard that."

"So." Natalie pursed her lips. "Ten years ago, when they found that spot on your mother's chest X-ray, I had to take a leave from my law firm, because I was so terrified." Her voice was calm and matter-of-fact again. "That was actually one of the factors that persuaded me to go to my friend on the town council—the one who was constantly trying to nominate me for municipal judge. I always used to ignore him. Maybe I've never told you that story. Well, this time, when they found the shadow on your mother's X-ray, I went and sought him out. I told him: The next judicial vacancy, I'll take it."

"Why?"

"I didn't want to argue any more. Legal arguments, I mean." Keeping her hand on Eleanor's, Natalie used her other hand to slide a short wave of greying hair behind an ear. "I wanted to be King Solomon, to make things right between people. It was pretentious, of course. Not to mention that being a municipal judge is only a part-time position, so I couldn't give up my legal 'arguing' entirely."

"You still felt that way, even after Ma's biopsy was benign? To be King Solomon?"

"It wasn't an impetuous decision."

"Yeah." Pulling her hand out from Natalie's grip, Eleanor pushed her chair away from the table and reached for the pizza box. "Well." Then she let go of the box but kept looking at it. "I'm sure it was a good decision. I'm sure you're a good judge." She shook her head. "It's hard to imagine Ma being the way you describe. The way she was with you."

"She's there for you, too."

One of the bedroom doors had flung open upstairs, banging against the opposite wall.

"I don't know, Natalie."

* * *

"Watermelon isn't dessert," Adam protested. "Ice cream is dessert."

"You had pizza," Eleanor muttered.

They were lined up at the kitchen table, next to Natalie's chair.

"What," Kate demanded, "does pizza have to do with watermelon?"

"Okay, okay." No, there was probably no way to avoid giving them yet more crappy food. Pizza. Ice cream. Nick would have baked organic homemade zucchini cookies or something, if he wasn't singlehandedly saving the world at the dinner hour.

Natalie patted Adam's arm. "How are you two dressing up for Halloween?"

"Um." Kate glanced at Eleanor before turning back to Natalie. "I'm twelve, actually. Twelve-year-olds don't go trick-or-treating."

"More candy for me!" Adam shouted. "I'm going to be Voldemort."

"That's actually pretty creative. Most kids are just Harry Potter," Kate added.

"Well, I could've been Luke Skywalker, but everyone does that too, so that's why I didn't."

"What's Volde—?" Natalie frowned at Eleanor.

"He's the villain of the Harry Potter books. Kind of like being the super-devil."

"No, he's a wizard," Adam corrected.

"I don't know. Mom, is he technically a wizard? Or an evil warped version of a wizard?"

"And he's half-Muggle, too."

By that point, Natalie had put both of her palms flat on the table and was just staring, wordlessly, at the other three.

* * *

"We need to prepare a list of questions in advance, for the doctor," Natalie declared, stopping just at the front door.

" 'When can she go home?' " Eleanor suggested.

"Actually, we should first ask: 'What do we need to do before she goes home?' " Natalie corrected. "Then we can ask 'when.' " As she spoke, she drew out of her black pocketbook a small leather notebook with a gold-plated pen attached.

"But we need to know when."

"Yes. All right. And also, what physical therapy will she need? How often will she need to return for checkups? What equipment should we get?"

"Why don't you just do it all?"

Natalie stopped writing and crossed her arms over her black leather coat. "Ellie. I'm trying to do this together. I'm not pushing you."

"No, I know. I'm sorry." Steepling her hands in front of her mouth and chin, Eleanor breathed in and out. Was she supposed to count to ten? Her big mouth. No, she didn't need to fight with Natalie now. "Thank you for telling me about Ma and your mother and all. I'm glad Ma helped you." She lowered her hands. "King Solomon."

"I wish! But I think the doctors are the kings in this case. Anyway, do you have anything else for our list of questions? I'll do my best."

" 'Would it be too much stress to ask her more about Poland?' " Eleanor said immediately.

* * *

Eleanor knocked quickly—two quiet taps—on Kate's closed door. "How's it going?" It was almost ten o'clock. Kate ought to be in bed already. She wouldn't have gone to bed without saying good-night.

Thank goodness: Kate called out, "You can come in," and she didn't sound annoyed.

She was at her desk, which meant her back was to the door, but she rotated around in her swivel chair when the door opened.

"Still doing homework?"

"Yeah. I've got a science test tomorrow. I know, I know, it's past my bedtime."

"Oh boy. Do you think it's going to be tough? The test?"

"Yeah. Sort of."

"What's it about?"

"Astronomy. It's okay."

A mother couldn't do something as simple as smooth the blue hair of a twelve-year-old girl. If Eleanor sat down—which would have to be on Kate's bed, since there was no other chair—would that be like she was inviting herself to stay?

Carefully, Eleanor eased half of her butt onto the edge of Kate's bed, where the blue-and-green duvet was bunched.

Kate was tapping her pencil. Time's up.

"You know that I went to visit Grandma today?"

Kate stopped tapping. "Is she really sick?"

"Well, she's having a lot of trouble walking. But you know what else? All of a sudden, she's started talking about Poland."

"Yeah, you told us." Kate turned back to her desk.

"You know, she was about your age when the Nazis invaded."

Kate winced.

Oops, bad idea. A twelve-year-old girl with Nazis. Switch topic. "I know you're busy. I'll tell you some of Grandma's stories another time. They went to a kind of farmers' market and poured milk from big cans." That was an equally stupid example. What would interest Kate? The Catholic girls who spat at Salka? The old witch-lady? So many stories they could share. Like Ma sharing with Eleanor, finally.

But Kate was already eying the book on her desk. "Can we talk another time? I've got a test, Mom."

* * *

It was three hours earlier in San Diego. Not too late to phone Steven. She should have updated him on their mother's condition days ago.

Steven asked all the expected questions. What did the doctor say, and was there any change in the prognosis, and how would they know when Rose was ready to go home? And then he said, the way he always did: "It's hard for me to give you advice, Ellie. You have a much better idea of how she is and what she needs, being right there with her. I'm sure you'll make the right decisions."

"And she's been talking about Poland."

There was a brief silence from San Diego. "It looks like you've got a full plate, Ellie. I'm sorry. Is Nick any help, or is he all caught up in his computer work?"

"Ma talked about a Nazi pharmacist. And there was a little Catholic girl who spat at her best friend, but another little girl she played dolls with."

"I'm sure Natalie has all the answers, right?"

"Aren't you listening? She's talking about Poland, all of a sudden. Poland! Our grandparents. Her friends. Her—her food. Don't you care?"

"Not really."

"Our grandfather was beaten up by Nazis!"

"What am I supposed to do about that?"

"It's our family's history. How can you not care?"

"I've gotten through forty-five years of life without knowing about Poland. What difference does it make after all this time?"

Chapter Nineteen

Jessica, Jessie, Meaghan, Sara, and Zoe ran into Eleanor's classroom just before first period on Monday. They had revised the script of their Thanksgiving skit yet again. It was still going to be a cook-off between Marie Antoinette and Pocahontas, but they needed to add cheese, in addition to Marie Antoinette's cake recipe, Jessica explained. And they wanted to bring in some real cheese and French bread for the audience.

Cutting Brie with a tiny guillotine? Cute idea, but wouldn't it smear on the guillotine blade?

How about a hard French cheese like Etorki instead? And probably the principal would insist that Eleanor do all the guillotine parts.

Had they ever heard of the Vichy government in France?

The five girls glanced among themselves, wrinkling their noses and eyebrows.

"*En même temps que Marie Antoinette?*" Jessica asked.

"*Non, non.*" Eleanor shook her head. "*Pendant la deuxième guerre mondiale. En même temps que les* Nazis. Hitler." Boy oh boy. These were her Advanced French students, and they thought the Vichy government was somehow connected to Marie Antoinette and the French Revolution? Clearly, Eleanor needed to do a lesson on Vichy. She would definitely talk to the principal about this. And check all her cartons of old books at home. And ask Susan. Maybe Mark knew something about French art history during World War Two. France had a lot of art.

Jessica blew her a Gallic air kiss on their way out, and later, during class, Zoe asked, in garbled French, some more about that Vichy thing.

* * *

Adam would be going to Tad's house again after school on Tuesday, to finish their science project.

"You should bring a snack to share," Eleanor pointed out. "His mom made that powdered dough last time."

"And the chocolate chip cookies."

She could ask Rose for the recipe for the Polish cheesecake! Or that *pierniki*-gingerbread thing. Hmm, would Maria be pleased or insulted if Adam showed up with a traditional Polish dessert? Cheesecake versus powdered dough: Rose's mother apparently was a hell of a lot better at Polish baking than Maria was. Well, it didn't matter, Rose wouldn't know the recipes anyway.

"Can we make brownies?" Adam shouted. "And then I can decorate them."

"Why is it always dessert? What if I make carrot-raisin salad?"

"Mom!"

From the cupboard, Adam brought Eleanor a package of brownie mix — never mind what his great-grandmother the famous baker of *sernik* and *pierniki* would think of cooking pastries from a powder pre-mixed in a plastic bag; he poured the water and vegetable oil each to the exact line in the measuring cup, according to the recipe on the brownie box, and he cracked an egg without letting any bits of shell fall into the bowl. Too weakly, he stirred the wooden spoon around and around the dough, while Eleanor turned on the oven.

So, when she picked Adam up, she could casually ask Maria:

Did you like the brownies? I would have made pierniki.

Yes, my mother is Polish. Jewish-Polish.

No, she doesn't talk much about the war. How about your parents?

Okay, okay, as Natalie had said, Maria's parents had just been teenagers during the Holocaust. They couldn't be blamed.

But they had eyes.

"We are not Jews."

Hadn't they noticed anything? The Germans arrested non-Jews and tore up their farms, stole their livestock and sent them to Auschwitz, too. Why hadn't Maria's family suffered more? How did they manage to hold onto their pharmacy?

Well, in fairness, that might be exactly why her parents didn't talk about the war years. Maybe they suffered so horribly that it hurt too much to remember.

Or they were collaborators.

The pharmacist in Rose's town had been the ringleader of the gang who beat up Eleanor's grandfather.

Of course that didn't mean that Maria's father or grandfather had also been Nazis just because they were pharmacists! This was getting ridiculous.

But even Catholics who weren't Nazis, little Catholic girls like Agata, spit at little Jewish girls.

But Maria wasn't even alive then.

But she'd giggled.

"We are not Jews."

The smell of chocolate was already seeping through the kitchen and beyond. "I'll make you super-brownies for your birthday, Mom!" Adam promised. "Kate, will you help me? How old will you be?"

"Speaking of birthdays," said Kate, who had somehow wandered into the room, "when can we talk more about my party? For my bat mitzvah?"

The bat mitzvah party. The eight-thousand-dollar bat mitzvah party.

Eleanor really, really needed to call Ben's dad, to talk about that drug stock. At least she should find out more details about its success record. Just to ask the guy. Asking didn't have to mean that she would actually buy it.

"This is agony, memorizing all this Hebrew stuff." Kate was leaning against the table, picking up and putting down the squirt guns of cake-decorating goo. Green. Yellow. White. No pink, not when Adam cooked. "What if I mess up in front of everybody? I will be so totally mortified."

"Oh honey, no one will know the difference if you get anything wrong. Adam, do you want to use the rainbow sprinkles, too?"

"It's just gibberish. I don't even understand a word. What's the point of reciting gibberish? Why is that spiritually meaningful?"

It would be so nice to give Kate a reassuring hug right now. Was that forbidden, too? "I know you're working hard."

"Yeah, *you* never had to do it. *You* never had a bat mitzvah."

Dammit. So much for hugs. "That's true. But you know, the bat mitzvah is only a small part of being Jewish."

Kate was eyeing her, frowning.

"It's all part of who you are, even if it doesn't make sense. Your heritage. Like Grandma's stories. I'm just beginning to learn that myself."

"No, it's not like Grandma's stories. Those are kind of interesting. This is just boring, boring, boring, meaningless junk that you force me to do for no reason!" Kate slammed the green squirt gun onto the table so hard that the flimsy plastic cracked, and green began seeping onto the white surface.

"Hey!" Adam shouted.

"You want me to waste my time on this? Then let me get my nose pierced. Then we're even." Kate crossed her arms and glared.

"No, Kate, it's not a trade-off. Mangling your body—"

Swiveling, Kate strode out of the kitchen.

"Mom, she used up all the green!"

Forget the damn eight-thousand-dollar party.

* * *

Rose's left leg, in pale blue sweatpants that dripped off her bones, was extended almost parallel to the floor while she sat straight up in a chair, hands gripping the armrests, lips and arm muscles taut, her other leg bent normally, and her eyes focused on the extended leg.

"Now down," said the therapist's voice, from slightly behind Rose's left side, and Rose's left foot thumped to the ground, but her body relaxed only slightly. She exhaled.

"Very good, Mrs. Ritter. Now can you do the right leg?"

Grimacing and re-clutching the arm rests, Rose stretched out her right leg and began to inch it up.

"Hey, Ma." Eleanor tugged her windbreaker off of her shoulders. "How're you doing? Are you almost done?"

"Eight more." Rose bit off the words with a sharp breath. "Of these."

"We'd like to do about fifteen more minutes," the therapist amended.

But fifteen minutes was fully half of all the time Eleanor could stay here, before she'd need to leave to pick up Adam at the Wysockis' house. What was she supposed to do, watch Rose move her leg for fifteen minutes? Would Rose talk about Poland in front of this therapist? "So how's she doing?" Eleanor asked the therapist.

The therapist nodded, as Rose's leg stretched out almost straight. "Now bring it down. She's making progress. Of course, it's slow."

Rose's knee bent, and the foot settled back on the floor. The other leg began moving up.

"So, Ma, I was thinking about how your father was a teacher—"

"Please, Miss Ritter," the therapist interrupted. "Your mother needs to concentrate."

Rose exhaled deeply, as her leg barely moved higher.

Eleanor took her cellphone out of her bag, although of course there were no messages, because she hadn't turned it on. "Is the doctor in? Maybe this would be a good chance to talk with him."

"No. He's only here on Thursdays."

Rose's other leg was back up now. Seven more? Six more?

"Is this too much for her? Ma, do you want to take a little break?"

"Please, Miss Ritter—"

Rose glared at both of them. "How many more?" she whispered, between breaths.

There was a second chair in the room. Eleanor pulled it closer and sat down. She stretched out one of her legs, too, and flexed her toes ballet-style.

Now the therapist had brought a large, padded footstool and was lifting Rose's legs onto it, so that they stretched flat, almost as if she were lying in bed. Rose didn't seem to be actually doing anything with her legs, yet her eyes and fists were still clenched tightly shut. Another minute.

Standing up, Eleanor strolled around the room. A set of five small, brightly colored weights was stacked on the floor by one window. Further down that wall was a desk, then a folded-up wheelchair and a folded-up walker, plus an open walker. Rose's walker?

One of Rose's feet was now arched, toes pointed. Slowly, she reversed and flexed it back. How many of *these* exercises?

"So, Ma. Are you tired?" Eleanor was at her mother's chair again.

"We're almost done, Miss Ritter."

With so little time left until Eleanor had to leave—and Rose so exhausted—if there was only one thing Eleanor might have a chance to ask, what was that one single most important thing? The Nazi pharmacist beating up her grandfather? The recipe for cheesecake? The name of the town and whether it was one of those with the pogroms? Or would a nice memory work better, to get Rose going? Stories of her best friend Salka and the little Catholic friend Krystyna?

Finally, thank God, Rose waved a limp hand. "Rest," she said to the therapist.

"We'll finish later, Mrs. Ritter?"

Rose shrugged.

The therapist helped her sit up a little higher, keeping the stool as a footrest. Rose closed her eyes, then opened them, while she took long breaths.

"Wow. It looks like quite a workout." Eleanor brought her chair right next to Rose's. "I wished I had your mother's cheesecake recipe yesterday." She smiled, but Rose let her eyelids fall shut again. "So I was wondering, you lived in a town near Warsaw, right?"

Rose moved her head slightly to the right, then left, just an inch or two each direction. Shaking "no."

No? She hadn't lived near Warsaw?

"Are you too tired to talk?"

Another shake. So did that mean no, not too tired, or no, don't want to talk?

"Tell me more about your friend Krystyna. You said you played— "

Rose pulled herself up sharply in the chair. "Enough stories!"

"Ma—"

"I don't want to talk about Poland anymore."

What? That was it?

"Ma?"

They would never learn anything more about Eleanor's grandfather getting beaten up, or Avram playing soccer—or how Rose escaped? No!

"Talk about your own life," Rose was saying. "Did Kate get a dress for her bat mitzvah?"

"Why don't you want to talk about Poland?"

"Enough already."

"Maybe another time?"

Eleanor had wasted all these hours and days and weeks since Rose broke her hip, asking the wrong questions, instead of asking the key one: *How did you survive the Nazis?*

They were probably talking too loud, because the therapist looked over at them, from her desk on the far side of the room.

"Maybe, Ma, you know, to tell Kate and Adam some—"

"*Ellie!*"

It was so loud and sharp that the therapist actually rose halfway off her chair.

"*Fine.*" Rose pinched her lips between her words and stared at her daughter. "What do you want me to talk about? Do you want me to say that I was skin and bones in a concentration camp? Do you want me to say that I wrote a diary like Anne Frank? You want a story about Polish girls that you can tell Kate? Okay—Here's a story: One day I knocked on my friend Krystyna's door, and Krystyna said, 'Go away, I don't play with Jews.' And she threw a doll at me, with the arms ripped off." Rose waited a beat. "Now you know all about Poland. And now I really need to rest, please."

* * *

"I'm so sorry I'm late. I got delayed with my mother—and then there was some construction on Edgewood Avenue, so that tied up—"

"Oh, please, don't worry." Maria held open her front door while she called over her shoulder to Adam.

He was at the doorway in a minute, clutching his backpack and his book about sharks, with Tad jogging in place beside him.

"Thank you for the chocolate desserts," Maria added, while Adam tugged at Eleanor's bag.

I would have made pierniki.

Did you ever ask your father why he survived so well and the Nazis didn't take over his pharmacy?

It was too late. There wasn't enough time.

* * *

Susan waved her over in the parking lot after school on Wednesday and began talking breathlessly while Eleanor was still a yard away. "I had the world's worst date last night. Oh my God, it got so bad that I hid in the bathroom of the restaurant for ten minutes." She didn't even know why she'd gone out to dinner with the guy—she'd met him on the plane returning from her archeological dig in Arizona over the summer, he was some sort of store manager, and somehow people were always more interesting on airplanes, but he was so incredibly, incredibly boring. Fixated on whether his electronic appliances would work after Y2K. Which he then enumerated one by one. Would his alarm clock work? Would his answering machine work?

"Was the dinner good, at least?"

"Ugh, no. Cold shrimp scampi. I swear, Eleanor, I'm going to give up on this dating scene. I'm going into a convent." Susan had opened her shoulder bag and was pulling out a huge key ring that consisted of a broken piece of black-and-white pottery encased in Lucite, plus three keys. "Can you teach me Latin?" she asked, speaking into the bag, as her bushy, pale-blonde hair fell over her eyes.

"Sorry, I never studied Latin—but listen!" Now it was Eleanor who was speaking in a rush. "You're a history teacher. What do you know about Poland in World War Two?"

With her free hand, Susan brushed away her hair and nudged her extra-large, tinted eyeglasses higher up on her nose. "Not much. I teach American history, mainly."

"Don't you also do world history? For eleventh grade?"

That drew a cheerful laugh. "Oh yeah, world history. In one year. The entire world. Starting with Mesopotamia. Not much time for World War Two. Sorry." Susan jangled her key ring.

"Because—there's this family I met—and the mother's parents were in Poland, in World War Two—and they giggled!—and my mother—What do the Poles tell their kids about the war?"

Susan undoubtedly had piles of papers to grade, maybe another big date waiting. Like Eleanor, she'd probably been up since five-thirty or six, at school since seven-thirty. She didn't know anything about Poland. Of course she had to hurry off.

But she seemed to be seriously pondering the question. She was standing in place, without fidgeting very much, only scratching the back of her head. "That's a fascinating topic, actually. In a lot of Eastern Europe, under Communism, there was very little discussion of the war, you see, because then they'd have to acknowledge awkward things like the Hitler-Stalin Pact of 1939 and various Soviet massacres. So the official Communist line was that Hitler was mainly targeting the valiant Socialist resistance, not the Jews. But I don't know much more, I'm sorry, Eleanor. I never specialized in that period. Maybe someone at the community college?" Nevertheless, Susan still paused, poised on the balls of her four-inch heels.

So Maria honestly wouldn't have known anything, growing up in Communist Poland? Under official government silence, her parents would have been reluctant to talk about the war years, no matter what they had, or hadn't, done to resist or collaborate? Quickly: "What if you met a family from Poland?"

"I don't get your question. But listen, I—"

"How would you feel about them?"

"I don't know. Why would I feel anything?"

"Wouldn't you wonder what their parents did in the war? And what they told their kids? If you were Jewish?" Eleanor's words couldn't come out fast enough.

Susan wasn't Jewish. She wouldn't get it.

However, Susan had pulled off her glasses and was staring at Eleanor with her green-grey eyes. "Whew, that's a heavy question when I'm standing in the middle of a parking lot. Second-generation guilt."

She did get it! After all, she was a history specialist.

Puffing her cheeks into a long exhale, Susan leaned against the closest car, which happened to be a dark-blue minivan. "You've hit on a perennial debate, girlfriend. This is a debate that history teachers and students have at every NEA convention and every college dorm." She waved her prison-jailers' key ring.

Eleanor rested her own back against the car next to the minivan, some sort of dirty-white sedan. "So what do you teachers usually say?"

"I'll try to give you the short version. Teacher A says: If the parents were truly horrible—hell, let's take the worst extreme, let's say they were SS guards at Auschwitz, something like that—then they probably raised their kids with all sorts of horrible ideas. Right? There certainly are plenty of neo-Nazis in Germany and the U.S. today. And Klan parents, likewise, they're going to raise new generations of little racists. You read about all these—they have these family gatherings of white supremacist groups, right? Like summer camps? So you can't blame the second generation. That's Teacher A, with Argument A, okay?

"Now," and Susan was leaning forward, her voice getting more excited, "over here is Teacher B, with Argument B: He says, it's fine to make Argument A when the second generation are still kids. But how about when they grow up? Yes, they were raised in that warped way, but shouldn't they realize at some point that it's warped? Shouldn't they ask questions? They live in the modern world; they can read newspapers. Don't they bear some responsibility for their own beliefs? Now back comes Teacher A: Well, if they've been surrounded by that whole racist-Klan-neo-Nazi community their whole life, maybe they never had a chance to see any other viewpoint. And Teacher B retorts: So now they're going to raise their own kids that same warped way? How do we break the cycle?" Grinning, Susan twirled her key ring another time. "So you see how this goes on and on? And you want me to give you my three-second solution, here in the middle of the parking lot, about some hypothetical Polish family?"

"Well, what side do you take in those debates?"

Susan shrugged. "A and B. And C."

Eleanor shook her head repeatedly. "No, no, not fair!" She waggled her index finger at Susan. "You can't cop out."

"Okay. Mostly B. But that's self-serving, because it's my profession to teach history to all those potential little Nazis, right?" With a good-bye laugh, Susan pushed herself off from the blue minivan. "Listen, I'd love to continue this—"

"Would you ask the Polish family? What their parents did in the war?"

"Hell no! Well, only if I knew them really well."

Susan's heels clacked like woodpeckers on the asphalt as she strode toward her car, sending a wave over her shoulder in Eleanor's direction.

Chapter Twenty

Mark was kicking a soccer ball, perfectly straight and moderately fast, down a narrow patch of scraggly grass and rocky dirt at the edge of the soccer-field parking lot. As the ball headed right toward Josh in his white Hornets shorts and royal-blue shirt, Josh pushed out his foot to kick it back. He missed, and the ball rolled past him.

Eleanor waved but Mark wasn't looking anywhere near her, so she called out, "Hi!" Then Mark turned and smiled at her. Adam was still inching out of the car.

While Josh chased the ball, Mark trotted over to the passenger's side of Eleanor's car. He held out his hand to Adam. "Thanks for joining us."

"Yeah." Adam stared at his sneakers. "I don't know if I can. . . . "

Mark was already resting his hand lightly on Adam's shoulders, guiding him toward the grassy patch. A few dots of green paint sprinkled his knuckles like freckles. Would his fingers be callused from clutching paintbrushes or throwing soccer balls? "Hey Josh!" Mark called out. "We've got a team now!"

"Hi, Adam!" Josh yelled back, waving while he ran in a sort of jerky but fast rhythm toward the group. Within a minute, Mark had organized a relay that placed Josh at the far end of the patch, Adam halfway, and Mark closest to the cars.

There was obviously was no place for Eleanor at this little soccer session. Which was fine, of course; the point was for Adam to gain practice and therefore self-confidence. In fact, she should have brought a book to read. Or better yet, the business section of *The New York Times*, so she could check the price of her stock.

Her stock. One hundred and fifty shares of Drugtrials-dot-com.

However, Mark was motioning to her, to come stand next to him.

"I'm glad you two joined our little practice."

"Adam didn't want to."

"Then an extra thanks for bringing him. How did you persuade him?"

"Like you suggested. I made it sound like a treat, not a punishment."

They spoke without looking at each other, staring diligently at their sons, straight black hair and curly brown hair, short and thin, taller and chubbier. Mark called out occasional instructions. "Block this one, Adam!" he ordered, as he pulled back his leg and then, with barely any visible effort, kicked and sent the ball directly to Adam's feet. Not an inch too far to the right or left. Not a second too fast or slow. Under his jeans, Mark's thigh and calf muscles stretched and flexed and worked at just the perfect combination.

There was about six inches between his shoulders and Eleanor's.

Adam's left foot managed to connect with an edge of the ball and, feebly, push it a few inches to the side.

"Great job," Mark called. "Now get right over to that ball. Don't give the other team a chance. Kick it to Josh. Remember he's your teammate, so you want him to get it."

Adam gave another kick-push. The ball rolled for a yard, and he looked over at Mark.

"Follow it!"

Adam ran after the ball, kicked it again, more powerfully, and this time it went bouncing into the parking lot.

"I've been meaning to ask you," Mark said, still eyeing the boys. They had run to the parking lot and were kneeling and peering around the parked cars, searching for the ball. "Why did Adam miss the first game?"

The first game? The first soccer game ....*Hey, Adam, hasn't soccer season started already?* Nick had asked at dinner. "He, uh, he wasn't sure he wanted to play at all. He had a so-so time last year. But all of his friends were doing it."

Mark nodded. "Josh played Little League for a season, and soccer for the past year. I'm sure I've been overdoing the father-son sports-bonding. Taking him to Mets games since he was four. That's when his mother and I split up, and I was a classic case of Disneyland Dad. You know what I mean? Each parent tries to get the kid to love them more by taking them to bigger and more elaborate places. The problem was that his mother took him to the actual Disney World when they visited her parents in Florida. So I took him to Mets games and stuffed him with Cracker Jacks. Too many, obviously." Mark gave Eleanor a quick glance that verged on a smile.

She returned a full smile. "Well, there are worse sins. Anyway, you don't look like you eat too many Cracker Jacks."

"Oh, there's always ice cream and funnel cake at the shore in summer. Disneyland Dads do that, too."

Mark in swim trunks at the shore. Or a Speedo. Blue and white like the soccer uniform? Would he have a hairy chest or a nice smooth one?

The boys must have found the ball, because they were racing back to their spots on the thin spread of grass. Mark walked quickly toward them, away from Eleanor, blowing his whistle and gesturing, and then all three were in a new configuration, with the two boys side by side in the narrow dirt lane and Mark taking turns kicking to each of them. He was practically Fred Astaire, as his feet kept dancing and hopping to catch a rebound, kick it, pivot, and sprint for the next one. And Adam was actually kicking a lot of the balls—maybe even half of his tries?—fairly straight to Mark. He was running a little back and forth, as though he truly wanted to meet the balls. After a few minutes, Mark eased away, calling out for the boys to relay with each other, and walked back to Eleanor.

His face was slightly flushed a dark pink, a few beads of sweat dotting his hairline, and his blue shirt flapped a little against his chest as he walked. It would make a person want to take a cloth and wipe his hot face, along the temples.

"I bet you're exhausted. How do you keep it up? Your energy level. It's incredible. Do you want some water?" Amazingly, Eleanor had remembered to bring a couple of water bottles. She was very careful the way she offered one to Mark, holding just onto the edge of the bottom, so their fingers wouldn't brush. She was not flirting. How could she be, when she always wore her wedding ring? Coming here today was for Adam's sake.

"How do *you* manage?" Mark retorted, swallowing a long gulp of the water and wiping off his mouth with the outside of his hand. Standing so close, he smelled the tiniest bit of sweat and a hint of peppermint. "Juggling two kids and a bat mitzvah and soccer and homework."

And my husband is so busy with Y2K that he can't help much.

It would be so awkward if she said that right now. So obvious. So

Eleanor just shrugged. "Not juggling well enough, I'm afraid. However, my daughter knows that when soccer season is over, I'll be dragging her to temple on Saturdays a lot more often."

When soccer season is over...

Mark reached the water bottle toward her. She waved it away. His arm lingered in the air another moment. "You're not signing up for winter soccer?" he asked.

"Oh. I hadn't—I don't know if Adam—"

Winter soccer?

Did that mean they could keep coming to games in winter? With the same team? With the Wysockis? Would Mark still be the coach?

"I don't know if Josh will want to do it," Mark was saying, "but he really seems to like the game. Even though, as you can tell, he's not the most talented kid on the Hornets." With a laugh, he half-turned away again, keeping watch on the boys' feet as they kicked and ran.

"Well, Adam isn't exactly the star of the team, either."

"No, no, with Adam a lot of the problem is self-confidence, that's all."

"It's more than that. You know." Certainly, she could talk to Mark about Adam's misery. Wasn't it Mark's job as coach to deal with these kinds of issues? "How does the rest of the team feel about him? You know, especially since he—well, you know—blew it? When he scored the goal for the other team?"

"Honestly?" As Mark swung back toward her, his royal-blue eyes gazed right into her eyes. His face was serious, concerned. Caring. "Sure, they were furious at the time. But I really think they've forgotten about it. It was two games ago. And anyway," and his expression shifted into a grin that was a little playful—"we won that game in the end."

A bigger grin must have been spreading across her face, because something was sending darts of warmth and relief through her veins. In fact, her knees buckled a little.

He was standing right next to her.

She touched his forearm. Only a couple of fingers.

To say thank you.

His arm tensed. Maybe shivered. Slightly.

Quickly, she pulled her hand away and said cheerfully, "You just made my day. Thanks. And luckily we've got some good players to compensate for Adam's mistakes. What do you think about Tad Wysocki? You know who I'm talking about? The skinny blond kid? He runs really fast?"

"Oh yeah, he's great. Fast. Accurate. With him, the problem I have to worry about is him being too dominant. Not giving anyone else a chance to score."

"How about his family? Do you know them?"

Mark didn't answer, staring down the length of the grassy patch toward Adam and Josh.

"You know," Eleanor prodded, "the dad who always stands right at the sideline? The mom is usually sitting by herself in a beach chair?"

"I don't—" Mark interrupted himself to gesture to Adam, who was racing to intercept Josh's wayward kick. "I don't really know much about the families. It's not my job. All I get on the team list is the kid's name and phone—Hey, Josh, keep your eye on it!"

If Mark didn't know anything about the Wysockis—and he was the coach, with the complete team list—then who would?

Still, it was okay to stand there for another minute, not talking, comfortably next to each other, a half-foot apart, or less, watching their two clumsy, earnest sons. Off in the soccer fields, beyond their little patch of privacy, there were occasional shouts and whistles from the real-world games. Soon, they would have to join that world.

"So I think you said you teach art history?" She glanced briefly at the side of Mark's head, then at the boys.

"Yeah?" His voice definitely perked up.

That was a good beginning.

Adam called out something. From the distance, a whistle screeched.

"Well, of course, I don't know what your specialty is, and really my question doesn't have much to do with art, it's more like history, actually, but I wonder if you know much about World War Two? Looted Nazi art? I was thinking of teaching my Advanced French class a little about Vichy France."

He obviously thought she was an utter airhead for rambling on about France—and she was—why the hell would a painter of Barbie dolls know anything about French Nazis?—he was already reaching into his pocket, probably for his whistle—but a new sound had suddenly arrived in the parking lot: the sound of a motor slowing down. A car was driving in.

And as though that ugly noise had lifted the lid of a clamorous music box, the air was filling with more vibrations, and the shouts and whistles from the far-away soccer fields had gotten louder. Mark glanced at his left wrist. "Believe it or not," he said, "it's almost game time. Everyone's going to start arriving any minute."

So it was over.

Mark waved to Josh and Adam, waving and pointing to himself. Then he looked straight-on at Eleanor.

"I was actually an art history major as an undergrad," and he wasn't frowning, and his voice wasn't annoyed; he was just giving her his usual big smile. As though they were continuing a perfectly normal conversation. "I focused on the medieval period, but I did take some overview courses on European history."

There was the sound of another car invading.

The two boys were a few yards away.

"We could do this again next Saturday," Mark said. He added, "I would enjoy talking about French history with you."

Just beyond their little dirt patch, a boy in white shorts and a royal-blue Hornets shirt was opening the passenger-side door of a car.

"Josh and I practice every week."

The new boy had run over to Adam and Josh, and Adam was laughing.

Laughing? At a soccer practice?

So Adam might want to come back on another Saturday with Josh and Mark?

Noise was now streaming from all directions, people leaving the old games that had just ended, cars arriving for the next set. Like autumn leaves drifting into a pile, kids in blue and white were moving toward Adam and Josh, or toward Mark, and their parents were stopping to say hello to each other.

"Hey," Eleanor said hurriedly, "I meant to tell you, I saw your paintings at the library."

Mark was actually blushing! And not just a little flush, like when he'd been overheated, but a sudden rush of blood all over his face and neck, as though a can of his own red paint had been poured over his skin.

Why the hell did she keep saying these stupid things to Mark?

He was gesturing to someone. "So," he asked, not looking at Eleanor, "what did you think? Of the paintings?"

"Well, they were really, uh, unusual. Really interesting. How, um, you take everyday objects. Barbie dolls."

"Yeah, yeah, that's one of my trademarks. Trying to get people to think about ordinary objects in a new way, and then hopefully that will lead the observer to think about social assumptions in new ways, too. For instance, in that particular painting that you mentioned, 'Bikini with Ketchup,' did you notice the contrast of the pink bikini and the red of the ketchup?" He had turned so that he was fully facing her again, still blushing as red as his ketchup, and talking faster and faster. "The ones at the library are oils, but I've started experimenting with watercolor and acrylics, because they react with canvas in a completely different way."

However, their time together truly was over. The Hornet parents had finished parking and chatting and were swarming in the direction of Mark and Eleanor, their sons racing ahead in a mass of blue and white. Matthew and his mother were among them, although so far not the Wysockis nor Ben's dad. Jack; Eleanor really ought to use his actual name, if she was now doing business with him. Mark waved and called out, high-fived the new boys, slapped Adam's shoulder, and then he and Josh did some kind of fake-punching of each other in the stomach before he slapped Josh's shoulder, too. Josh reached up and dug into Mark's shirt pocket, emerging with a pack of gum.

And Adam was laughing.

It was true, what Mark had said. The other teammates seemed to be including Adam in their laughter and shouts, as though he'd never kicked a ball into the wrong goal.

"Hey, Adam." Mark crouched down. "That was a great practice. You're developing a nice, strong kick. Next time we'll work a little more on how to control the direction, okay?"

Adam nodded, vigorously and promptly. "Okay."

"Are you trick-or-treating tomorrow?"

"Yeah. I'm Voldemort."

"Cool."

"From Harry Potter."

"He made the costume himself," Eleanor added. "I just bought one of those standard black witch's robes, and he attached all kinds of stuff. Lightning bolts. You know."

"Come on over to our house. I've got M&Ms." Standing, Mark smiled at Eleanor, as always, no longer blushing. "Voldemort. Now that's different." He leaned toward her, and then all of a sudden he had cupped his hand over his mouth as his mouth brushed her cheek and he whispered into her ear, and his hand wasn't callused, and his breath was a little warm and a little wet, and he still smelled of perspiration and peppermint, "Josh just wears his soccer uniform and pretends to be Pelé. No imagination."

By then, more kids and parents had arrived. They had to have seen the whisper. Matthew's mother? Maria and Janek?

It was just a whisper. A conspiratorial whisper between parents, so as not to hurt Josh's feelings. Eleanor could have whispered the same to—to Joanna's mother, or Matthew's mother. Brushing their cheeks with her lips. It was hard to avoid that sort of thing, when you whispered. Though maybe it was a little too-friendly of Mark, in front of all the other parents.

Her neck and cheeks were getting warm, probably almost as red as Mark's had been.

* * *

The whole atmosphere around the field was more juiced-up than usual. Adam was so clearly excited, slugging down water, running to Mark, then running to Eleanor to ask, "Did you see that long kick I made to Josh in practice?" and running back again to add, "Maybe I can be a forward this time."

Matthew's mother strolled over to Eleanor. "You were here early. Talking with the coach?" Betsy. That was her name.

Betsy was not smiling. She was staring into Eleanor's face.

"Well, you know, Mark—the coach—he thought it would be a good idea for Adam to have some extra practice. After the way Adam totally screwed up the other week." Eleanor gestured airily. "You know, kicking the ball into the wrong goal?"

"Oh, kids make mistakes in soccer all the time."

"I guess. Sure."

"Perhaps," Betsy said, "the coach might invite us all for an extra practice." She still wasn't smiling.

Eleanor lifted up her hands, dropped them, shrugged, and glanced around.

She waved to Jack, who flashed her a huge grin before he bent down to say something to the red-haired boy next to him. His son Ben? The boy ran off, and Jack immediately strode toward Eleanor, calling out, "Hey, rich lady!"

"What do you mean?"

"Don't you check the stock pages? You bought Drugtrials-dot-com on Thursday, right? It's up half a point already."

Half a point? That was good? Maybe she could tell Nick soon.

"Listen, I've got another great stock you might—"

"I think one at a time is enough for me."

Were all the Hornet parents jerks? If only she could speak more with Mark. Of course he was busy. Betsy, by now, was chattering with a few other mothers. Was one of them staring at Eleanor? She had to get away from Jack before she spent another zillion dollars on the stock market.

Maria was sitting alone in her chair with the cooler.

"Tad is amazing," Eleanor began brightly. "Doesn't he ever get—"

As Maria turned in Eleanor's direction, her face, for a flash, looked worn-out. Worried. Instantly, however, her mouth switched into a wide, proud smile. "Thank you. Yes. But I think too much he runs crazy."

"Maybe." Did Maria look tired because she was worried about Tad and his ADHD? Were she and Janek having a fight? She was still ridiculously perfectly turned out, with purple boots and her smooth page-boy haircut.

"And Adam, such a beautiful drawing of the sharks!" Maria was now all smiles, any hint of problems totally wiped off her face. "It's okay he comes to our house on Wednesday to finish science project with Tadek? I will drive them from the school."

In light of that invitation—in light of the fact that this would be the third time that Adam would have gone to the Wysockis' house, and Tad had never been to their house—clearly it was Eleanor's turn to reciprocate. "Would Tad like to go trick-or-treating with Adam tomorrow? You know what Halloween is, right?"

Besides, if Eleanor were the host, rather than Maria again baby-sitting while Adam mooched the Wysockis' food, Eleanor would perhaps be in a stronger position to ask a few questions about Maria's parents. Maria would owe her a favor.

And then the game was over, their team had won four-to-nothing, thanks to three goals by Tad, of course, and Adam was standing smack in the middle of a group of teammates, laughing and eating some kind of packaged peanut-butter-on-crackers junk—oh, who cared what chemical crap was probably in that snack? Who cared what Betsy thought? Some parent had brought Cokes instead of Gatorade and water; who cared? It was a perfect crisp fall day; the Hornets had won; Eleanor's stock was up half a point—whatever that meant; she would soon be able to ask Maria more questions; Adam was laughing, and his teammates weren't mad at him anymore.

"Great game, everyone!" Mark called out to the group. "Next Saturday, nine o'clock."

He was leaning over, whispering something to Eleanor.

His fingers lightly on her shoulder.

He shouldn't have leaned so close again.
She couldn't hear. She nodded.

* * *

She wasn't going all that fast. It was just a right-hand turn. But somehow, maybe she hadn't judged the distance to the curb accurately. Maybe she didn't see it.

Maybe she was still thinking about Mark.

Or maybe she was thinking about the Wysockis and Halloween. Or even her new stock, or Betsy and Matthew.

She swerved for the right turn—it should have been a right turn—but the curb and a mailbox were there instead, and she hit the brakes, but the car screamed—no, Adam screamed, as his body lunged forward against his seat belt and his hands instinctively jerked toward the glove compartment to stop himself.

* * *

"I'm okay," he insisted. But his voice was too quiet, and he was still sniffling, and his face was still wet. "I'm okay. It just hurts."

There was no blood or gashes, and none of his fingers seemed to be sticking out in the wrong position. He could move them all without too much wincing. The hands might be starting to swell, a little. Turning black and blue? It was hard to tell.

So nothing was broken?

He was breathing. His eyes were open.

He had been wearing his seat belt. Thank God. Thank God Eleanor had done something right, she'd made her son wear his seat belt.

His hands hurt, and also he yelped a little bit when she tried to touch his chest and stomach where the seat belt had held him in. But his pale little hairless chest looked normal, when he lifted his blue Hornets shirt. No bruises or cut along the line of the seat belt.

He didn't have a headache, and his eyes weren't bloodshot. He hadn't banged his head, which was the most important thing. Not like that time when Nick had let baby Kate fall off the table in the bagel shop.

She hugged him, but he yelped again, so she stroked his hair instead. Over and over. "It's okay. It's okay," she whispered. Her own chest heaved. "It's okay."

She'd hit, what, the mailbox? There was probably a huge dent somewhere on the car. As long as Adam was okay. As long as the engine still worked. She took a deep breath and turned the ignition key.

Yes! The engine kicked in. Thank God.

Maybe — maybe it wasn't too bad, then? A sprained wrist, maybe? That could happen in a soccer game.

But it hadn't been a soccer game. It had been because of Eleanor's driving. She had injured her own son.

But maybe not too seriously.

She needed more deep breaths. Before she dared start to drive again. She patted Adam's thigh.

"You're sure it doesn't hurt?"

She would look him over more carefully at home.

It would be okay.

Chapter Twenty-One

By Sunday morning, the last three fingers on Adam's left hand and the last two on his right were definitely swollen and reddish, and his chest felt a little sore. Nevertheless, he insisted that he was fine, that nothing really hurt unless he actually touched the particular part of his body. That he could certainly go trick-or-treating in the afternoon.

Because it was Sunday, the pediatrician's office would be closed. Which meant they'd have to go to the emergency room. Which would mean sitting around for hours. Which would undoubtedly cut into trick-or-treating time. Which would make Adam even more unhappy. Which would also mean they'd have to cancel their plan with Maria and Tad, and Kate would obviously realize there was a problem, and despite her supposed independence from all things related to her family, she would be worried. Were a few swollen fingers serious enough to drag both of the kids through all that?

She should have asked Nick what he thought. But of course he got home late last night, tired of course; Adam was watching his videos and went to bed, and the fingers weren't so swollen then, so there really hadn't been a chance to talk. And Nick was gone in the morning before Adam woke up. After all, Nick had no more medical knowledge than Eleanor, so what could he say that she wouldn't already think of? And then she'd have to explain, a car accident, on top of the other accident with that woman driving the Malibu, which she hadn't told Nick about yet. And the drug stock. And Kate's bat mitzvah. There was just too much to fight about. If Adam's fingers would get better on their own.

He could move his fingers, hands, and body normally. Almost normally. A little stiffly, maybe. If something was broken, wouldn't it hurt more? Of course Eleanor wanted to get her son treated if there was something serious, but honestly, before running to the hospital, she ought to give the Tylenol more time to kick in and try harder to get Adam to keep ice on the swollen areas. Didn't the experts all say that people flooded the ER unnecessarily?

This was, after all, nowhere near as critical as Rose falling down at age seventy-two and fracturing her hip.

"But you need to take it easy," she told Adam. "No drawing today."

His face wrinkled.

"And no basketball."

"Huh? Oh—" He grinned. "That's a joke."

What about carrying the bag of candy for trick-or-treating? Eleanor could let Adam use one of her canvas shoulder bags. That was easily solved!

There was just one new dent on the car, plus some scratches. In addition, of course, to the dent from Eleanor's other accident, which she really ought to get fixed before Nick noticed.

She and Nick had taken Kate straight to the emergency room at North Jersey Hospital after Kate fell off the table in the bagel shop. They sat on rounded yellow-and-orange plastic chairs that were welded together in rows in the concrete-walled waiting room, clutching each other's hands, and they stared at the triage nurse through the window of her office. They stared at the candy machine. At the round clock on one wall. At the TV set mounted on another wall. At Kate, taking turns stroking her forehead, while Eleanor held her. And four years later, when Adam was two years old and had a fever of 103, and he wouldn't stop screaming, and then he started throwing up—then, too, they'd waited endlessly in the hospital. He screamed for almost the entire two hours that they sat in the ER waiting room, in the same stupid plastic seats, rocking him, kissing him, patting his forehead with wet cloths, taking the cloths to the drinking fountain for more cold water, while five-year-old Kate kept fidgeting, moving, flinging away the picture books they'd brought for her, spitting out the crackers, climbing down from the chairs to tug at their legs and demand to go home. The clock inched forward just as slowly both times, and they sat just as tensely, and they strained each time for the sound of their name being called, terrified that Kate was losing brain cells each second they waited, that Adam was growing weaker and weaker, that each of the kids might—No! Every ten or fifteen minutes, during both of their long visits, Nick strode over to the triage nurse, although he never returned with information.

"If it was something to really worry about, Kate would be showing symptoms by now," Eleanor had reassured Nick, the first time.

"If 103 were something to worry about, they would have seen us right away," Nick had said, the second time.

And in both of those cases, after they had waited all those hours, nothing horrible in fact had been diagnosed. Kate had taken a fall. Adam had strep throat, easily treated with antibiotics. "The human body is very resilient," the first doctor had told them.

No, there was no harm in letting Adam's body have another day to heal itself this time, as long as Adam showed no real signs of severe injury. If anything still hurt tomorrow, then Eleanor could call the pediatrician.

* * *

Tad rang the doorbell at three o'clock wearing a polyester Superman costume and swinging a plastic pumpkin with a handle. Maria had a costume, too. She'd actually found an adult-size Disney Snow White outfit, complete with a long yellow skirt and a blue, puffed-sleeve blouse with a stiff white collar, plus a black-haired wig, which she'd decorated with a red bow on top. Or maybe she'd gone so far as to dye her hair. However, she was not carrying a plastic pumpkin.

"Halloween's my favorite holiday except Christmas!" Tad yelled. "Let's go!"

"Can you tell who I am?" Adam started to run after Tad to the house next door, then winced, paused, and resumed, Eleanor's canvas bag flapping against his black robe. "I'm Voldemort."

"But you have not costume?" Maria asked Eleanor, with a worried look on her face.

Supposedly, Kate was doing her mother a big favor by staying home with Joanna and Rachel to give out candy, since she was, of course, too old for trick-or-treating. Or maybe the girls planned to siphon some of the candy for themselves while Adam and Tad were out. Eleanor offered the stainless-steel candy bowl to Maria, and Maria selected a Nestlé Crunch mini-bar.

"With bites in chocolate!" she declared.

"So," Eleanor began, alternating her attention from Maria to Adam, already three houses down the street. The flapping robe and darkening night ought to do a good job of hiding his ugly-looking hands. "Do you have any holidays like this in Poland?"

"Ah, tomorrow is All Saints' Day, but that is very serious. We do not ask for candies." Maria shook her head, frowning. "We go to the graveyards."

"Graveyards? That does sound like Halloween."

"Oh, no, no! It is very serious. It is to visit the graves of our parents, you see. We clean them, we sweep and then we put flowers. Also candles. And also in November is Saint Andrew's Eve." Now Maria's words were barreling forward, nonstop, and she waved her hands around to mimic the movements of sweeping and planting flowers, and as she kept talking her grammar actually got worse, as though she hadn't been living in the United States for twenty years. "That is more like your Halloween, I think. We are telling fortunes. We have candles—yes—we light candles, and then, in water—"

"Water?"

"Yes. Into water. And then fortunes!" Maria beamed.

"How does putting a candle into water tell your fortune?" Perhaps Eleanor could talk about Shabbat candles and Hanukkah candles. That could be a way to ease into the World War Two discussion. *Yes, my Jewish mother is from Poland.*

"And for costume, yes, we have costumes, for very old custom. We sing for Christmas songs with *turoi*, yes? And we must wear costume of animal. And then is Saint Nicholas Day, for children."

"Mom!" Adam called out. "Can we go around the corner?" He had shifted the canvas bag to his right shoulder.

"And of course most important is *Wigilia!* This is Christmas Eve but much much bigger than American Christmas Eve, yes? We have very special dinner with twelve—twelve—foods? Plates?" Maria didn't wait for Eleanor to answer. "For Christ and the apostles, yes? Everything you can eat, but not meat. Never to eat meat at *Wigilia.* And also the fruits for the apostles. But first my father must break the *oplatki*, yes, and we all break a piece?"

Oh. Eleanor could compare that to breaking off hunks of challah bread on Friday night. *Yes, the oplatki bread. We Jews also break special bread.*

"And the *kolaczki!* This is special cookies my family always has at *Wigilia*, with sweet jellies in it. You must try!"

"Wow, that sounds like the *hamantaschen* at—"

"And I must make for you *kopytka*—my potato dumplings!" Maria exclaimed. "Of course with mushroom sauce."

* * *

After an hour, Eleanor yelled down the street to the boys: "Time's up! Let's go home and eat candy!" Tad managed to dart to two more doors on his way back, but Adam walked slowly, hugging his arms and the canvas bag to his chest. "Does it hurt?" Eleanor whispered to him. He quickly shook his head No.

Kate and her friends even volunteered to continue giving out candy, while Tad and Adam poured their collections onto the kitchen table for analysis and Eleanor set up coffee in the living room.

"I got five Hershey's!" Adam shouted, through a candy-stuffed mouth.

"Can we trade? Do you have any Snickers?"

Adam was in candy-heaven. True, he was using only the thumb and pointer of his right hand to sort and pick up his stash; his left hand rested on the table, obviously swollen. But he was so happy, and really, he was okay.

"So. Tell me more about your family and Janek's family in Poland." Eleanor offered Maria a mug.

Maria smoothed her yellow Snow White skirt before sitting and taking the mug. "Yes, my father and grandfather were in pharmacies. I have told you that, yes? Janek's father has worked at Nowa Huta in Krakow. You know it? Oh my goodness!" Maria looked disappointed, maybe even a bit insulted, when Eleanor shook her head. "Yes, so, Nowa Huta is very big steel factory. It is built by Russians near Krakow after Second World War, and so many Polish families come to live there and to work there. So Janek's family comes. It is very good jobs, but the air becomes very dirty. Such shame, yes? Because Krakow is such beautiful city."

Oh yes, the Krakow civic pride. Maria discoursed for several minutes on the history of Krakow, and Wawel Cathedral, and Poland during its glory days in the sixteenth and seventeenth centuries, and the Commonwealth of Poland and Lithuania...

It would have been rude for Eleanor to interrupt and say that she already knew much of that, even if she'd never heard of the newer parts of Polish history like Nowa Huta. But how could she nudge Maria's monologue over to World War Two?

...Not just Janek's father, but also Janek's three older brothers and then Janek himself all worked at the Nowa Huta steel factory. However, Janek was ambitious, he wanted a better life, so he studied chemistry books, and a science teacher at the school befriended him. The teacher gave him special lessons and let him help out in the school labs, and then encouraged him to apply to the brand-new Krakow University of

Technology. And from there, other professors were so impressed with him—Maria gave a big, happy smile—that they made the connections for Janek to go to England to study more, and from there to America.

As Maria swallowed a gulp of coffee, her smile closed up into a frown. "But our son Konrad, he is not like Janek. He wants only to play the video games. All day long. It drives me crazy, as you say in English."

"It's a rebellious age. I think my daughter is one year older than Konrad. She keeps nagging us to get her nose pierced."

"Ugh!" Maria grimaced. "So ugly!"

"Would you talk to my daughter, please? Maybe she'll listen to you, if you tell her that it's ugly. She doesn't listen to me."

"Yes, I know. Konrad does not listen also. He will not come to soccer games any more. He will not do homework. We fight all the time."

"Tell me about it. With my daughter, we're fighting constantly over her bat mitzvah."

Bat mitzvah.

She'd said it.

Chapter Twenty-Two

The typeface in the newspaper was so tiny that it was hard to read the long column of random letters. DRTR. That was what Eleanor was searching for. The abbreviation for Drugtrials-dot-com.

"Hi," Nick said, walking into the kitchen and heading for the coffee-maker.

"Hey." Eleanor glanced up briefly and waved at him with her left hand, while her right index finger remained planted on the column in the newspaper, which she'd spread out on the table. If she had bought the stock at twenty-seven and three-eights—that was how Jack-the-stock-dad had put it—and then he'd said on Saturday it was up half a point, what did half a point mean?

"Where are the kids? Did they leave for school already?" There was the waterfall noise of coffee going into Nick's cup, followed by the vacuum-swish of the refrigerator door opening. His footsteps sounded closer to the table. "Since when do you read the business section?"

Quickly, Eleanor shut the page. "I was looking for the weather. Sometimes it's in this section."

Nick was standing almost next to her. Inches away. She shuffled the sheets of newsprint on the table until she found the main news section, keeping her gaze focused on the pages. Were her cheeks flushed? Nick swallowed some coffee with a small gulp. His breathing —directly on her neck—didn't seem noticeably loud or fast or slow. He was wearing a pine-smelling aftershave.

"You didn't buy that stupid stock, did you?" he asked quietly.

There had to be a good way to manage this. To be honest with him without getting into a fight. To admit, yes, that she should have talked this over with him more, that would be a good way to begin. But also to remind him that they could use a little extra money—without getting specifically into the topic of bat mitzvah expenses. Or car repairs. Two repair jobs, now. To point out that she'd done her research before putting any money into this. DRTR was up half a point already!

"Why—why do you call it stupid?"

"You did buy it, didn't you?"

"What's so terrible about the stock market?"

"Without discussing it with me?"

"We did discuss it."

"And did we agree?"

"I did a lot of research, Nick. You know, it's my money, too."

"This is a bubble, Eleanor. Did your research tell you that? I see it constantly with technology stocks. Everyone's gone crazy, they're either sure stocks are going to keep rising forever or else hysterical that the world is going to end—"

"This has nothing to do with Y2K—"

" — and it's all going to crash."

"I'm tired of being wimps."

"How much have you lost already?"

"I haven't! It's up half a point!"

"Great. Sell it now before we lose it all."

Eleanor had maybe three seconds before she had to reply. She could let the fight end here, pretty much the way their fights always ended. Agree with Nick. Maybe apologize. Promise to sell the stock, take the winnings. The situation could have been a lot worse. They weren't even yelling too loud.

However, she'd waited half a breath too long, and Nick grabbed the opening. He spit his words out in controlled, quiet bursts: "It's not even losing the money, Eleanor. It's that you unilaterally risked our money without talking with me. No—even worse: Knowing that I disagreed."

Thank goodness she had the excuse of needing to make Adam's American-cheese-and-peanut-butter sandwich for lunch. She could turn her back on Nick while she busied herself walking to the refrigerator for the cheese, then to the cupboard to get a knife, bread, and peanut butter. That could delay the need to look at Nick or answer him for a few more seconds.

Okay, so she could call Jack today and sell the stock.

And then feel like a fool as Drugtrials-dot-com kept gaining points.

Not only that, but she would have to face this embarrassment every Saturday, at all of the remaining soccer games, as Jack teased her, or maybe glared at her. Or ignored her, while he and the other parents eagerly compared their winnings. And even if she did all that, sold the stock, endured the embarrassment, watched the hypothetical money she could have made float up into the clouds — even after all that, she and Nick would still need money for Kate's bat mitzvah.

No! Giving in and selling the stock would be a completely stupid thing for her to do. Nick was being a jerk.

"I've got an idea." Eleanor finally turned around. Nick was still standing in the same spot by the table next to where Eleanor had been and staring at her with lips pressed together in a thin, flat line. "How about if you read about the stock a little bit, and see what you think? It's not a technology company. It's called Drugtrials-dot-com. And then we'll talk? I didn't put in much money," she added.

He actually glanced down at the table and picked up the newspaper. As though there might be an article about Drugtrials-dot-com on the front page.

"You're right, I should have talked to you first." Eleanor tried to spread the peanut butter, but she had slathered too much on the knife and it was making a mess. Then she dropped the knife on the floor. "It's just—well, you know, you're so busy with Y2K, and I'm worried about my mother."

Even with the mention of Rose, Nick didn't respond.

Eleanor bent down to retrieve the knife.

This wasn't Nick, not her husband Nick. He could get angry, for sure, but never ice-angry like this. Did his extra-long silence mean he was trying to find a way to reduce the tension? Or was he too furious to speak? The regular rules of their fights seemed to be all out the window.

"How did you get suckered into this stock?" Nick finally asked, tonelessly, still staring at the newspaper.

"I didn't get suckered. One of the parents at Adam's soccer games works on Wall Street …." That sounded terrible. As if she'd fallen for some fast-talking sales pitch, rather than a recommendation from someone she knew. Sort-of knew.

Nick was now gazing at her with his eyes unusually widened.

"And wait till I tell you about the other parents I've met at these games," Eleanor said quickly.

"From some huckster in a Florida boiler room?"

Each word of his slapped the air between them.

What was a Florida boiler room?

Never mind that. "There's one family from Poland—can you believe it? My mother starts talking Polish all of a sudden, and then I actually meet a family from Poland!"

"What's that got to do with—"

"And I'm trying to be open-minded, you see? Of course not all Poles were Nazis. Not all Poles cheered when their Jewish neighbors —"

"Eleanor— "

"But then she giggles about the Holocaust, and how come the Germans didn't take over their pharmacy? —and I don't know what to think. Janek and Maria Wysocki. But their son is a really good soccer player, and he and Adam have kind-of become friends."

Maybe Nick had forgotten about the stock now. He had pulled out one of the wooden chairs from the table and sat down, still keeping his gaze on her, but there was definitely less tension in his body. He was leaning back a little in the chair.

Abandoning Adam's half-made sandwich, Eleanor walked the few steps to the table and sat down across from Nick. "They're from Krakow, and she works at CVS and he—" Oops, better not mention that Janek worked at a drug company "—he used to work at some big steel mill in Poland."

"Eleanor, why would I care about these people?"

"Because—you know. They're from Poland."

"Are they friends of your mother's?" His voice lifted slightly, almost like it was showing some interest.

"Well, no. But they're from Poland."

He was looking at her, waiting.

"And my mother ... "

"And ten million other people."

"Thirty million," she mumbled.

"What?"

"There were thirty million Poles. Jews and Catholics combined. When World War Two began."

Nick let out a sharp breath. "Why do you give a fuck about this family?"

"Because they're from Poland. Maybe they can help explain."

"Explain what?" Nick crossed his arms on top of the table.

Explain what? In fact, exactly what did she want to ask Janek and Maria? She had to dig out the answer word by word from her brain, before Nick switched back to the topic of the drug-company stock. "They're the only people from Poland I've ever met besides my mother and Aunt Chana. The closest I can come to the people my mother grew up with. Maybe they've asked their parents about what happened back then, and they can explain why their parents' generation did things like spit at Ma's best friend, even before Hitler came. Or beat up my grandfather. And why Ma hasn't talked about it all this time."

Slowly, Nick shook his head. His voice tone was crisp, as if he was at work sudying a broken computer. "You're making no sense. Why would these people possibly be able to explain why your mother —who they've never met—does anything?"

"They wouldn't explain *her*. They'd explain themselves."

"If you want your mother to explain something, ask her directly."

"I told you: It's to explain Poland, not her."

"Two people aren't Poland."

"They're part of it."

"You're going to make a fool of yourself."

"I'm only being friendly."

"No, you're obsessing over them. Leave them alone."

"You don't understand."

"Why you're obsessed with them?"

"Because you're not Jewish!"

His chair clattered to the floor as he jumped up. "That's always your trump card, isn't it?"

Eleanor had to look away. Nick was standing right over her, hovering, breathing loudly. "I'm sorry," she whispered into the table. "That was—you're right—"

"How can I be right? I'm not Jewish."

If she'd thought his voice was icy before, this was permafrost.

How were they supposed to get out of this? And Kate and Adam would be arriving any minute, seeing this fight. And she needed to finish making Adam's lunch. And there was no way to stand up without looking almost straight at Nick. Inches away from her. And she needed to talk, to say something, quickly, before Nick spoke.

Apologize. Change the subject. Talk about Rose.

A fast glimpse: He was still glaring at her, his mouth a slash.

And then Kate pounded in, pushing past her father in her race to the refrigerator. Her hair was blue again. "How come we never have anything I can just take to school with me, like a granola bar?" she demanded, tugging open the refrigerator, which promptly began to buzz. "I'm going to be late."

Okay. Thank goodness. Kate could be handled. "Take an apple." And with Kate now between Nick and the table, Eleanor could move over to the counter and finish making Adam's sandwich.

"I need to go to Abercrombie with everyone on Saturday," Kate continued, her neck craning inside the refrigerator. "We need to get Will's birthday present." She emerged with a Granny Smith apple and a little carton of orange juice. "What else can I eat?"

"How are you going to fit in bat mitzvah services—"

"Not the goddam bat mitzvah again!" Nick slammed his hand on the table. Kate jerked back from the refrigerator, leaving the door hanging open. Cold air shot straight at Eleanor's cheek.

"M-o-m-m-m-m!" Adam wailed, his voice preceding him into the kitchen. "I can't find my markers!"

"Hey, save me some cheese!" Kate swiveled toward Eleanor. "Why do we only have yucky processed cheese?"

"Do you know where my markers are?" Adam asked, finally appearing in person and almost choking on tears.

Eleanor's fingers were shaking as she dug the knife into the jar of peanut butter. "Did you leave them at school?"

"WHAT THE HELL?" Nick shouted.

Eleanor's hand froze, partway inside the jar. Kate's mouth dropped open. Adam shut his mouth.

What now?

"What the hell is wrong with his hands?" Nick demanded. He strode closer to Adam, extending his right arm and index finger straight toward Adam's swollen, reddened fingers.

Adam gazed at his hands. Kate made a face of disgust.

"I was planning to call the doctor today," Eleanor said quickly.

"But what happened?"

"He just banged them. Against the dashboard."

"Hell of a bang. Does it hurt?" Nick's voice softened as he turned to Adam, who shook his head, then nodded. Gently, Nick took Adam's left hand in his own palm.

Of course: Nick was worried about Adam. Like any good dad would be. It was okay. They could get back to a normal fight.

"But I still trick-or-treated," Adam added.

"Wait a—" Nick looked again at Eleanor, dropping Adam's hand. "So this happened before Halloween? AND YOU NEVER TOLD ME?"

The shout shook the knife out of Eleanor's grip, and the peanut butter jar toppled over, onto the white-tile floor.

Kate backed up against the buzzing refrigerator. Adam tucked his hands under his arms and then clutched his arms around his chest, breathing rapidly, and he and Kate both moved their heads like owls, staring at one parent, then the other. Peanut butter was oozing down Eleanor's skirt. Nick's face had no softness, no love, no openness. His shoulders were rigid, and every tendon in his neck stood at attention.

What kind of monster was this? A Nick who swore and screamed and hit the table? This was not the man Eleanor had married. Not the man who brought salmon mousse to meet her parents, and who hugged her and baked cookies for her when she wasn't getting pregnant all those months, and who even two weeks ago had let Adam think that Adam had figured out the secret of the movie *Sixth Sense* before Nick did, because Adam needed to feel good about himself after messing up the soccer goal.

Eleanor was stumbling, drowning, lost in a forest, thrown from a rocket ship into outer space. This was way beyond an apology. Yes, she had screwed up badly, buying the stock behind Nick's back, driving too fast, not taking Adam straight to the doctor, playing the Jewish card too often with Nick. Still, did all those actions deserve this? Whatever was happening here, this moment, in the kitchen, all this was a planet she'd never ever been to.

Was Nick overworked? Was he cheating on her? Was he so furious that he wanted a divorce? Was Y2K somehow driving everyone nuts, terrified that the world was going to end, even guys like Nick who were supposedly fixing all that computer stuff?

She had to control this scene. Rewind it. Apologize. Replace this Nick.

Carefully.

"It only happened on Saturday—the accident—and it really didn't seem that bad yesterday. And the doctor's office was closed, for the weekend." She waited. "Do you think we should have gone to the emergency room?" She picked up the peanut butter jar and turned toward Nick, because now she could look at him, because he was no longer looking at her. He had squatted down nearer to Adam's height and was very intent on studying Adam's hands, poking his own finger here and there near the swollen parts, wiggling some of Adam's fingers. "I was just remembering how horrible those emergency rooms were, when we took the kids the other times."

Adam shivered and let out little mews after a couple of the pokes. Nick gave him a small smile and patted his head before straightening up. He was breathing more steadily. "I don't think anything's broken."

It was going to be okay. Or a normal fight, anyway. The whole room was relaxing. Kate scooted over to the counter and grabbed a slice of cheese.

"Can I have some breakfast?" Adam asked.

"I have to go to work," Nick said. He spit out his words, but at least he seemed to be at room temperature. "Can you call the doctor this morning?"

"I'd need to get a substitute—" Why the hell had she said that? Did she want to start another fight? "But it's okay. I'll get a sub. I'll call the doctor."

Nick was hesitating, fingers poised on the back of a chair.

"Try to rest your hands and don't use them today," Eleanor told Adam. "I'll write your teacher a note."

"Should I go to school?"

"Um, I guess so. Until I call the doctor. What do you think, Nick?"

"I'll probably have to quit soccer," Adam added.

"NO!" Eleanor shouted.

They stared at her, Nick and Kate and Adam. Her family.

"Since when," Nick asked, shoving the chair closer to the table, and his voice was ice again, "did you suddenly care so much about soccer?" He flicked at the newspaper. "Since you got suckered into that stupid stock?"

Chapter Twenty-Three

How could the soccer field have dropped from October-warm to November-chilly in just one week? And what kind of mother wouldn't think to bring a jacket for her son in November?

The kind who would break her son's finger.

There was no way to sugar-coat the fact: Because of Eleanor's reckless driving, Adam had fractured a bone in his pinky. And then, because she had put off taking him to the hospital, she had prevented him from getting the treatment he needed, for nearly two days. She had caused harm to her own son.

But it could have been worse. Ten fingers, twenty-eight bones, and Adam had broken only one.

"Most likely, it has to do with the angle at which his body moved forward," the orthopedist at the hospital had said Monday morning. "It was a car accident, correct? And the way his weight shifted." He patted Adam's shoulder. He didn't criticize Eleanor. In fact, he praised them both because Adam had been wearing his seat belt. "It's a very simple fracture of the distal phalanx—that's the bone farthest from the palm. We can easily treat it with a basic splint."

One finger. One bone. Just one.

Even the soreness in Adam's torso was, apparently, just soreness, probably the result of the seat belt restraining and squeezing him so tightly, of all weird things. He had no broken ribs and no internal injuries, according to the X-rays. The doctor watched Adam walk a few steps, to make sure.

Then he strapped Adam's finger into a small splint made of aluminum with foam padding the same shade of blue as his Hornets shirt, which Adam was to wear for four weeks. He wrote out prescriptions for two different painkillers, in case Adam had a bad reaction to either one—super-strength Motrin and also Advil—and he told them to return in a week for another X-ray. And no strenuous exercise for six weeks.

Six weeks. Way past the end of soccer season.

Eleanor went to the local pharmacy, not Maria's CVS, to fill the Motrin prescription, saving the second one as a fallback.

She stayed awake to talk with Nick when he got home, close to midnight. "It's a very simple fracture," she repeated. "The doctor said it's easy to treat."

"Okay. Guess we'll see how it goes," and he rubbed a washcloth over his face.

* * *

Since he was liberated from all the risks of playing, and therefore of screwing up, Adam hadn't objected to coming to the soccer game. He bobbed his head up and down when Eleanor suggested that it would not show good team spirit to stay home. That he might learn some pointers by listening to the coach's half-time analysis. That he could cheer on his friends and hang out with them afterwards.

All he asked was, "Could you please just say I was in a car accident? That sounds more exciting than saying I banged my finger, okay?"

However, no one seemed to notice the two of them when they first walked toward the soccer field from the parking lot, until Mark waved. Even before Eleanor could explain, Adam ran over to show Mark the splint. Then a few other boys crowded around, but the splint probably wasn't very impressive, because the huddle quickly dissolved. Mark briefly ruffled Adam's hair, glanced at Eleanor with a palms-up, what-can-you-do shrug, and turned to the team. As he had to do.

And thus Adam was standing by himself, shivering in the flimsy white polyester soccer shorts and Hornet-blue shirt that Eleanor had said he should wear as a sign of solidarity, another motherly duty she'd gotten wrong. If he wasn't playing, then he wasn't going to work up a sweat and get his circulation going, and he'd be a lot colder than the other kids, wouldn't he? Duh.

He trailed after Mark while the coach strode up and down the edge of the field, eyeing the plays and taking notes. A couple of times, when Tad chased a ball toward the goal, Adam cupped his hands around his mouth, splint and all, and shouted, "Go Hornets!" But it was a slow game. None of the parents seemed to be paying much attention. Even Janek, at his spot at the sideline, was mainly standing still, except for his head moving back and forth. Nor was Jack anywhere in sight, haranguing potential stock customers. In fact, Eleanor damn well needed to find him, because if she'd been reading the newspaper correctly this week, her stupid stock had actually lost points, or dollars, or whatever it was, and what was she going to tell Nick when he asked if she'd sold it yet?

Well, she had never specifically promised Nick that she'd sell it.

Adam's legs and arms were pockmarked with goose bumps now. He couldn't go on like that. Could he borrow a jacket from someone?

From Maria? She always had so much stuff with her, her bags and chairs and cooler. Would she bring spare jackets? Eleanor waved toward her.

Maria's hair was blonde and in its perfect page-boy, non-Snow White style again. She waved back.

But was it a less vigorous, smaller wave than usual? Almost pro-forma?

Because Maria now knew that Eleanor was Jewish and no longer wanted to talk with her?

For Heaven's sake, Eleanor was getting carried away again. Maria had probably waved as cheerfully as always. In fact, she might not even have realized Eleanor was Jewish, even after the Halloween slipup. She hadn't said anything at the time. Did a Catholic girl from Krakow know what a bat mitzvah was?

Or maybe, now that Eleanor's Jewishness was out in the open, they could actually talk more candidly about Maria's parents and the Holocaust, without worrying about who knew what.

Or, if Maria really was being a little standoffish, the reason could have nothing to do with Eleanor. Maybe she'd had a fight with Janek.

Anyway, obtaining a jacket for Adam was certainly more important than worrying about Maria's arm movements. For once, maybe Eleanor could do the correct, good-mother thing. Smiling and waving as though all was normal, Eleanor walked briskly toward Maria and her chair.

"Adam does not play soccer today?" Maria asked, with a slight frown, when Eleanor was a few feet away.

"Oh, well, he was in a car accident."

"*To niemozliwe!* He is not hurt?"

"No, no, he's okay, thank you. Well, he broke a finger. Um, maybe— do you possibly have a spare jacket he could borrow?"

From her bag, Maria immediately pulled out a dark-blue hoodie as well as a faded denim jacket, both approximately Adam's size. She also gave Adam a juice box and a granola bar when he ran over to try on the jackets; he chose the hoodie. He sat cross-legged on the grass a couple of yards away from them, drinking the juice and watching the game, while Maria patted the chair next to her, gesturing for Eleanor to sit down. As friendly as ever, certainly.

"I can ask you question?" Maria queried, leaning toward Eleanor.

"Sure."

"You have bat mitzvah, you said. So you are Jewish? But on Saturday is your Sabbath, no? You play soccer on your Sabbath?"

Okay then, yes, Maria did know what a bat mitzvah was.

So, there was nothing wrong with a simple factual question. Just like Eleanor had asked about the Polish holidays while they were trick-or-treating. No reason to overreact. "Well," Eleanor replied, pushing her mouth into a smile, "some Jews are more religious than others. I'm sure that's true of Catholics, right?"

"And you do not eat sausage?"

Okay, okay. Maria probably didn't know many Jews. There were damn few Jews left in Poland any more, and the Jewish population of Edgewood wasn't very big either. "Like I said. Some Jews are more religious."

Maria was nodding. Good; maybe the Grand Religious Inquisition was finished. Maybe Eleanor could thank Maria for the hoodie and leave now. Or even better, maybe it was Eleanor's turn to ask a few multicultural-exchange questions.

But Maria was saying something about the art project. The boys were almost done? "Adam, I think he is doing more work than Tadek."

"Oh, I don't know."

"Of course Adam is very smart. You Jewish people always are." Maria smiled.

* * *

Maria was still talking. "He knows so much about the sharks, he is telling Tadek all about them. He reads many books?"

You Jewish people.

Salka's father, too, had been a smart Jew, who helped Agata's family read a contract. Before Agata and her friends spit at Salka.

Maria was smiling at Eleanor. Waiting.

Eleanor should stand up. She should throw Maria's damn chair on the grass. She should shout at Maria: *What the fuck did you say?* She should slap Maria's face. She should grab the juice box away from Adam and fling it at Maria's face and walk away.

Nazi bitch.

But she sat in the chair, Maria's chair, and she stared at Maria, and her throat froze. Just like, maybe, her grandparents had frozen, in their little town near Warsaw, when the Nazis knocked on their door.

She had to say something. She couldn't let Maria get away with this. Thinking it was okay to say "you Jewish people."

How could Eleanor explain? Maybe Maria didn't realize what she was saying. Did she mangle her intentions because her English was so poor, as Natalie had suggested? (Even after twenty years in the U.S.?) Maybe Maria figured that she was praising Adam for being smart—the same way Eleanor so often praised Tad for his soccer ability. It wasn't, after all, as though Maria had said, "Of course Adam likes money. You Jewish people always like money." Or, "Of course Adam is dirty, just like a little Jewish girl wearing a dirty pink birthday dress."

But.

The silence was hanging too long.

What words could Eleanor possibly say?

In the middle of a soccer game? She couldn't make a scene, with everyone watching. Mark. Betsy.

Maria—it's a little insulting—

How would you feel if—But it wasn't the same as praising Tad! Even if Susan and Natalie were right, even if Maria's family hadn't been a bunch of Nazis during the war, even if they were only ordinary people surrounded by everyday knee-jerk anti-Semitism, and they didn't think twice about it, and they raised Maria that same way—It was still stereotyping, wasn't it? *You Jewish people.* You Jewish people are smart but you don't play soccer on Saturday and you don't eat Polish *kielbasa,* and you're just not *us.*

That was what made Maria's words so icky, and so different from simply praising one particular Polish kid like Tad.

And even if it wasn't her fault that she'd been raised that way, why hadn't Maria unlearned any of those stereotypes, after all her years in the U.S.?

"Yes," Maria was saying, "I think they turn in the project next week to the teacher? I am sure they are getting an A."

No! No, Eleanor didn't want to make a public scene, but she also could not let this be just about the sharks project. La-de-dah, sharks, boys, smart Jew, how nice, let's have some powdered dough.

Adam had stood up and was wandering toward toward their chairs.

Smart Jew. Who didn't eat sausage.

"Adam, you like more juice box?" Maria called out to him.

Who didn't play soccer on Saturday, like everyone else.

Eleanor also stood. She leaned over Maria. "That's very nice, that you think Adam is smart, and I know you didn't mean to insult him, but of course that doesn't, you know—I mean—I'm sure there are some Polish people who are smart, too."

Shit. No, that wasn't what she meant.

Maria was staring at Eleanor. Mouth open. Eyes narrowed. Not smiling any more.

"Mom," Adam asked, shivering as he hopped from foot to foot in front of them, "when can we go home?"

"I mean—What I'm trying—No one is all smart or all stupid—No group of people —We should go," Eleanor abruptly answered Adam, and she shoved the hoodie at Maria with a blurted "thank-you."

* * *

"You're leaving already?" Mark asked. Suddenly next to her.

He was standing so close that if she turned to look at him, which was of course the polite thing to do, her arm or shoulder might brush against him. She turned.

This time there was a faint smell of spearmint gum, not peppermint, and maybe leather. From his jacket? His aftershave? His jaw had a slight grazing of stubble again.

But she had to leave. She had to get away from Maria and this whole soccer game.

No, she had to go back and apologize to Maria for calling all Poles stupid.

No, Maria had to apologize.

There were only a few inches between Mark's chin and her cheek.

"So if your son isn't on the field, you don't want to stay?" He was teasing. Smiling. Pretending to shake his head reproachfully.

Had Mark forgotten that Adam had broken his finger? That was a little more serious than whether Eleanor was being a good sport and watching a soccer game. Still, she could joke along with him for a minute, before she fled. It would be nice to relax. To have a friend. She smiled back. "Oops. Sorry, I guess I should have more team spirit. But Adam's getting a little chilly. And, to be honest, I think he's bored."

"Okay, you're excused this time, but I expect you to pay more attention next week. And we'll find something to keep Adam busy."

"Yessir. I'll be cheering every move from now on."

"Good. You can be my backup. Let me know if I miss anything."

"I'm sure you don't miss much."

"I hope not."

Mark's gaze finally dropped away from her face, to his clipboard, but there was a little smile on his lips.

"Do you still want to talk about Vichy France?" he added.

Oh.

"Maybe we can meet after school one day?" he went on. "There's a new little French *boulangerie* in Edgewood that might make an appropriate milieu, so to speak."

However, Mark taught an art class at the library Monday and Wednesday afternoons, and Friday was the beginning of his weekend with Josh, while Eleanor had a faculty meeting after school on Thursday and had promised the Advanced French girls that she would help with their Marie Antoinette skit on Tuesday. The week after next, then? Tuesday? Quarter past four? The place was called La Petite Baguette.

Chapter Twenty-Four

"How is Adam's finger?" Rose asked, the minute Eleanor walked into her room on Sunday.

"How did you—?"

"Your husband told me. He's very worried."

Yes, I know he's worried. He screamed at me.

"It's just a little fracture, a very simple one, but I kind of wish Nick hadn't said anything. I didn't want to worry you. Your hip is enough injuries for our family right now." And no need to get into exactly how Adam happened to break that finger. With her mother sitting in her usual armchair, feet flat on the floor and a book in her lap, Eleanor eased herself into the second chair and pulled it closer. She arched her back to stretch, catlike. "How's your progress? How many steps did you do today?"

But when Eleanor lowered her neck from arching and looked at her mother, Rose's lips were pinched shut.

"None," Rose snapped. "I'm taking a vacation."

Rose? Taking it easy? "Why are—"

"He said it was a car accident."

"Yes. Okay. Enough about Adam! Why didn't you do more walking?"

"And enough about walking!"

From the hallway, two women's voices called out in rounded, rich Caribbean cadences. The elevator bell clanged. Rose adjusted the small throw pillows on her chair, one on each side. "It's okay, you know, if Adam breaks a bone sometimes," she said, more quietly. "People break bones."

"Sure, I know. So when did you see Nick?"

Rose looked down at her hands, folded over her book. The wedding and engagement rings. The wrinkled skin. "Feiga," she said.

A few beads of sweat pooled on Eleanor's upper lip, and she wiped them.

"My baby sister Feiga," Rose continued. "She must have been, I don't remember exactly, three years old. Four." Rose uncrossed her hands, then crossed them in the opposite direction. "We were at home. It was snowing, and it was late afternoon, after school, and I was supposed to mind Feiga. My mother was cooking in the kitchen, and my father was sitting with her—I suppose he was preparing his lessons for the next day, whatever you teachers do after school. The apartment was warm, and it smelled of my mother's wonderful cooking smells, I remember that. Probably chicken, kasha; who knows? My brother Avram would have been at *cheder*—Jewish school. Or maybe he was outside running around with the other boys. Well, he wasn't home right then. And Chana was already gone to America."

Rose's voice had gained energy. "Feiga, I think I've already told you, she was a little bit—well, a little mischief-maker. She never listened to the word 'no.' What she particularly liked to do was to climb. Maybe because she was the littlest in the family, and she wanted to be as big as the rest of us? Who knows? One of her favorite places was to climb onto a chair and from there up onto the dining table, which was a long, sturdy, wooden table. It was in the front room, not the kitchen." Finally, Rose stopped for a breath, although she barely paused. "So, on that afternoon, I wasn't paying attention—yes, I confess this —you see, Krystyna's mother had given me some scraps of beautiful soft blue wool, and I wanted to make a dress for my doll. Yes—" She glanced at Eleanor. "Yes, Krystyna and I were still playing together. At that time. So I was in the front room with Feiga, trying to push the sewing needle through my beautiful blue wool without pricking myself and getting blood on the dress—and I have to tell you, I have never been good at sewing. Not then, not later. And Feiga kept shouting, 'Look at me! Look at me!'

"And then she screamed. You see, she had come up with a new idea: After she got on top of the dining table, she was going to take the chair up onto the tabletop with her and then climb on it up there, I suppose so she could be even taller. Maybe you can guess what happened?"

Rose paused again, this time to pick up a Styrofoam cup of cold tea that was sitting on the little table next to her. She frowned, tasting it.

"Feiga fell off the chair from the top of the table, all the way to the floor?"

Rose grinned. "I knew you would say that. No! She was only three or four years old, how could she possibly be strong enough to pull a heavy wooden chair up on top of the table?" Triumphantly, Rose put down the Styrofoam cup, leaned back, and set her arms on her chair's armrests. "But she tried. She leaned over too far, trying to pull up that big heavy chair, because she was so determined. And so she lost her balance. She fell right onto the floor with a loud crash, and she screamed — and you have to realize, Ellie, in Poland we didn't have wall-to-wall carpeting. It was a hard, wooden floor."

"Oh boy." Eleanor smiled gently at her mother. "Did you get in trouble, for not watching her?"

"I was terrified, believe me. Feiga was screaming, and my mother and my father ran into the room. She was lying on her side on the floor with her leg twisted underneath her the wrong way. And there was a big, scary pool of blood next to her, let me tell you.

"In those days" —Rose sat forward all of a sudden, her voice now pouring out—"you didn't go running to the doctor or the hospital for every little thing, the way Americans do today. You took care of most problems at home. Maybe you called the *feldsher*, if you were old-fashioned. Or you went to the pharmacist, if you were modern, like we were." Briefly, she grimaced. "I told you about that pharmacist in my town. So, only if it was something more serious that a pharmacist could not take care of, then you might need the doctor. Of course we didn't know with Feiga. Maybe she had broken a bone? She was screaming, and all that blood.

"The problem was how to go fetch the doctor? We didn't have a telephone, of course. Or a horse. Or certainly not a car! No one had cars. And Avram wasn't home at that point, and I was too little to send. The doctor wasn't next-door, you know. And it was snowing.

"So: There really was no choice. My father wrapped up Feiga in layers and layers of blankets and coats as warm as he could, and they left. To walk to the doctor, carrying her. What else could he do? We watched them out the window as long as we could, in the snow, my mother and I."

Rose's voice faltered, then. She gave a quick glance at her own window as she scratched her hair for a moment.

Was that all she was going to say?

"Wow," Eleanor said softly. "How far away was the doctor?"

"My poor father. He was no *shtarker*—not a big strong man, like a farmer. He was a schoolteacher. Carrying her in the snow …. When Avram finally came home, my mother even thought to send him after Feiga and my father, but Avram complained that he was tired and hungry. I remember that, because it made him look bad, you understand? That he was too lazy to go help my father and Feiga? So we waited. For hours Or it seemed to me like hours. And then, the most amazing sound: We heard the neighing of a horse!"

At that point, as she paused, Rose laughed. "You don't understand why that was amazing, do you?"

Eleanor shook her head.

"Because who had a horse? We didn't have one; no one in our building did. It turned out," and Rose patted her skinny lap, "while my father was walking, trying to carry Feiga, a farmer came by with his horse and cart. He had been delayed at the market by the snow. A *goyisher* farmer, of course. The Jews weren't farmers. And the doctor, too, of course, was Polish. So the farmer gave them a ride. Even in the snow and the dark, and in his hurry to get home, he took my father and Feiga to the doctor, and not only that, he waited for the doctor to finish. I don't know exactly what the doctor did for Feiga, except that she came home with her leg in white bandages. But my point is, the farmer waited all that time with them and brought them home in his cart."

Her voice was quieter, and she stared at her hands in her lap. "You see, he was the farmer we had always bought the milk from. First when I went with my mother, and then when I got too big and had to go to school, then Feiga would go, and the farmer recognized her. And—" Placing her palms on the pillows around her, Rose wiggled her shoulders and her hips slightly. The pillows shifted position. "A few days later, I was walking home from school, and I saw that there were pieces of paper stuck to some of the buildings. So I walked over to read one. It was a list of prominent 'Jew-lovers' from the town." She ran an index finger down the armrest of the chair. "That doctor's name was on the list." And then ran her finger up the armrest.

"Now I just want to get the hell out of here and home to my own apartment." She waved her cold Styrofoam cup. "Can you get me some fresh tea? There should be some in that common room."

Once upon a time there was a little girl in a town in Poland named Feiga who fell down and maybe broke her leg trying to climb up on a table, while her sister Ruzia sewed a doll's dress from a beautiful piece of blue wool given to her by her Catholic friend Krystyna. Who later stopped playing with her. And a farmer gave Feiga a ride to the doctor, along with her father who was a schoolteacher, and then later the townspeople called the doctor a Jew-lover. There were so many stories. Would Rose keep going? How much more could Eleanor push?

"Ellie? Can you get me some tea?"

"Ma." Eleanor swallowed. "Why didn't you ever talk about this before?"

Rose looked toward the window, than across the room to the door. She let out a breath. She was staring at her knees.

"What makes you think I haven't talked?"

But—

Who—

"You think you're the only person in the world?" Rose added.

Eleanor swallowed again. Then she coughed. "Who did you talk to?" Her voice wobbled.

"My sister. Your father." Finally, Rose looked at Eleanor. "You're surprised?"

Eleanor nodded, then shook her head. "Aunt Chana never told Natalie…?"

Rose shrugged. "Of course not. I said to her, and she agreed, that these are my stories, not hers. For me to tell, not her."

"So why didn't you tell me and Steven and Natalie?"

Rose sucked in her cheeks, one side, then the other. "You mean when you were nagging and nagging me?"

Eleanor shut her eyes.

When she opened them, Rose was smiling very, very slightly. "It's complicated, Ellie."

There were footsteps in the hallway, the brisk snap of rubber-soled shoes, the mumble of a man's voice, the reply of a woman's Caribbean accent. A quiet bump; maybe a wheelchair banging against a wall? The man shouted.

"When I first came to the United States, you know, I didn't want to talk. Not to anyone. Not anything. And once I finally was ready to talk, a little, after a few years, of course I had Chana. And then your father, until two years ago." Rose wrapped her fingers together in her lap. "And you know, in our family, in many families, the parents protect the children. Right? We don't tell them the bad news And then the children protect the parents sometimes, when they get older. My parents, in Poland, they pretended that Chana was only going to America for a little vacation. They must have seen that conditions were getting worse in our town—you know, that list of 'Jew-lovers' didn't come from nowhere, so? So they probably sent Chana to America to be safe. But that's not what they said to my brother and my sister and me." At that, Rose tilted her head, studying Eleanor. "Like you not telling me about Adam's broken finger, hmm? Protecting me?"

"I didn't want to put my painful memories on my children."

"But we're not children any more."

"So? What was the point of telling you?"

"Because it's my history!"

"No, Ellie. It's mine."

Facing her mother, across the span of only a small square table, Eleanor leaned forward an inch or two. She opened her mouth.

"You see, Ellie? You pushed me as if my life was a — a dress of yours that I had taken, and I should give it back. You pushed whether or not I was ready. Whether or not it was painful. I mean, yes, sometimes I wanted to talk about it. That's true. I knew I would tell you and your brother eventually. I needed to find the right way, and the right time."

"I'm sorry," Eleanor whispered. "I did stop pushing sometimes, you know."

"Yes. Well, I probably made it into too much of a big secret. You know, we all have stories. All of us 'survivors' —ech, that's the fancy name they give us. I hate that name. Yes," —she nodded toward Eleanor—"I went to one of those 'survivor' groups. A few times. Nonsense."

"So why did you start talking now?" Immediately, Eleanor clamped her left hand over her mouth. "I mean—Am I pushing you now? Should I stop?"

With her palms flat on her face, Rose ran her fingertips along each eyebrow, away from the top of her nose, and down each cheek, meeting in a prayer clasp under her chin. "Why? Maybe it was time. The anger piddles away after a while, you know. And then your father died. And then this"—Rose pointed to her hip. "At my age, broken bones make you realize how old you are. Next time it could be a stroke, and I wouldn't be able to talk at all." She sighed. "Because you asked, and this time I was ready." Turning toward Eleanor, she offered a little smile. "I don't mean to shut you up, Ellie. Go ahead."

"Go ahead?"

"Ask. But maybe not too much?"

"I don't know where to begin." Eleanor reached out her hand, across the little table.

"Actually," Rose said, "you could ask your husband."

Eleanor frowned. "What do you mean?"

"You know, after your father died." Rose licked her top lip, bringing her front teeth down to bite her tongue for an instant as she released a breath. "He was so helpful, you know. Nick. Bringing me meals that he cooked, and, you know, I was so used to talking with your father. So. I started talking with him, a little. Nick. And he didn't nag me, Ellie." Rose drew in and released another long breath. "Oh Ellie, you're like me, you know. Sometimes a little pushy. And I'm hard to take, aren't I?" Rose held out her Styrofoam cup. "Could I please get some tea?"

* * *

"So, ask," Rose declared, when Eleanor returned—with tea, although she'd spilled the first cup and then forgotten the sugar. "What do you want to know?"

What did Eleanor want to know? Everything. What games did Ruzia like to play in Poland? What was her favorite subject in school? What did her school look like? And her bedroom? Her family, the schoolteach-er-father, the baby Feiga who loved to climb, Avram, her mother—what did they all talk about together at dinner? What signs of anti-Semitism had she seen and did it get worse? What was the name of her town? What had Rose told Nick already—and why hadn't that fucker told Eleanor?

"I guess—begin with your family," Eleanor stuttered. "Tell me something about each person in your family."

Rose wrinkled her forehead a moment as she massaged her right earlobe between her thumb and index finger. "I remember my mother brushing my hair and tying a big white ribbon in a bow." Her face morphed into a wistful smile. "Her name was Necha. I was very little, and I sat in her lap and held the mirror by the handle, so I watched while she brushed. The mirror was oval, with a pink handle. And my hair was very wild and curly, so it always got tangled. Like yours, but dark blonde. I told you that, right?"

Eleanor nodded.

"Chana," Rose went on. "She gave me a pink dress from one of her dolls and helped me put it on my doll. I remember the dress. It was a long gown with puffy sleeves.

"Avram, I don't know. Mostly I remember him telling me to stop bothering him. And watching him play soccer, of course. Well—no, I do remember nice times." She glanced down as she tapped her lap. "He must have just learned to read. And I hadn't started school yet. So he let me sit next to him at the table, the big dining table that Feiga tried to climb, yes, and he turned the pages of his book very slowly, and he pointed to each word as he read it. It was *Hansel and Gretel*." Then she rubbed her thumb against her lower lip. "The first time my father took me to Pani Helena's house, and I was pulling on his arm, trying to stop him. But I didn't dare say anything. Because you know, if I told him that everyone said she was a witch, he would say I was being an ignorant peasant."

Her favorite toy.

Her favorite food.

Something she studied in school.

What Salka looked like.

What her mother and father looked like.

"Why did you talk Polish to the EMT in the ambulance?"

"I did? When?"

"You know— when you fell in the bathroom."

"Polish? Oh, I don't know. I don't remember. I was in pain, who knows what I was saying?"

What games she played.

What kinds of shops were in the town and what she bought there.

What books she read.

What signs of anti-Semitism she saw.

"How did you survive the Nazis?" Eleanor asked, finally.

Rose slowly shook her head. "I'm tired, Ellie. I need a break. Next time."

* * *

From Rose and the rehab center, Eleanor drove to the CVS on Edgewood Avenue. Just to fill Adam's prescription for Advil.

True, Adam was doing fine on the Motrin. Nevertheless, it couldn't hurt to have an alternate painkiller around the house, in case he suddenly developed a bad reaction to the first one.

Of course, Maria might not even be working at CVS today.

But if she was, well, Eleanor certainly had to apologize for yesterday's soccer game and for all but saying that all Poles were stupid. And then. . . Maria was there.

Standing alone behind the "Drop Off" window of the pharmacy section, wearing a white, short-sleeved, imitation-doctor jacket, gazing down at the counter, reading something. When she first looked up, at the sound of Eleanor's footsteps, her face briefly had the sober, tired appearance that had once shown up at the soccer field, but it disappeared promptly into a formal smile. "Ah, Eleanor. Hello." Her tone hovered between businesslike and pleasant.

"Oh. Hi, Maria. I didn't realize you were working today."

"Someone is sick and you need medicine? I am sorry to hear that."

"No, no." Eleanor opened her leather bag wide to search for the small prescription slip. "I just wanted to fill a—uh—a new prescription for Adam. It's for the same finger that he hurt." Digging out the paper from her wallet, she handed it to Maria. "No, listen, I need to apologize, Maria. For what I said at the, um, soccer game. Yesterday. About smart Polish people—I didn't mean it the way it probably sounded."

Maria shook her head with a tiny smile.

"It was totally rude of me, after you were so nice about Adam. Giving him a jacket."

Maria was studying the writing on the paper and typing something on her computer keyboard. "You can pick up in one hour?"

Well, what else could Eleanor say? She had tried to apologize. She should just leave now.

She would only be asking for trouble if she asked Maria about her parents and the giggling. Being too pushy. Hadn't she insulted Maria enough by now?

And yet: What if Eleanor had said "enough" and stopped asking her mother about Poland? Look what she would have missed!

Maybe one more try with Maria?

"This must be so different from your grandfather's pharmacy in Poland. So much bigger. Did you ever help him at his pharmacy? Or your father?"

"Of course. That is how I am interested to work in pharmacy."

"That's so nice. The grandfather-granddaughter pharmacy."

They both tittered. Finally, Maria was loosening up a little.

"I suppose you had many different types of customers, in a big city like Krakow."

Maria furrowed her brows. "Why do you ask about Krakow?"

"Isn't that where you're from? Near Krakow?"

"No, no." Maria laughed, more naturally now. "Janek is from Nowa Huta. From the steel mills near to Krakow. I meet him here in New Jersey."

"Oh. So where are you from?"

"Ah." Maria waved dismissively. "It is a little town near Warsaw. You will not know it."

A little town near Warsaw.

A town where a mother and daughter bought milk from big metal cans in the market, and the farmer might give them a ride in his horse and cart to the Jew-loving doctor. Where boys played soccer in a field near the *gimnazjum* and a Jewish Socialist sat on the town council. Where the pharmacist was a Nazi. Which was probably why his family didn't suffer during the war.

This was ridiculous. Coincidences like this didn't happen. There had to be dozens of small towns near Warsaw.

"What"—Eleanor cleared her throat and closed her eyes, then opened them—"what's the name of your town?" She forced her lips to continue smiling.

"Ah, it is just a little town. Not famous."

"That's okay." Eleanor's voice was as bad as Rose's cigarette voice.

Maria smiled in response.

"Tell me."

And Maria said a name. Three syllables. With an S sound and a K and a W and ending in an "ooff" sound.

Why the fuck hadn't Eleanor stuck with her studies of Polish in college? Why did she switch to stupid French? S and K and what the hell?

"Repeat it!"

"What do you ask?"

Eleanor swallowed. "I'm sorry. It's, uh, so interesting. Languages. You know. Because I study languages. Could you, um, repeat the name?"

Fucking unpronounceable Polish.

Saw-kaw-woof. Eleanor nodded, in time to the syllables. *Saw-kaw-woof.*

As soon as she was in the vitamin aisle, heading toward the front door, beyond the sightline from the pharmacy counter, not even waiting until she was outside the store, Eleanor scrambled in her bag for a pen. But she didn't have one. Not a pencil nor a crayon nor a marker.

In the car, speeding home to pen and paper, she repeated the litany in her head, over and over. *S — K — W — ooff. S — K — W —ooff.* Were the vowels a sort of short A or more of an "aw"? *Sah-Kah-Wooff? Saw-Kaw-Wawff? Saw-Kaw-Wahff?* Or even an "ow"? How had Maria said it, dammit! What had happened to Eleanor's ear for languages? *Sah-Kah-Wowff? Saw-Kaw-Wowff?*

Chapter Twenty-Five

But Rose wanted to complain about her doctor.

"He never shows up. Once a week, that's it. And all he says is, 'You're doing fine, keep going.' 'Keep going.' I've been here a month now, and I think I'm entitled to some better explanation. When do I go home?"

How about your home in Poland?

How did you survive the Holocaust?

Is it really okay to keep asking you questions?

What was the name of your town?

There was already too much to absorb, and yet so much more to know. Eleanor even had her marble composition notebook with her, so that she could take notes properly. But what if Rose decided the timing wasn't right any more and clammed up again? There wasn't time for complaining about doctors. Rose could complain later. How bad could the doctor be?

What was the name of the Nazi pharmacist?

No: Even if Rose knew the guy's name, what good would that do? It wouldn't prove whether he was or was not Maria's father or grandfather, because Maria's father's and grandfather's last name wouldn't have been Wysocki. It would have been Maria's birth name.

Besides which, Rose had said there was at least one other pharmacist in the town. So Maria's grandfather could just as well have been him. If Maria was, in fact, from the same town.

"And the nurses don't know anything," Rose was saying, tapping her armrests. "All they know is how to tell you to do their *meshugeh* exercises. Slide your heel. Lift your leg. Blah blah blah."

The lamps on the nightstand, the dresser, and the little table next to the armchairs cast cones of varying shades of yellow light into the late-afternoon grayness of Rose's room. Although the building was too warm, as always, Rose wore a matching cardigan sweater over her dark-blue tailored blouse.

Did the pharmacist have a granddaughter?

That would be an even more useless question. Maria hadn't been born yet, when Rose was still living in Poland. No, the more accurate questions were: *Did the Nazi pharmacist have a teenage son? And was that son dating a local girl? And did they giggle?* And how could Rose possibly know any of those answers?

Rose held out her right hand, gesturing toward the door. "Can you go to the office, please? Get me the name and telephone number for the doctor, and I will call him myself, instead of waiting for his convenience. Thank you."

Did the name of your town begin S—K—something?

"And if they try to tell you I should wait, he'll be here in a few days—feh! Just get the telephone number."

"Doctor's name. Okay. I'll be back as fast as I can."

What have you been telling Nick all these years?

"Wait. Slow down." Leaning back in her chair, Rose flicked her eyelids shut for a second or two and breathed deeply.

Eleanor sat down and put her leather bag on the floor. Rubbed her own forehead. Picked her bag up, to dig out a pen and her notebook.

Once upon a time, in a small town near Warsaw, there was a little girl with wild, dark-blonde hair that sometimes was tied back with a white ribbon, and her big brother read *Hansel and Gretel* to her, and her little sister came back in a farmer's horse cart after she broke her leg and the Jew-loving doctor fixed it, but the Nazi pharmacist hated them all.

Had Rose told Nick the name of her town? The pharmacist's name? How many stories did he know about Feiga and Avram and her grandfather the teacher? About Salka and the Catholic girl Krystyna whose mother made beautiful dolls? Or maybe Nick and Rose had shared recipes, Grandma's cheesecake and Nick's salmon mousse.

Why hadn't he told Eleanor that her own mother was telling him all these stories?

If he would ever be home from his stupid goddam job saving the world, maybe Eleanor could ask him.

"And also," Rose continued, turning again to Eleanor, "please see if you can find some fresh tea. Okay, go. Thank you."

Eleanor backed out of the doorway and half-ran down the corridor.

* * *

"I was just wondering, Ma, after we talked yesterday, what was the name of your town in Poland?"

It sped out of her mouth in a tumble of words, and Rose frowned. Eleanor held up her marble notebook and pen. Rose crossed her arms.

"Now, all of a sudden, you need to know everything about Poland in five minutes."

"Now, all of a sudden, you're talking."

It was almost four-thirty already. Soon it would be dinnertime at the rehab center. Soon Eleanor would have to go home to make her own family's dinner.

"Ma, you've left two messages for the doctor's answering service. There's nothing else you can do today."

"You couldn't pronounce the name," Rose said.

"I'm a foreign language teacher, remember?"

Rose stared into the Styrofoam teacup, curling the edge of her lips. She blew into the water, which wasn't even steaming. "S-O-C-H." She put the cup on the square table. "Aren't you going to write it down?"

Eleanor dropped her pen as she fumbled open the notebook.

Rose finished spelling it out, letter by Polish letter.

And there it was: Sochaczew.

Eleanor's roots.

Once upon a time there was a town in Poland called Sochaczew where four children named Chana, Avram, Ruzia and Feiga had grown up. Or started to grow up, before they fled or were killed. In a second-floor apartment, in a town with a little girl named Krystyna, whose mother made beautiful dolls, and a Nazi pharmacist.

"Say it," Eleanor demanded.

Saw-khah-cheff.

Was that what Rose had said?

"Again."

"Again."

Eleanor looked up. Her mother was smiling a little sadly at her.

But was Sochaczew or *Sawkhahcheff* anything like the name Maria had said?

Maria's town's name also had three syllables, beginning with an S-ah-K, right? Or S-aw-K. And ending in "ff." Except hadn't there been a W? Or was Eleanor confusing that with the Polish W that was pronounced "vee"? Damn, she'd been speaking French all day at school, and now her mind was too confused by too many different languages, with too many different sounds.

What kind of a lousy foreign-language teacher was she, that she couldn't even get one name straight?

She would have to ask Maria to spell out her town's name. Somehow, she would have to concoct a reason why she needed to know that. And also ask her what her birth name was. While Maria was probably still insulted over Eleanor's comment about stupid Poles. And if she could ever convince Adam to go to another soccer game.

And she had to ask Nick. What stories had Rose told him already? Why hadn't he told her?

And talk to Rose's doctor.

And tell Natalie, Kate, and Adam everything she'd learned. And call Steven.

First, though, there was one more question for Rose that couldn't wait.

"How did you get out of Poland?"

Chapter Twenty-Six

Already, by 1936, things were getting worse. Even a nine-year-old girl could sense it. One day, walking to school, Ruzia and Salka saw a gang of teenage boys beating up an old man with a shaggy white beard and long black coat. They recognized the old man from the synagogue.

After that, their parents wouldn't let them walk to school alone. One of their mothers always went with them.

The phrase "dirty Jew" was heard more often. After church on Sundays, the peasants would march out in a line, singing and carrying crucifixes. Jews began staying home on Sundays, with their doors barred.

Each week, more Jewish stores were vandalized. At the tailor's shop, tough-looking boys hovered around the entrance slapping heavy branches against their thighs. On the butcher's window, someone scrawled: *Zyd*. Yid. Jew.

A year went by, and another.

There was a time when Salka's father had to go to Warsaw, but none of the horse-coach drivers would give him a ride to the train station, and he finally had to walk. Of course Krystyna had already stopped playing with Ruzia.

The Nazi pharmacist refused to serve Jews at all. Wouldn't even let them in the door. When Feiga got sick, their mother sent Avram and Ruzia to another pharmacy, which was much farther away.

You heard names, sometimes. In whispers. The grownups mentioned Hitler, certainly. A pogrom in a Polish city somewhere. Jews beaten in Germany, their synagogues and stores ransacked and burned. Although they stopped talking as soon as Ruzia or Avram or their friends came into the room, you could hear the fear hiding behind the whispers.

Still, they were kids, so they didn't pay all that much attention. School rolled on, as did the holidays. Pani Helena continued to invite Ruzia into her cottage for her dreadful *makowiec* poppy-seed cake. If Ruzia's mother whispered about Hitler and pogroms, Salka's mother acted normally. Another year came and went.

Hitler was in a foreign country. Pogroms were something from the eighteen-hundreds.

Ruzia celebrated her twelfth birthday on July 17, 1939. Her grandmother, aunts, uncles, and cousins came to her apartment; her mother baked the special cheesecake as always, and her parents gave her a fancy hair ribbon with flowers. Six weeks later, on September 1, Hitler invaded Poland.

Within days, the war was in Ruzia's town. There was fighting very nearby, you heard and saw and breathed it. Airplanes screeched overhead day and night, pummeling the ground with bombs as if they were shaking dirtballs from a rug. The synagogue burned like a towering Shabbos candle.

One day the town was swarming with German soldiers carrying their terrifying swastika flags, the next day the Germans were gone and Polish soldiers filled the streets. But then the Germans returned, and stayed.

Some people fled to Warsaw. Ruzia's parents debated.

Salka's parents left but came back. Everywhere was chaos, they said. Homes were bombed and burning. The roads were so crowded with carts and people that you couldn't move anyway.

And then it was too late to decide.

The Jews weren't rounded up and sent to concentration camps immediately. The Germans started by setting fire to dozens and dozens of Jewish houses. Not Ruzia's apartment building, luckily. So far. However, that meant that all the burnt-out families had to crowd in with those who still had homes. Two families—teachers who worked with her father, plus their wives and children—suddenly were living with Ruzia's family in four rooms.

Feiga slept with Ruzia in her bed. There were two other girls in Chana's bed, a third on a pile of clothing on the floor, and two boys with Avram in the front room, along with the big table. All the adults shared the second bedroom.

Next, Jewish families were ordered out of the homes that were still in good shape, and these families, too, squeezed into the remaining Jewish apartments. Three new strangers somehow moved in with Ruzia's family.

And yet more: Apparently Jews were being kicked out of many cities, and hundreds of them abruptly arrived in Ruzia's town in January.

But jam-packed as it was, the apartment was better than being outside. One of the teachers who now lived with them went out one morning to hunt for food, and he didn't return until two days later, filthy, starving, barely able to drag himself through the door. German soldiers had grabbed him to go work repairing the bridge over the Bzura River, he said.

They cornered a group of Hasidim and made them dance in the marketplace, wearing their prayer shawls. Nonstop. Over and over. No, not the Germans. This was done by their Polish neighbors, as they were leaving church.

Some of the non-Jews suffered, too, it was true. In the first week, the Germans had arrested the doctor who had taken care of Feiga's leg, along with the town's other doctor, the mayor, the town council, the *gimnazjum* principal, and pretty much anyone else who had an education or a position of authority, Catholic or Jewish.

At the beginning, the grown-ups' whispering had been loud, excited. The big rich countries like England and France would be coming to the rescue with airplanes and soldiers. That talk quickly ended.

In December, all Jews were ordered to wear a yellow Star of David on their clothes, which was a problem for people like Ruzia and her mother, who didn't sew very well. If only Krystyna's mother could help.

To match the Jews' yellow stars, the Nazi pharmacist had a red armband with a swastika. As did an amazing number of other people in their town. Farmers. Teachers from the Catholic school. The baker where Ruzia had sometimes bought rolls for a treat. And his bakery now had a sign: "No Jews or Dogs Allowed."

Not that it really mattered any more. Food was rationed to almost nothing. The birthday cheesecake was a long-ago memory. So were milk, eggs, chicken, and butter. Also soap. You traded jewelry, plates, anything you could at the few stalls that opened, sometimes, in the deserted marketplace. The *goyim* were hungry and rationed, too, but not as severely as the Jews. Once Ruzia's mother sent Ruzia to buy something—potatoes, maybe—and the Poles already in line spat at her and yelled at her when they saw her coat with the yellow star, and finally, when one woman picked up a rock, Ruzia ran home.

The schools were all closed. The kids cheered at first, as though they could have a permanent vacation; however, Ruzia's father and some other parents quickly organized small, secret classes in their homes. Her father taught Avram, Ruzia, Feiga, Salka, Salka's older brother, and the seven other children living with them.

And he was a tough, mean teacher. Although he didn't yell or hit them with a leather strap, his voice grew very cold when Ruzia got an answer wrong.

Even playing, it seemed, was not for Jews. No one dared leave the apartment building unless it was absolutely necessary, mainly to search for food and firewood. The braver ones scrounged for mushrooms in the woods and scraps in the street. Playing inside, though, was still allowed. Playing with dolls, reading the Brothers Grimm, giggling with Salka, tickling Feiga: Those bits of pleasure remained.

One day, abruptly, Salka's brother was not with them for their lessons. He had run away, somehow, Salka whispered. To safety? Where was that?

Now, hissing through the adults' strained whispers, they heard the word "ghetto." Wasn't a ghetto something from the Middle Ages? By Hanukkah time, the whispers had shifted and became about escape and hiding. Especially, hiding children.

Sometimes Ruzia, Avram, and Salka would huddle together, to try to figure things out.

The pharmacist had been named to some sort of official position by the Nazis, and he was posting notices everywhere with his signature and a big seal, under the salutation "Heil Hitler." All Jewish stores must be turned over to the government. Jews may not ride horse carts. Jews may not ride the train. Jews may not walk on the sidewalk. Jews may not speak to Germans.

The tiny cache of food shrank further. There was no coal for the stove, and they started burning furniture. The books went last.

Eventually, the grown-ups stopped whispering. What was the point of pretending to hide anything from the children?

Then their home-school lessons ended, because the chief teacher, Ruzia's father, was gone. Along with the two other teachers, and the seventeen-year-old son of one of them, and the man who had moved in with them when his house was taken over, and all the Jewish men in all the apartments.

And the winter went on and on, dragging out the cold and hunger with it, until one day their mother pulled Ruzia, Avram and Feiga into a corner of what had been Ruzia's bedroom and was now the multiple girls' dormitory. She explained: The best plan at this point —what a lot of Jewish families were doing—was to split up. Only until these bad times were over. To find a nice Polish family, or two families, who would let the children live with them, while their mother protected the apartment. Or perhaps—their mother's mouth made a smile that even a twelve-year-old could tell was fake—perhaps just Ruzia and Feiga would leave.

Why not me? Avram demanded.

I need you to help me, their mother said quickly.

Salka clarified the matter the next day: It was impossible to hide a Jewish boy and pretend he was Catholic, because of the circumcision. Her brother had described this to her, in some detail.

Salka, herself, had no hiding place yet.

But Feiga and Ruzia were safe! The farmer with the horse and cart who had given Feiga a ride to the doctor—the one who had always poured their milk from his big metal can at the market—he had agreed to take the girls. He could hide them on his farm.

Except that two days later, the farmer's wife panicked. Hiding two Jews was too hard. She would take only Feiga.

Why Feiga? Why not Ruzia? You didn't ask. Maybe because Feiga had been the one who had been going to the market with their mother most recently. Or maybe because she was younger, cuter, more likely to forget her real parents.

Krystyna will hide me! Ruzia suggested to her mother.

Her mother had already asked. Krystyna's family had refused.

* * *

"After the war, I went back to our town, to try and find them," Rose said. "I asked everyone I saw. You couldn't have any pride or shame; they stared at you with faces full of hate, or they turned their backs and spat on the ground. Or they were suddenly all phony smiles, painted on like lipstick. They said to you, 'How come you didn't die?' None of them had seen anything during the war, of course not. None of them had realized that all the Jews had disappeared. Oh, and they had never liked the Nazis, none of them. So you nodded, you didn't argue, you just kept asking. Did they know what happened to your mother, your father, your brother, your sister? They were living in your best friend's house, and you pretended not to notice, and you just asked: 'Do you know what happened to the people who used to live here?' I asked Krystyna's mother —Krystyna herself had married and moved away. I asked someone from the volunteer fire brigade who had known my father."

"How did Krystyna's mother treat you?"

"Eh. She opened the door a crack. She said she didn't know anything. And then she wished me *dobranoc*—a very polite good night—before she shut the door in my face."

"God, you must have hated her!"

"At that point, Ellie? You did what you had to do. You didn't have the time for hating or for crying. And you know, Ellie, when I finally could talk about it? Yes, they were cruel. But what am I going to hate now, after all this time? Krystyna was a little girl. Her mother did what she had to do, too."

Rose was sitting straight up in the green armchair, staring at the bed, her voice like the recitation of a teacher reading a math book aloud, her red lipstick in place. Only her fingers moved. Clutching the armrests; sometimes twitching. "After a few days, I saw Salka's brother, standing next to a building with broken windows. I had hardly known him before the war, he was much older than we were. He told me how he had hidden in all kinds of different places. Haylofts. Attics. He joined the partisans at the end. They allowed him in because he didn't tell them he was Jewish."

She let go of the armrests and ran her palms down the legs of her sweatpants. "So Salka's brother and a couple of his friends took me with them, and we walked away from the town and into the forest. To the west. Through the fields, through villages, through more forests. It took days and days, until we could sneak across the border into Germany and reach a DP camp. That was the only way to get out of Poland, to America. HIAS—the Jewish immigration group—they helped me find Chana in New York." With one hand, she brushed some hair away from her ear and forehead.

"So what happened to your family? Our family."

Rose's hand dropped into her lap. "Most of the Jews from our town were sent to the Warsaw ghetto, and then Treblinka. We found a lot of their names through Yad Vashem in Israel, Chana and I. We found Salka and her family there, too." Her fingers, all ten laced together, squeezed her palms shut, then open. "The pharmacist didn't waste a minute. As soon as the Germans showed up, he gave them a list of every single Jew.

He had already prepared it." She paused, to blow a breath out of her pursed red-lipsticked lips. "But I can't blame it all on him. He wasn't the one who turned in the farmer who had hidden Feiga; that was the baker, who did that. The Germans gave him a hundred zlotys and a bottle of vodka, so they said."

Eleanor waited.

"But how about you?" she asked.

Rose raised her eyebrows. "You haven't guessed?"

* * *

The evening after the farmer said he wouldn't take Ruzia, though before he actually came to get Feiga, Pani Helena walked into their apartment building. She hobbled up the stairs and stopped, hovering right outside their front doorway, leaning on her too-short cane. The cane that Ruzia's father had shaved free of splinters. She had never come to their building before.

The other children who were living in the apartment at that point ran screaming into the bedrooms and kitchen at the sight of the witch, except for Avram and a couple of the boys, who were out scavenging for food.

Pani Helena beckoned to Ruzia's mother, who walked over, tugging Ruzia with her.

"Pack up a bundle," Pani Helena said sternly, staring into Ruzia's mother's face. She was wearing a frayed grey shawl and a brown cotton kerchief that was tied under her chin. "I will save your daughter," she said. Just like that. No hugs, no tears. Her voice sounded almost angry. Ruzia was the one who started to cry. Her mother slapped her. Then her mother looked at Pani Helena and whispered, also without emotion, without tears or hugs, "*Dziękuję.*" Thank you.

While Ruzia stood, frozen, by the door, her mother ran to the big oak cupboard in the front room and yanked at the bottom drawer. It took a few tries before she could open it; the drawer was heavy, and her fingers were shaking. Her dress was dark blue, gathered at the waist with a cloth belt.

Her shaking fingers pawed through whatever was inside the drawer until she finally pulled out a black carpetbag. All the time, Pani Helena stood in her spot, frowning, leaning slightly forward with both hands on the top of her cane, as the big clock on the table ticked loudly.

Everyone else watched from the doorways to the other rooms.

Ruzia's mother strode back to the door and dumped the bag into Ruzia's arms. It was scratchy and heavier than Ruzia had expected. Her mother told her to pack warm clothes and spare shoes, but Ruzia still couldn't move. Couldn't cry, couldn't talk, couldn't think about what her mother was saying, until her mother finally had to take her hand and drag her into the bedroom that she now shared with Feiga and all the other girls, and that she used to share with Chana. The girls in the doorway scattered, some deeper into the bedroom and some into the front room.

Inside the bedroom, her mother let go of Ruzia and seemed to scrabble at clothing from the wardrobe at random, nonstop. If something looked too small she threw it on the floor and went to the next one, and if it looked big enough she shoved it into the carpetbag, woolen stockings, underwear, skirts, sweaters, a pair of shoes from beneath the bed. She took a step toward the front door, then back, to grab two books. A pause again at the bedroom doorway, then to the kitchen, and she wrapped a towel around a few rolls that, too, were squeezed into that scratchy, heavy bag.

Finally, putting down the bag, her mother gripped Ruzia's shoulders and wrapped her arms around Ruzia, folded Ruzia to her chest, sank her face into Ruzia's curly, almost-blonde hair. Ruzia locked her arms around her mother's back so that no one could unlock them. Into her hair, her mother whispered, haltingly, stuttering. In Yiddish, not Polish: "I love you, Ruzieleh. We'll see each other soon. When this is over. I love you." And: "Stay alive."

But then her mother stood up and pushed Ruzia away, so hard that Ruzia's hands instinctively ungripped from behind her back before Ruzia realized what the hands were doing.

Her mother shoved Ruzia at Pani Helena.

Even worse, her mother kissed Pani Helena's hand. The witch's wrinkled, dirty-peasant hand. Picked one hand up from the top of the cane and kissed it. Ruzia felt a scream coming out. Feiga, standing by the bedroom with the other girls, actually did scream. Maybe, then, Feiga realized what was happening.

Pani Helena nodded at her mother, took the bag, and clutched Ruzia's fingers along with the bag in that dirty, wrinkled, kissed, witch's hand while the other hand held the cane. And pulled her to the door.

Ruzia wriggled to turn around.

Maybe she started to scream.

Feiga came flying from the bedroom doorway, but their mother caught her before she could reach Ruzia.

"You must be quiet," Pani Helena muttered.

Ruzia's mother slammed the heavy front door shut as soon as Ruzia's feet crossed the doorway. Ruzia could still hear Feiga's screams through the wood.

And then, whether it was because Pani Helena was pulling her, or gravity was helping, Ruzia's feet were stumbling down the staircase behind the witch and the bag and the cane and away from her home.

Outside, it was dark. Pani Helena's grip was strong. Ruzia was wearing her woolen coat but had forgotten to put on her cap or wrap a scarf around her throat, so the bitterly cold air slapped her face the way her mother had. And maybe, at that point, deep within her frozen brain, Ruzia knew. She didn't try to scream, nor did Pani Helena really have to drag her any more.

In the darkness, they walked close to the sides of buildings, ducking any light that might flicker out of a window. That is, they limp-walked, slowly, both of them at Pani Helena's leaden gait. Set the cane in place, put the left foot forward, drag the right leg to follow. Left foot forward. Right leg drag. Left foot forward. Right leg drag. Slowly. Stooping over the cane that was too short. Silently, except for the soft scrape of the right foot in the dirt. The soldiers patrolling on the main streets were louder.

It must have taken an hour to limp through the town, past the marketplace and then past the brick factory beyond. They were nowhere near Pani Helena's cottage. They kept walking. Out in the open wheat and cabbage fields, there were no buildings to hide them from the chubby moon's light, although of course there were also fewer soldiers patrolling. They walked more. Left food forward. Right foot drag. The cane stumbled often in the uneven dirt. Then the fields ended at an abrupt wall of trees, and Pani Helen simply kept walking forward into a space between two of the trees.

There was no path, merely more such spaces between trees. The air was the slightest notch warmer within the huddled protection of the tall, thick tree trunks, but the sky was darker, as the tangled branches and their early-spring leaves blocked the moonlight. Pani Helena's witch-eyes could see through blackness. And they kept walking.

They didn't stop to eat or drink, nor to seek out a path or change their route. Pani Helena never shifted the bag to her other hand or let go of Ruzia, and she never asked Ruzia to carry the bag. The feet just moved forward.

At some point, Pani Helena's old body must have given out, because all of a sudden she crumpled to a seated position under a tree. From a pocket in her wide brown skirt, she dug out two boiled potatoes. She held out one toward Ruzia.

Ruzia considered, for a quick second, running away. But she was too lost and too scared of the night, and then she fell asleep instead.

Pani Helena shook her awake even before the sky held any hint of pink. This time Ruzia ate the apple that the old lady offered and even ate a piece of her poppy-seed cake, which was as dry and hard as ever. And then they were limp-walking again. Shivering from the left-over night chill, her back sore from sleeping on the rocky ground, her legs aching, dragging almost as badly as Pani Helena's right leg, Ruzia walked.

Until, with a step forward, there were no more trees in front of them.

They entered the rough rectangle of a clearing surrounded by forest, facing two long furrows and a thatched-roof cottage far more bedraggled than Pani Helena's. A half-dozen scrawny chickens pecked tiredly in the dirt of a fenced-in yard next to a second, smaller shack. Three goats were tied to different sections of the wooden fence, and a filthy pig lay in the mud in one corner. A woman with pale blonde hair stood in the cottage doorway watching them limp closer.

When they were only steps away, a little boy darted out from behind the woman and ran back into the cottage, screaming.

Pani Helena limped until she and Ruzia stood in front of the blonde woman. A short man in a torn brown vest, striding from the side of the cottage, abruptly halted.

The woman swallowed visibly. "Hello, Mother," she whispered.

* * *

The girl was her brother's grandchild Janina, now orphaned, Pani Helena sternly told her daughter and son-in-law, shoving the carpet-bag toward them. A little Polish-Catholic girl with curly, dark blonde hair whose papers had gotten lost.

The daughter never said: "You don't have a brother. I don't have a cousin Janina."

Janina would remain here at the cottage until Pani Helena came to retrieve her, and meanwhile, she would earn her keep doing whatever chores needed to be done.

She did earn her keep. For nearly five years, she washed cabbages, she boiled cabbages in a huge iron pot, she took bowls of rotten cabbage ends to the pig, and in the spring she dug into the hard earth of the clearing to plant more cabbages. Also beets. She milked the goats. She carried heavy wooden buckets to the stream in the woods, and she lugged the filled buckets back, even heavier, her arms dragging down almost to her feet as sharp waves splashed over the sides of the buckets and against her legs. Then back to the stream with dirty clothes to scrub, and again to the cottage with sort-of clean clothes. In the freezing winter, in the snow, in the summer, in the spring.

The little boy was named Bogdan, and it turned out that there was also a little girl, Eva, his younger sister, and they worked too. Everyone worked. Bogdan and his father cut branches and laid traps in the woods for rabbits and birds and maybe — if they might be very, very lucky — a wild boar. Little Eva gathered eggs and fed the chickens and pig. Pani Helena's daughter cooked over the big iron pot at the hearth, filling the cottage with black smoke from the logs that her husband chopped and Bogdan and Ruzia-Janina dragged in, and the kindling that Ruzia-Janina and Eva scrounged in the woods, smoke so thick that Ruzia-Janina never stopped coughing, not summer nor winter, for those long five years.

The second shack was a kind of barn, and that was where Ruzia-Janaina slept. There was plenty of straw, reeking of urine and cabbage. But there was no heat, so when the first big snow came the following autumn, the family finally let her sleep with them in the cottage, on the kitchen floor. They all slept there during the winter; they dragged a straw-filled mattress and a stack of torn quilts into the kitchen every evening and huddled close to the smoldering heat of the smoky stove, Pani Helena's daughter and son-in-law on the mattress, Bogdan and Eva on the quilts. For Ruzia-Janina, they made a bed out of a pile of dirty clothes. Many nights, Ruzia-Janina heard movement from the mattress. She heard low grunting noises and high-pitched squeals and a steady pounding of the mattress against the floor.

As soon as it was warm enough to start planting, the sleepover ended. The daughter and son-in-law were back in the bedroom, Bogdan and Eva went to the tiny attic, and Ruzia-Janina returned to the barn-shack.

When she wore out the shoes she'd brought, she went barefoot like the others in spring and summer, and the son-in-law fashioned some sort of footwear out of boar skin in the fall. When she outgrew the two skirts she'd brought, the daughter showed her how to rip the hem off of one of them in order to sew it onto the other for extra length, and then Eva got the remainder of the first skirt. No one cared if she pricked her finger with the sewing needle and got blood on the skirts.

For a few months, Ruzia-Janina tried to read the two books her mother had packed at the last minute, but it was so hard in the smoky cottage, and too dark outside or in the barn after she had finished her chores, and she was so tired. And by wintertime, the books were gone anyway. Probably taken for the stove.

There was too little food and even less laughter. Every day was endless: Get up, bring in kindling, stoke the fire, lug buckets to the stream, stir the pot in the smoky hearth, wash cabbages, cut cabbages, gather mushrooms in the forest, skin any meat Bogdan and the son-in-law might have caught, eat something, fall asleep.

She had to train herself to speak only Polish, never to slip into Yiddish. Never to mutter an annoyed "*oy vey*" or an angry "*shmendrik*." But after a few months, it got easier. She hardly talked anyway. And after a few months more, she stopped dreaming about her family.

Still, the daughter and son-in-law obeyed Pani Helena. They let Ruzia-Janina stay in their cottage, they fed her, and apparently they never reported her.

They could have told the neighbors. Many days you could hear faint noises from other tiny, threadbare farms. The crash of a tree being felled. Someone shouting at a recalcitrant goat. A baby wailing. A farmer might come by for help, if his thatched roof had caved in during a storm. Ruzia-Janina was told to hide in the barn when they saw anyone coming. And when the family went to church in the little nearby village, on Easter and Holy Thursday, she did not go with them.

Even when some German soldiers marched through the clearing one time, the daughter and son-in-law didn't turn in Ruzia-Janina.

They also hid the goats and the chickens in the root cellar with her, although the Germans took the pig.

In the fall, conditions always cheered up a bit. Every week there was something ready to harvest. The daughter would take Eva to the village market—without Ruzia-Janina, of course—and they would return red-cheeked and giggly, with baskets of tin dishes, knives, cloth, maybe strawberries or a bottle of vodka or a small lump of tobacco for the son-in-law's pipe. Then they might all sit around the wooden table after dinner, even Ruzia-Janina, and the son-in-law might light his pipe, or perhaps whistle, while the daughter sewed and Eva wrapped a scrap from her mother's sewing around the lump of wood that was her doll.

When she was in a good mood, the daughter made the same *makowiec* poppy-seed cake as Pani Helena, in a long rolled loaf with dark poppy filling. It was not as tough as her mother's version, but still dreadful and dry.

The daughter and her husband never hit Ruzia-Janina. Even though they slapped their own children, almost every day.

Nor, even as Ruzia-Janina grew into a teenager and almost a woman, over the five years, did the son-in-law ever touch her. There were the grunts and squeals all those winter nights with his wife, instead.

Bogdan, once, toward the end, came up to Ruzia-Janina as she was walking back from the stream with the heavy buckets of water. "Lift your skirt!" he commanded. However, he was still a boy, younger than she was, and she threw water in his face.

A few times, Eva sat down next to Ruzia-Janina, maybe on the ground while she was mending her clothes. The older girl wrapped an arm around the younger one and tried to remember fairy tales to tell. Hansel and Gretel and the witch. Eventually, Eva got bored.

Pani Helena visited twice. She showed up toward the end of the first spring and again in the late summer. She must have made the grueling, limping, all-day trip, and then back, alone with just her cane, because there was never any sign of a cart or horse bringing her. Then the visits stopped. But they could have started again, any time, and so the daughter did not kick out Ruzia-Janina. For nearly five years, Ruzia remained in the cottage and the barn. From the bare beginning of spring of 1940, when Pani Helena brought her, into the most bitter high-winter days of 1945. Then, one day, the church bells rang, and people were running from one farm to the next, to announce that the Germans were gone. Russian soldiers had entered Warsaw.

The next morning, the son-in-law told Ruzia to come with him. Almost all day they walked through the forest, the forest where she and Pani Helena had limp-walked five years earlier, until they were at the very final wall of trees, and through the spaces between the trunks she could see the winter-bare wheat and cabbage fields outside her town and maybe a building that might be the brick factory. Pointing vaguely toward her town, the son-in-law then turned around and left.

In the town, Ruzia learned that Pani Helena had died. But no one was really sure when, because who would ever dare knock on the witch's door? Not even the Nazi pharmacist would touch her. And why would anyone ask a witch what she knew about some Jew girl?

* * *

"You still haven't figured it out?"

Eleanor looked back at her mother, frowning.

Rose shook her head and pursed her lips.

Slowly, Eleanor shook her own head in response. "What — what else is there?"

Rose's lips were curling up slightly at the corners. "Your brother," she began, "is named for my father. Steven, for Shulem. And Chana named her daughter Natalie, for our mother. Necha."

So Eleanor for Feiga? For Avram? No, neither of those worked.

Stupidly, there was some waterering at the edges of Eleanor's eyes. Maybe a sniffle. As she rubbed her nose, Eleanor turned to her mother.

Eleanor. Helena.

Chapter Twenty-Seven

At the front door, Natalie hugged Eleanor, and Gary kissed her cheek, and Natalie hugged Kate and Adam, and Adam showed Natalie his finger-splint, and Kate examined Natalie's nail polish, and then Kate ran back inside the house to resume her phone call with Joanna.

"Is Mom really forty-two?" Adam demanded of Natalie and Gary.

"You shouldn't cook on your own birthday," Natalie ordered, handing Eleanor a big plastic bag that smelled of fried rice, "and I gather that you don't like it when I bring pizza, so I hope Chinese is acceptable."

Gary, for his part, held out a large, pink, cardboard box. "Nick asked us to pick this up from the bakery. I'm sure it's a birthday cake for you."

Natalie cocked her eyebrows at Eleanor.

Once upon a time, on a long-ago birthday, Nick had baked Eleanor the most incredible chocolate cake. It had flirted with her taste buds like rich cream.

"I guess he, uh, had to work," Gary added, still presenting the box. "And he couldn't be here." He quickly kicked the front door shut behind him.

But Adam was staring at the box. "I told Dad," he mumbled. "I told him I was making special brownies for your birthday."

Once upon a time, Nick would have baked brownies with Adam.

"Mom?" Kate was standing in front of Eleanor, also holding out a box, although a much smaller one, made of white cardboard. "I got you a birthday present."

"Oh, wow." With all the hugging going on, maybe it would be okay if Eleanor gave Kate just a tiny squeeze? "Thanks, Kate." Inside the box, nestled in fluffy cotton, were two pieces of green-and-black met-al, shaped like very slim and elongated diamonds. A pair of earrings. Although Eleanor never wore earrings.

"Hint, hint. Like, maybe, a hint for my next birthday present?"

Eleanor dangled one of the earrings against the side of her nose. "Kind of looks like a big piece of snot, doesn't it?"

"*Mom!*" But Kate giggled. "Well, of course, for nose piercings, you would get me much smaller earrings, like little—"

"No."

* * *

"But she told Nick!" Eleanor smacked a palm flat on her bedspread. "He's been hearing Ma's stories for two years and he never told me?"

Leaning partly over the edge of Eleanor's bed, Natalie carefully placed her coffee mug on the wooden floor, behind one of the feet of the bedframe.

"How could he—It's *my* mother, not his. It's my family and my sto-ries! And yours, of course. And Kate's and Adam's. We have a right to know."

"Maybe she told Nick not to tell you. For the same reason that she told my mother not to say anything, don't you think? Because it's her story to tell."

"Even so." Eleanor shifted her seat on the mattress. "He could have told me just the *fact* that he was talking to her. Even if he didn't tell me exactly what she said. He could have told me the magic secret for getting her to talk."

"Maybe he doesn't think there's a magic secret."

"That's not a good enough answer. He could have told me she's will-ing to talk now. That's all he had to do!"

"Well, that's a fair point. Are you going to ask him why he didn't?"

"When? He's never home."

Natalie pulled Eleanor's hands together so that she could wrap her own around them. "Are things okay with you two?"

"Yeah, yeah, of course. It's just this Y2K crap, he's so busy."

Natalie nodded.

"And Adam's finger. You know, we're worried about it."

Natalie still didn't say anything.

"And I kind of, well, I've had a couple of car—Hey! Stop doing your judge-silent thing."

Natalie grinned.

Just as Eleanor stood up, Adam shouted something from downstairs.

"Is it time for Adam's brownies?" Natalie bit her lip. "I told Gary to hide Nick's cake, so we only serve the brownies. Do you think that will help Adam feel better?"

"Mom!" Kate shouted, this time. "Grandma's on the phone."

"Maria Wysocki's grandfather," Eleanor added, "could have been that same Nazi pharmacist. Who turned in the names of all the Jews."

Halfway bent down toward retrieving her coffee mug, Natalie paused, sat back up, and rested a hand on Eleanor's forearm. "Maybe it's not a great idea to keep thinking that way, Ellie."

"But it could be the same town."

"Even your mother said she doesn't hate Krystyna's mother."

"Krystyna's mother wasn't a Nazi ringleader."

"Ellie." With both hands, Natalie rubbed Eleanor's upper arms. "It's truly wonderful that you've gotten your mother to start talking, after all these years. You were right to ignore my advice, and push her. And I hope we'll get to hear more of her stories. But please keep some perspective. Maria wasn't even born back then. And your mother's alive now. That's what matters."

In return, Eleanor squeezed Natalie's elbows. "Natalie, I know you mean well. I know you love Ma. But I've done okay so far on this, haven't I? Even you said so. Trust me."

* * *

"Of course I remembered," Rose scolded, over the phone. "You think I don't remember going into labor with you forty-two years ago? But I'm the one who's getting the birthday present today." She actually laughed. Maybe it was her first laugh since she'd broken her hip. "I finally talked to the big *makher* doctor."

No, the doctor still wouldn't promise how well she would ever be able to walk, but he and the rehab center were preparing to send her home, possibly in two weeks. "There's a whole list I'm supposed to do in advance, I have to get it from the nurses, things we have to do to my apartment to—what's their nonsense word for it? 'Fall-proof' the apartment. 'Fall-proof'! The landlord has to install handrails in the tub, and we have to tape down the rugs. A whole long list. You and Natalie and Nick will help me with that?"

"Of course."

"And I should clean up spills promptly, they said. As though I wouldn't?"

Eleanor stroked the phone receiver. "So for my next birthday, Ma, after you're back home: Will you make me that Polish cheesecake that your mother always made for birthdays?"

Rose was silent.

"If I'm not being too pushy?"

"It was a delicious cheesecake," Rose said, and her voice sounded like she was smiling.

Chapter Twenty-Eight

La Petite Baguette was barely wider than its door and two front windows, which were framed by white lace curtains. Three small, round, marble-topped tables, each hosting two heart-shaped chairs, squeezed between the windows and the display counter. The room was warm, cocooned in the sweet, buttery smell of croissants.

It was not on busy Edgewood Avenue, but tucked quietly away on a dead-end side street, across from a vacant store that used to sell auto parts.

At four-fifteen, the bakery was almost ready to close. "Ouvert: 6 AM—5 PM" the sign on the door promised. Other than a half-asleep teenage boy with a scrawny goatee at the counter, Mark was the only person inside the shop when Eleanor tugged open the door, which sent the "Ouvert" sign swinging.

A smile flashed on Mark's face, and he stood up quickly from his tiny table, stepping sideways over the dark-green knapsack on the floor by his chair, to pull the second chair out a few inches. A mug with cinnamon-speckled milk foam sat on the table in front of his chair, next to a basket nestling two croissants in a red-checked cloth napkin. The rest of table was nearly filled with a stack of hardcover books.

"I didn't think about it, when I suggested this place, that it would close so early," he was saying, as his smile creased into worry. "Do you want to go somewhere else? Do you want to go to the diner? We can stay here for almost an hour, anyway. I didn't order you any coffee because I wasn't sure exactly what you want. I hope you don't mind. What would you like?"

The top book on the stack had a title that included "Holocaust" and "Jews" and "Marseilles."

"No, no, this is great." Eleanor bent her knees to sit in her chair — Mark began to ease the chair toward the table—he leaned into her, on her right side. She stopped. She half-straightened up, setting her leather pocketbook and her own canvas bag of books on the floor in order to drag off her wool coat, starting with her right shoulder.

Mark's hands were on her shoulders. On the shoulders of her coat. On her right hand, resting on her right shoulder. Then his hands moved her coat down her arms.

His palm was warm. A little moist.

He breathed out chocolate-flavored coffee.

His breath was shaky. Loud.

His Adam's apple pulsed.

His hands paused. The coat was caught under her butt as she half-crouched over the chair seat.

Eleanor stood up straighter until the coat was freed and then she let it slide off of her and draped it over the back of her chair, which Mark was already pulling out again.

"Can I get you anything? Cappuccino?" he asked immediately.

She was reading the first chapter of the top book when he returned with her coffee. "This is incredible," she muttered, not looking at him or the coffee. "Pure evil. Worse than I remembered from my college classes—You know, I don't teach French history at my school." She looked up briefly. "Just grammar and conversation, that sort of thing. So I've forgotten a lot."

He nodded as he placed her mug on the marble tabletop and sat down. The table was so small that even sitting opposite, he had to extend his legs into the narrow aisle space, rather than underneath the table, to avoid touching her legs.

"Thousands of Jews fled into France from the rest of Europe before 1940, assuming they'd be safe, right? After all, good old civilized France, the Louvre, the Mona Lisa. Camembert. *Liberté, egalité, fraternité.* How could a land of such wonderful cheeses ever send people to Auschwitz?" She was turning pages as she spoke, pushing aside the first book and flipping through the next. "Look at this!"

He nodded again, lifting his cup toward his mouth. The frothy milk painted a few delicate dots on his upper lip.

"Do you know what the Vichy Commissar for Jewish Affairs said at his trial, after the war?" Slowly, Eleanor read: "He couldn't be guilty of collaboration, because he'd always been anti-Semitic." She turned back toward Mark. "The guy didn't collaborate with the Nazis, you see, because he would have been happy to kill the Jews on his own."

"Isn't that kind of an extreme case, a Vichy leader?"

Eleanor was already reading another page. "Did you know that three-quarters of the Jews who were deported to Auschwitz were arrested by French police. Not the Germans. The *French!*" She fanned the book open in front of his face. "I mean, I knew the image of the brave French Resistance was exaggerated, but— "

"But wasn't there also a long historical French hatred of Germans?"

"I don't know how I can teach this." She slammed the book on the table. "I'll get too riled up."

He smiled at her, with his usual, warm smile. "I've always admired that about full-time teachers. How do you manage to go a whole day with a classroom full of kids and never lose your temper?"

"Oh Mark." She leaned forward, halfway across the pile of books. "How can I teach French at all now?"

He put his cup down, and his smile dropped away. He leaned forward, too.

"It was almost a fluke that I ended up teaching French. I think I told you that I started out majoring in history, kind of as a way to study my mother's story, how she survived the Holocaust in Poland. Right? Then after I gave up on that and switched majors, well, I could just as easily have chosen Spanish, or who knows? Italian. Russian. But I had a wonderful high school teacher who taught French, so that's what I decided to do. And I suppose it happens with everyone who majors in a foreign language, where the language becomes *your* language. You know? You kind-of adopt the country that speaks that language. And in my case, I'm sure I took all my fascination with my mother's history and transferred it to my new major. So I fell in love with France.That's not hard to do in the case of France, right? The wine, the art, the food."

Mark looked at the croissants.

She waved toward the basket. "Yes, thank you for choosing this place in honor of my career. So, I lived there for a summer during college, studying at the University of Dijon and traveling around the countryside, and then I've been to Paris twice. And I lived with a French family for a month, as an au pair. I spent days and days sitting in cafés holding onto an empty cup of espresso and ostentatiously reading Proust—in French, of course—pretending to be *très parisienne*. I took my little string bag to shop at my favorite *boulangerie* and *boucherie* every day.

"Of course I learned about Vichy France while I was still majoring in history at NYU, but, you know, I didn't focus on it. I was specializing more on Poland. And then when I switched my major to French, well, history was just a small part of the course load, and the professors kind of skimmed over the World War Two part of that."

Mark had tilted his head slightly to his left as he watched her.

The buttery-smelling warmth of the shop and the heat from the coffee seeped into her cheeks and, gradually, down her neck and arms.

"What I'm trying to say" —and Eleanor took a breath. She kept her gaze on Mark. "I took France *personally*. I love the way the language sounds, with its crazy mix of long rounded vowels and ripples and grunts. I love the streets, I love the art, I love the food, I even love the snobbishness that won't ever let me forget that I will never truly speak French properly because I'm a mere American. I love teaching all this, to those two or three kids a semester—if I'm lucky—like Zoe and Sara and Meaghan and the Jessicas in my Advanced Class—those kids who maybe might share my excitement." She let out another long, exhausted breath.

"You can still love all that."

Mark's eyes were such an intense royal blue, not a wishy-washy, water-color light blue. Adam could paint a gorgeous ocean with the blue of Mark's eyes. His pale lips, dotted with the milk foam, were slightly open, as if he was ready to say something, or smile; his eyebrows were thick and light brown like his hair. There was a little pimple at the edge of his jawline, near his left ear.

"And now my mother is suddenly talking about the Holocaust! She's talking names, people in her town, people she knew, people who beat up my grandfather. So now Hitler and the Nazis—and any kind of collaborator—all that's become more personal to me. Maybe that's why the evil of the Vichy regime is hitting me so hard." One hand made a fist on the table, and her other hand clutched it. "How do you feel," Eleanor whispered, "when you meet someone from Germany?"

Without moving his gaze from her face, Mark nodded slightly.

"Who might have been old enough to be alive in World War Two," Eleanor continued. "Or whose parents were."

Mark laid his hands flat on the table, next to the stack of books.

"Or from, you know—wherever anti-Semitism was really bad. Poland."

"I know."

There was a short scratch on his left hand, near the thumb.

The hand quivered.

"Do you ask—?"

" 'What were your parents doing during the war?' "

Now she was the one who nodded.

"How can you not think that?" His fingers toyed with the book at the bottom of the pile.

"So you don't think I'm, like, stupidly prejudiced to feel that way?"

His fingers crawled one book higher. "I've talked about that with a lot of other Jews, actually. Yeah, we often have these automatic angry reactions when we meet people from Germany and Poland and, you know, other places. Lithuania. Ukraine. Like you said. And then we feel guilty about feeling angry. We sit there and tell ourselves it's unfair of us to blame the next generation, *n'est-ce pas?*"

Stupidly, Eleanor's mouth was moving into a grin. Why? Because he was mixing a French phrase with talk of Poland?

Because he understood.

"Josh shouldn't be blamed for the dumb things I've done, should he?" Mark was saying.

"Yeah, but how about when he's twenty? Should we expect him to challenge you then about all your dumb things?"

"Hey, I don't want Josh challenging me!"

As Eleanor opened her mouth, Mark put up his hands, palms facing her. Surrender. "I know, you want to be serious about this. I'm sorry for joking."

"No, it's okay. Jokes are good, too." Her coffee was already disgustingly cold. She lowered her cup.

Mark's index finger was making little circles on the spine of the bottom book.

"How about when you see the Wysockis?" she added.

"Who?"

"You know, from soccer. Their son, Tad, is the one who scores all the goals."

Mark tapped the stack of books. "What's that got to do with anything?"

"They're from Poland."

"Oh." He shook his head. "I don't know anything about the families on my teams. I just get a list with the kids' names. If Tad's from Poland, well, I don't know, I never really talk to his parents."

He wasn't looking at her, so Eleanor stared at the table, too. Mark really didn't notice the Wysockis' accent?

"These aren't easy questions, what you were talking about before," he was saying. "Historical blame. Think of all the generations of Americans who grew up being told it was fine to have separate water fountains for blacks and whites. Or to call people wops and kikes and fags."

His arms were crossed on the table, with his shirt sleeves partly rolled up on his forearms. The brown hair on his arms was dark and thick, stopping just above his wrists. His skin, under the hair, was still a little tan, maybe from those summers at the shore with Josh, or all the Saturdays coaching soccer.

"So." Eleanor lifted her glance back to Mark's face. "Do we let some eighty-year-old racist get away with saying that kind of garbage, even today, because that's how he was raised?"

"Isn't that what most people do? I think we tend to cringe and ignore it. We figure we're not going to change the guy."

"We don't try to change him?" Maria Wysocki couldn't be changed?

"And you know, if he's old, well, then we probably worry that we'll give him a heart attack, if we challenge some eighty-year-old racist too strongly." An almost-smile played at Mark's lips.

"Okay, but how about a seventy-year-old? Sixty?" Her tone was getting too shrill. "At what age do they become responsible for their words?"

"It's partly solved by general social mores, isn't it?"

"What do you mean?" She managed to lower her volume.

"If we've gotten to the point where we're cringing at that person, then we can be pretty sure he's an outlier."

Mark was leaning so far forward at the tiny table that his chin was resting on the top of the stack of books, and the chocolate-coffee breath that blew out of his lips brushed her chin.

Eleanor's lungs were having trouble getting enough air. She coughed.

"So we can more or less count on the people around the racist-outlier to ignore him," Mark continued, his voice calm, maybe tinged with a tiny laugh. "Even his own kids are probably rolling their eyes."

It would be so nice to smile back and agree with Mark. To smile with him. To imagine Tad rolling his eyes at Maria. But did Maria ever roll her eyes at her parents?

Coughing again, then swallowing, Eleanor pulled some more oxygen into her lungs. "I don't know, I think you're being too optimistic. Counting on social pressure. Plenty of second-generation Polish people say things like 'All Jews are smart.' " No; she actually couldn't get her next breath out.

Mark was still leaning on the books. "That's true. It probably takes more than one generation. And it depends on the community, too."

He sucked in his pale bottom lip.

He smiled.

Eleanor swallowed.

Were her hands still clutched in a fist? Were they on the table?

"So, Eleanor."

Eleanor.

Had he ever called her by her first name before?

"Have I helped you come up with a lesson plan about Vichy France? Or have I only made things worse?"

Eleanor.

She shook her head.

"Uh oh. Do we need more books? I might have some on European history, back at my apartment."

In the warm, quiet café, a cuckoo clock abruptly chimed from high up on the wall barely a foot away, and a wooden bird popped out. Three chimes. For three o'clock? That made no sense. And then, of all things, the stupid clock played the opening bars of "Frère Jacques."

Or was that Eleanor's cellphone ringing, deep in her bag? No, it couldn't be, because she'd turned the phone off.

The kid behind the counter shouted — with no discernable French accent — "We're closing in fifteen minutes. Ya want anything else?"

"Damn," Mark mumbled.

Eleanor and Mark looked toward the kid, then back toward each other, at the same time.

"Do you want a—" Mark glanced around. "An éclair?"

"No, no. But the coffee was good."

"They have good pastries, too."

"It's good to know about it. A new French bakery."

Eleanor half-turned, as though to get her coat from the chair.

"Let's talk outside."

Eleanor nodded immediately.

They scrambled to collect their belongings. Mark gathered his books into his knapsack. Eleanor brought the basket of croissants to the counter and asked the teenager to wrap them to go. Frowning, he thrust a white paper bag in the air toward her.

The bakery had no parking lot. Eleanor had parked down the side street toward the right, and Mark had parked on Edgewood Avenue around the corner. He walked her to her car.

She held the car keys in her gloved hands.

They stood next to the passenger side.

"So where were you and Adam last Saturday? I know Adam can't play, since he broke his finger, but I hope he still feels like he's part of the team."

"You know, he felt so left out at the game two weeks ago. Bored. He didn't want to go on Saturday."

"But you'll come to the soccer game this week? It's the last game. And there's the pizza party afterwards."

"Yes, of course, we wouldn't miss the pizza party."

"Good."

She blew out a puff of white air. It was getting too cold to just stand there, in her coat, by her car. "Thank you for the coffee. And the information about Vichy France."

"You didn't finish reading the books," he said quickly.

"Well. No."

"Maybe we can find something nice about the French. So you can stay in love with France."

He smiled down at her face. He tilted his head sideways, like before.

"Do you want to look at some more books, back at my place?" he asked.

His smile spread slowly, nudging his mouth wider, crinkling his eyes.

His eyes were so blue.

His lips parted, to let out a chocolate-coffee breath.

"That would be good," she replied quietly. "To see if you have other books."

* * *

She followed Mark's car in her own. It took about fifteen minutes, south one exit on Route 17 and then through a meandering series of side streets, going at Mark's turtle-slow speed-limit pace. Finally he halted, at a two-story stucco apartment building.

He waited for her at the front door.

They climbed to the second floor, Eleanor in front, clutching the steel railing, and Mark right behind her. One step behind. Inches behind. If she hadn't been wearing a coat, she probably would have felt his breath on her back. If she stumbled, she would fall against him.

She was only going to stay a half an hour. That was all. She had obligations, as a mother. And wife. She had to make dinner. Adam might need help with homework.

Just to skim a few books. Maybe he had books on Poland.

His hand was on her back.

Even through the coat, she could feel it. Firmly.

Her back quivered.

"To the right," he said.

And his hand was turning her body, guiding her in the correct direction, and after a few more seconds, the hand let go.

He was a single guy. Divorced. He probably brought women here all the time and put his hand on their backs.

But he would keep his hand on *their* backs longer. Probably put his arm around them. Hug them. Giggle, nuzzle their necks. Down the dimly lit hall, past other apartment doors. Although the floor had only a thin industrial carpet, it would undoubtedly muffle the tap of stiletto heels late at night.

Would he walk closer to those other women?

How close was he, in fact, behind her?

How much further was his apartment?

"Should I keep going—?" She turned her head barely a couple of inches, to ask, and his face was there. The bit of stubble on his jaw. The pimple.

He stopped. She stopped a breath later.

His chin bumped her head. Maybe.

He raised the arm that was farther away from her and pointed down the hallway ahead of them. "One more door."

At the door itself, the etiquette was easy. She stepped away to give him enough room to get his key in the lock, and then he gallantly held the door open, and she walked in. But then they were inside his apartment. He shut the door.

The last time she had been in a guy's place—not a family's house, not a couple's house, but the dwelling-place of a single man—how many years ago was that? Boyfriends ago, in college. In fact, the last time was probably Nick's college apartment. With the thick purple-and-green coleus plant hanging in his kitchen window, and blank paper stacked in an oblong box next to his typewriter, and the blankets neatly tucked along both sides of his bed.

In Mark's living room, a copy of *ARTnews* magazine lay open on a glass-topped coffee table. One wall was papered with posters and glossy magazine pictures of sports teams, some of them curling at the edges. Football players in blue uniforms, was that the Giants or Jets? A big orange-white-and-blue Mets banner. Dramatic photos of soccer players kicking the ball and running. The opposite wall displayed three framed paintings of jumbles like the still lifes at the library: A garden trowel, a tube of lipstick, and a single, worn-down sneaker. A rippling red curtain. There was also a black-and-white unfinished sketch, possibly a person. A girlfriend?

A bookshelf and a window filled most of a third wall. Clustered on one shelf, in front of a row of books, was a group of framed four-by-six photos plus two trophies. Even from the doorway, it was clear they were school pictures of Josh, marching upwards in age, ending with a large shot of him with Mark.

Good. Pictures of his son. That was an obvious, neutral place to walk to. Eleanor took a step.

But Mark was standing too close. Maybe he'd been expecting to do the thing with taking off her coat again. So as she took her step forward, he had to abruptly shift his weight out of her way, except that he was still carrying the knapsack full of all those heavy books about Vichy France, and it swung forward and thudded against her calf. And she muttered something like "Ow!" or "Damn!" and he mumbled something like "Sorry," and they bent their heads down by instinct to see what had happened. And when they looked up, also by instinct, their noses were definitely touching. With less than an inch separating their lips.

He swallowed.

She held her breath.

And he dropped the knapsack, and suddenly there was one muscular hand cupping her head, stroking her hair, pulling her face even closer to his face, and another hand pressed on her back.

Her right arm was trapped between their chests. Her left arm was dangling outside their bodies.

There was still a breath of space between them. There was still a nanosecond of waiting.

And then there wasn't.

* * *

His two hands pulled her through the breath of open space until her chin was against his chin, and his eyes were too close to see, and then her left hand found his back, and her right hand got loose and found his cheek, his nose, his eyes, his eyebrows, his hair, his ears, all of it, dashing from one to the other, while his tongue found her lips but it didn't have to push the lips open because they already were. He tasted of coffee, of chocolate, of foamy milk, of saliva, and why wasn't he pulling her closer? Closer! More! One of his hands was stroking her back, big strong strokes up and down and up and down, kneading deeper into her coat, and the fingers of the other hand were on her ear. Oh God. Her earlobe was on fire. Or firecrackers. His crotch was pressed against her. She had to, she had to, she had to wrap her leg around him. She yanked her tongue out of his mouth to lick the stubble on his jaw and his cheek, and then his lips were kissing her neck and oh God oh God she was going to fall down, she was going to pee in her pants right there. And then she would have to wash them.

Because she was a wife and a mother and she did the laundry.

She had to stop this.

But just another minute more.

Because dammit, she was never going to have this chance again, and maybe the world would end on January first anyway, and right now it felt so goddam good.

Goddam goddam goddam he was pulling her coat down.

He moved her hands and her arms off of him just long enough for the wool to slide down her body, and there was only her blouse and bra between him and her.

His finger, each finger, five fingers, ten fingers, each fingertip was on her shoulder blades, on her spine, against the silk of her blouse, and her back arched and her head bent back oh God oh God and her breasts and her blouse were rubbing right on his shirt, his soft cotton oxford shirt. Her nipples wanted to burst through her blouse.

She had to tell him to stop. In a minute.

If they didn't actually have sex, it wasn't cheating. It was just a lapse.

Because it was her own body that was grabbing him, demanding him, craving him, her hands that were trying to figure out how to tear off his cotton shirt and then clutching his hair and then back to his shirt, then grabbing his face from both sides and tugging his mouth back into hers and oh Jesus Jesus Jesus his tongue was whipping through her mouth like the fastest snake in the world. And it was her body that needed to get closer, to shove against him, to clutch his back and to suck in his tongue and coil her tongue around his and twist and coil and dance and never stop. Her own body that was telling her the truth.

His voice was barely a breath in her ear. Simply her name. "Eleanor."

Did he call the other parents by their first names? Or were they "Ben's mother." And "Tad's mother." And she was "Adam's mother."

But wasn't she also Eleanor?

And Nick's wife.

Nick was a jerk.

Wasn't her own body telling her? This, now, with Mark, this was what was real. Not Nick.

She hardly knew Mark, yet she could talk more to him in half an hour than she'd talked to Nick in years.

Nick who never came home. Nick who might be cheating on her all those supposed late nights at work. Nick who hadn't even bothered telling her that her own mother was talking to him.

But her hands must have slowed down, or stopped, because Mark had pulled his face slightly away. The vacuum between their skins was broken. He touched a fingertip to her chin and gazed at her.

"Are you okay?" he asked. Softly. Hoarsely.

Look at him: He was gentle. He understood. He wouldn't push. He was a good person. They could take this slowly, see where it went. It didn't have to be all at once, right here, this second. They had time. If the world didn't actually end at Y2K. She could talk to him.

Her voice was stuck. Her right index finger traced the side of his nose.

His finger toyed with her hair. Gently. As gently as a breath. As a baby's hair. As silk. When Adam was a baby. He lifted a strand, twirled it around, put it carefully back in place.

He kissed her eyelashes. Barely breathing.

She could give him a little kiss, and say that she had to go, and he would whisper, so gently, so gently, that he would call her in a few days. And they would talk again. And kiss again. She would come here again. Maybe they'd have coffee again at the bakery. Or wine. French wine. They would take time; explore. And then she'd see him at the soccer pizza party. Oh shit, that would be tough, to keep her hands off of him in front of all those other parents. And Maria.

His finger moved along the side of her mouth, gliding her lips a little up into the merest smile, and a shiver went straight down to her crotch.

Her legs were going to collapse any minute.

Here? On the floor?

In his bed?

Did he make his bed with the blankets tucked in?

He kissed the tip of her nose.

Was it a double bed? A queen?

A mattress and a stack of quilts on the floor of a smoky kitchen?

In a thatched-roof cottage in Poland, Ruzia-Janina listened night after night to the grunts of two Polish peasants doing what Eleanor and Mark were going to do. What Eleanor and Nick did.

Nick was a jerk, but once upon a time his face had been as white as a bed sheet when he handed the baby Kate to Eleanor and cried that he was no good as a father because he'd let their baby fall down on the floor of a bagel shop. And once upon a time a little girl named Feiga had fallen off a table in Poland and needed to go to the doctor who would take care of Jewish children, the Jew-lover.

And once upon a time, a college senior who was kind of a fuddy-duddy but also a really good cook, this guy had listened to his girlfriend's father ramble on and on about his stamp collection. And it was that same college senior, years later, whose mother-in-law had trusted him with the stories she had told almost no one else.

Good and bad, there were things in a family that were deeper than deep kissing, or even deep talking, and you didn't throw them out the window like a cigarette butt.

Eleanor closed her eyes. Squeezed back the tears that were inching toward the lids. Put her hands on Mark's face, gently, one hand on each side. Shook her head.

"I'm sorry," she whispered. "You know I'm married, I just—"

"WHAT??"

* * *

"I wear a goddam wedding ring all the time!"

"Women wear all kinds of rings."

"Like *this?* A gold band?"

"I don't go around staring at people's fingers."

"Well you should if you're going to hit on them."

"*Hit on? You* were flirting with *me!*"

"I was not!"

"Why would I possibly think a married woman would start flirting —"

"I was not—"

"*'Oh, Mark, let's talk about Vichy France.'*"

"Yeah. Well maybe I actually am interested, huh? I do teach French."

"You never mentioned your husband."

"Well — why would I? It never came up."

"You had plenty of chances."

"You could have seen it on the team list."

"I told you, the parents' names aren't on the list."

"You could have asked."

"Just get the fuck out."

* * *

In her car, when she turned her cellphone back on, there were eight missed calls. The five most recent were from Nick, increasingly angry. "Where the hell have you been? Isn't your phone working? We're at the ER at North Jersey now."

The three earlier ones were from Kate. The first had been about two hours ago: "Hey Mom, it's Kate. Um, could you call me? Like, I kind of—well, I just cut my nose. I mean, it's probably okay."

Eleanor peeled out of the parking spot in front of Mark's building, twice as fast as stupid Mark had driven there.

Chapter Twenty-Nine

It was the same emergency room where Rose had been taken, barely two months earlier. And where Nick and Eleanor had once brought baby Kate, after the fall in the bagel shop, and baby Adam with the high fever.

The waiting area hadn't changed much in all that time. It still had the rows of yellow and orange plastic chairs welded together and the reek of dried sweat, the TV mounted high on one concrete wall and the round clock on another, with hands that never seemed to move. There was the vending machine that dispensed tiny cups of watery coffee, and the other one with candy and chips. At the farthest corner was the office where Marion Hanks had told Natalie and Eleanor how funny it was that Rose had sworn in Polish. Maybe the same Nazi bitch EMT was unloading an ambulance at that very moment.

About a dozen people were waiting in the plastic chairs, but none of them were Nick or Kate.

"Kate Phillips?" said the triage nurse—who was not Marion Hanks. "Oh goodness, she went into the examining rooms an hour ago."

Through the double doors, past the fourth partition on the right, in a narrow cubicle, Kate was sitting on a hospital bed, cuddling against Nick.

With a big wad of white cotton shoved up one nostril. But her nose was all there, in one piece.

"Mom!" Kate jumped off the bed and ran to Eleanor, cramming her cheek against Eleanor's neck and wrapping her arms around Eleanor's back.

Her yellow T-shirt was splattered with red, in blobs and wide streaks, like ketchup on scrambled eggs. She was shaking, holding Eleanor tight against the side of her face that didn't have the cotton wad. Her face was wet on Eleanor's skin and her breathing, through the cotton, was an endless spurt of whistles. Adam jumped up from where he'd been sitting, on a chair next to the bed, seconds after his sister, and he, too, ran to Eleanor and found an available spot to hug the base of her back from behind. "Mom!" he shouted. His finger-splint dug a little bit into her side.

Eleanor pressed her two children against her, first Kate in front, then Adam in back.

Was it really possible? She had almost cheated on her marriage, and failed to realize that her daughter was planning to poke bloody holes in her nose, and also caused her son to break his finger, and nevertheless her children were okay and they still loved her?

"Your mother and I need to talk," Nick said.

Adam squirmed his way to Eleanor's front, squeezing next to Kate. "It was so gross! She had all this blood and snot pouring out—"

"Shut up!" Kate snapped, pulling a little bit away from Eleanor and glaring at Adam. The long, fat wad of cotton was a weird intrusion on her face, too-bright white against her puffy, pink-splotchy skin.

"It was so—"

"Adam, you don't even know what you're talking about. It really hurt, Mom."

Was there still some scent of Mark, lingering on her skin and her blouse? Cinnamon foam? Pheromones? Was her hair a mess? Was her face flushed? She hadn't even stopped to check in the car mirror.

Eleanor tugged Kate and Adam back to her. "What happened?" she whispered. Asking Kate; asking anyone. No one answered immediately.

"She cut her *own nose!*" Adam announced, at the same time that Nick began, more quietly, "Kate and her friends were trying to do their own nose-piercing."

Kate wriggled her cheek a bit harder into Eleanor's neck, as though she could pierce herself into her mother. An instant later, however, she did the opposite, drawing away and tossing her hair, which was pale purple, and then crossing her arms while she stared at Eleanor. "We did a lot of research, you know. Joanna talked to the earring place. And Rachel talked to her sister, because she pierced her friend's ears a long time ago, and she's never had any problems. We did everything just like Rachel's sister said. We sterilized the needle *twice!* We held it to a candle flame and then with a whole ton of alcohol, and we also, like, *drowned* my nose in alcohol. With brand-new cotton balls. And the earring was 14-karat. We weren't stupid."

"But you *were!*" Adam shouted. "You got cut."

"That's because—" Kate glanced away from Eleanor. "Well, I don't know exactly."

"You kept sticking the needle in and sticking it in— "

"Well, it wouldn't go through—you know, the nose skin is really thick—so first we tried a bigger a needle. And then Joanna thought maybe a knife—"

"I need to sit down," Eleanor interrupted weakly.

"But then we decided to use a safety pin."

But not to let go of Adam or Kate. Her children. Clutching them, Eleanor tried to crab-walk sideways to the bed. If Nick would just get up, there would be room on the bed for Eleanor, Kate, and Adam. Eleanor and her children. However, he didn't move. Eleanor made enough space so that she could sit with Kate as a shield between her and Nick. Adam had to take a chair.

"So—are you—we—are we waiting for a doctor or something?" Eleanor asked.

"No," Nick replied coldly. "The doctor finished. We were waiting for you."

Oh, well you can go back to work now. Don't let me stop you.

"What did the doctor say?"

Nick began answering matter-of-factly, as though he was analyzing a computer malfunction, and Kate and Adam kept interrupting, but the gist of it seemed to be that Kate had never actually succeeded in her goal of punching a hole completely through the cartilage on the outer side of the nose. However, what with all the jabbings from the needle and the safety pin—an extra-large safety pin, Kate pointed out—she and her friends had apparently done a pretty good job of cutting her skin in several places and even nicked a little into the septum. Which was the cartilage between the nostrils. Which was full of blood vessels. Thus, she'd ended up with some dramatic bleeding.

"But not enough blood to die from losing," Kate clarified.

Eleanor closed her eyes and swallowed.

That was why she had that cotton wad, which was called a "nasal *tampon*"—Kate giggled—just in case of continued bleeding. The biggest risk now wasn't hemorrhage but rather infection, since the nose is a fairly dirty part of the body.

"We were careful!" Kate muttered.

They should watch out for any signs of infection, such as redness or swelling. And dab the area a few times a day with hydrogen peroxide.

"But why—?"

"And it *hurt!*" Kate suddenly screamed, burying her head back into Eleanor's coat.

Even Adam was suddenly quiet, and all Eleanor could do was softly rub Kate's back and murmur, "Shh, shh, it's all right."

Nick was smoothing Kate's purple hair. Gently. Never quite touching Eleanor's hand.

* * *

Eventually, a hospital worker in burgundy scrubs came by with the discharge papers, and they had to leave the refuge of the little cubicle. "Kids," Nick ordered, "go wait outside. Right outside these doors, in the big waiting room with the TV where we were before. Your mother and I will. We'll be there in a minute."

"I've got to call Joanna and Rachel," Kate announced. "Mom, can I use your cellphone?"

Nick glared at Eleanor.

Eleanor fumbled in her leather bag, avoiding his face. "Yeah, yeah, sure."

"Oh? It's working now?"

Eleanor dropped the phone on the floor as she tried to give it to Kate.

"Where the hell were you?" Nick demanded, as soon as the double doors swung shut behind Kate and Adam, and he and Eleanor were standing by the nurses' station. "Kate said she kept calling you—"

"I know."

"While she was bleeding—"

"Yes, I know."

"Why didn't you answer?"

"Can we not argue in front of all these people?"

Nick gestured toward an emptier spot next to a metal table along a nearby wall but kept speaking, hissing in a lower tone, as they walked,

"Didn't you hear it ring? Why did I give you that phone if you don't use it?"

"I couldn't get reception."

"Where were you?"

"Just at my mother's ... " Damn, no, he might ask Rose if Eleanor had been there. "I mean, I was meeting another teacher. We were talking about Vichy France. For school."

"I had to leave in the middle of work—you know how hard that is for me."

For God's sake, why was it always about his stupid job? He was a jerk. He was a selfish jerk.

Nick was still hissing: "How could you let Kate get this far? She cut her own goddamn nose!"

Eleanor had just rejected a sexy soccer coach for this jerk?

"Weren't you paying attention to her?"

Maybe it wasn't too late, to go back to Mark.

"Why weren't you more firm with her? Why didn't you make it clear that it was *No!* No piercing. No nose."

"Well I never dropped her on the floor!" Eleanor screamed.

Nick paused only for a second. "Don't you dare throw that at me," he said quietly, between narrowed lips. "Don't you think I've hated myself for that for eleven years?"

She could barely keep her gaze on his face, but she had to. What emotions did he see reflected in her eyes? What sins? What lies? The stupid bag of croissants was still in her car. She swallowed.

"And if you want to throw stones," he added—.

What??

He couldn't mean Mark?

"—what's that insurance claim for rear-ending Ms. Frieda Stickland on October fifth?"

She grabbed the hard, cold edge of the metal table. "What?"

"Fifteen-hundred-something-dollars damage to the trunk of her car. And pain and suffering, of course. And that's not even the same accident where Adam broke his finger, is it?"

Oh Jesus. It was that woman whose car she'd rear-ended. The fender-bender.

"When were you going to tell me about that?"

The day she'd met Mark at the art-supply store.

"What the hell is going on with you, Eleanor? You're having car accidents right and left— "

She hadn't fixed the car yet.

"—and our kids are getting so many injuries that we're going to get investigated for child abuse—Where the hell is your mind? I know you're worried about your mother, and I am too, but I'm not having car accidents. I don't understand, is it because you're obsessed with this Polish family? or your stupid stock investment?"

"Nick—"

"You did sell that stock, didn't you?"

She managed to sit down on a wooden chair, next to the metal table. She stared at her lap. Then at him, looming over her.

The hell with both of them. Nick and Mark.

But Mark was right about one thing: Why the hell hadn't she been honest and told him she was married?

They were a family that didn't tell each other bad news, her mother had said; a family that kept secrets. Rose's secrets, Nick's secrets, Eleanor's secrets upon secrets, and now Kate was inheriting that family trait—but no, Kate had actually been honest that she wanted her nose pierced.

"Maybe," Eleanor said. The only way she could get words out was slowly and softly. "Maybe we should have been less firm with Kate. And more open to listening. We told her 'no,' but that's all we did. Maybe we needed to ask her why it meant so much to her. Getting her nose pierced. We should have talked about it more. All of us."

Nick stopped shouting.

He leaned back against the table that Eleanor had been clinging to a minute ago.

"Do you think," he asked, his voice very quiet, almost inaudible, "it was some sort of call for attention? Because I haven't been around very much?"

She could say yes. She could make him feel guilty.

"No," she said. "I think she just wants to pierce her nose because it's fashionable right now."

His breath, released, was louder than his voice had been.

"But we still should have asked her why," Eleanor went on.

"So if we'd discussed this more with her? We still would have said 'no.'"

"True."

From her left side, someone was trying to squeeze down the skinny aisle, past Eleanor and Nick. Eleanor tucked her legs under the chair. A whiff of rubbing alcohol, a slap of sneakers on the linoleum floor, then a set of slower feet. Then someone from the other direction.

"And it's also true that you haven't been available very much. For Kate or Adam."

If Nick had been available to take Adam to soccer, Eleanor never would have met Maria Wysocki.

She also never would have met Mark and made such a fool of herself.

Once. Just once in a marriage. And not even a full once. That wasn't so terrible, was it?

Nick's ankles were crossed in front of him as he leaned against the table, his arms braced and his fingers gripping the table edge. With a gold wedding band on his fourth finger. He was wearing khaki slacks and a denim shirt, tieless, his shirtsleeves rolled up, and the veins in his forearms stood out like suntanned ropes covered in dark hair. His face was thinner than Mark's, and his hair was darker brown and straighter. It flopped over his ears in the straggly way that she had always found sexy but he always said meant he needed a haircut. His chin was rounder and less stubbly than Mark's, which softened it. He had thick eyebrows like a brooding poet and dark brown eyes, which looked at her now.

"I'm sorry," he said.

He was a jerk, but so was she. He, after all, wasn't the one who had almost cheated on their marriage. Or broken his son's finger. Or lied, sort-of, about investing in a crazy drug-company stock.

"I guess I've been more stressed-out than I've admitted."

She focused on her shoes. Dark-brown pumps. "I'm sorry, too," she mumbled. "I've been kind of overwhelmed. With my mother and all." Neither of them moved, however. She still didn't look at Nick. "Maybe there is something to this Y2K paranoia in the air. Like our minds have been taken over by aliens."

Nick exhaled abruptly.

"But you're going to save us all from Y2K, right?"

Someone else in burgundy scrubs walked over just then and asked them to move, because he needed something from a drawer in the table Nick was leaning against.

* * *

"Joanna says everyone will be freaked at school!" Kate was laughing as she held out the cellphone toward her mother. Adam was kneeling on a plastic chair, his head tilted back, gazing up at cartoons on the TV on the wall.

Nick opened his mouth—Eleanor stared right at him while she took the phone—and he shut his mouth.

Instead, he ran his hand lightly across the top of Kate's head. "Wait until they see you with a bunch of big fat scabs on your nose."

"Dad!"

"What matters," he said, and he pulled her closer for a hug, "is that you're okay."

The Y2K panic would be over in January, and Nick would, supposedly, have more free time. To take Adam to soccer games — but only if Adam truly wanted to go. To cook dinner for Eleanor's next birthday. To tell each other the stories they'd gotten from Rose, back and forth. To talk.

But without pushing?

To listen.

They were so out of practice, but they had to start making sentences. Maybe they wouldn't share deep thoughts about Vichy France, okay. Nevertheless, a wife ought to tell her own husband if she'd had a car accident, and a husband darn well ought to tell his wife that her mother was starting to talk to him about her hidden past. They needed to talk about Kate's bat mitzvah, and Nick's feeling about it, and how they'd pay for it. And whether to sell the stupid stock. And how Nick needed to do more of his share of parenting.

And about Mark?

Well, maybe that topic could hold until things were a little more secure between her and Nick.

In our family, the parents protect the children. We don't tell them the bad news. For fifty years, it had been a family of not talking. It didn't have to be.

"You know, Dad." Kate pulled away from his hug. "I still want to get my nose pierced."

"Oh?"

"But I'll wait."

"You don't have any nose left!" Adam declared, without turning from the TV.

Walking over to Nick and Kate, Eleanor placed a hand on Kate's head, where it barely missed Nick's hand. "My mother mentioned to me that she's been talking to you about Poland."

"Well—yes… " Nick frowned.

"I know it's been good for her, to—to talk to you. She's started telling me some of her stories, too. Finally. She says she would've told me earlier if I hadn't pushed her so much."

"Well…" A slight smile lifted the edges of Nick's lips as he looked down at the floor. "I guess she did say something like that."

"So maybe we can, you know, share our stories? And we should tell Kate and Adam, too."

Nick nodded in reply. His fingers brushed back against hers.

Chapter Thirty

Of course Mark was at the soccer field. Standing at the sideline, surrounded by the usual clutch of devoted boys in blue and white, tilting his curly-haired head to talk to them. Probably giving them his warm smile. Patting someone's shoulder. With the fingers that had traced the side of her nose and twirled a strand of her hair.

Did he sense when Eleanor and Adam emerged from the parking lot? Did his back twitch?

No, that would be awfully unlikely. He was standing too far away, facing the wrong direction.

Adam ran toward a small gang of teammates who were hovering over something that one of them was apparently showing the others. At least Adam was willing to come this time, it being the final game of the season, with the pizza party afterwards.

The final game: Eleanor would never have to see Mark again. However, that also made it the final chance to ask Maria about her father and her town and her last name and what her parents had told her while she was growing up, unless Eleanor wanted to stalk her at CVS indefinitely. Therefore, Eleanor had to phrase her questions very carefully.

Isn't it silly, that I just assumed you're from Krakow like your husband?

Was the pharmacy named for your grandfather's last name?

Maria wasn't there.

No lawn chair on the grass, and no cooler. No shopping bags filled with spare jackets and junk food. No skinny blond boy racing back and forth past Mark. At the sideline, no big blond guy thrusting his fist in the air.

Was Tad sick? Considering Janek's obsession with every move of the ball, surely they would never skip a game unless something very serious was wrong. Maybe they were just late. A car accident? Yeah, Eleanor could identify with that. Or more likely, a Tad-accident; maybe he'd run around without watching where he was going one time too many and smashed into something. Right now the Wysockis could be waiting anxiously at the very same emergency room where Eleanor and Nick had been with Kate just a few days ago.

Maybe the Nazi-hunters had finally caught up with them?

Well, Eleanor was getting carried away now.

Whatever the explanation, the game would start soon, and Mark would be unhappy—all the Hornets would be unhappy—if they didn't have their star player.

Mark might know what had happened to Maria and Janek. But Eleanor could hardly ask him.

Who else? Did Maria and Janek ever talk to any parents besides Eleanor? How about trying Betsy? Hell no, she'd just make another snide remark about Eleanor and Mark. Maybe Jack? He was always gabbing with everyone, trying to sell his stupid stocks, so he might have picked up some information. Not to mention that Eleanor really, really needed to ask him about his lousy drug-company stock, which seemed to keep losing money, and which, in light of her new self-promise, she needed to talk to Nick honestly about.

On a grassy side patch further down the field, Jack was—no surprise—engrossed in a conversation with another Hornet dad. But he greeted Eleanor with his usual big grin, so perhaps the drug stock had gained money yesterday?

"Hey, friend!" He reached out for a high-five. "Dave and I— you know each other?—We were just talking about Y2K-dot-com. Did I ever tell you about that stock? It's kind of an insurance policy against computer meltdowns in the Year 2000."

"Yeah, listen, Jack. You know that blond family from Poland we once talked about? Their son is, like, the star of our team?"

Immediately, Jack's grin disappeared. "Oh yeah. Tough story."

"What story?"

"That's right, you weren't here last week, were you? How's your son's finger?"

"Fine, fine. Thank you. But what about the Wysockis?"

"Yeah. Well, you know, Mrs. W. has cancer."

Maria—There was a whistle from the Hornets field. Or maybe from another field. Far away, parents were clapping; too far away to be Hornets parents.

A quick slap of cold wind hit Eleanor's cheek.

"They found a clinical trial for her, which is a damn good thing, let me tell you. Her husband—Johnny?—he and I got to talking a few weeks ago, when I was telling him about Drugtrials-dot-com. That's the company you're in, right? Of course he was very interested, and we got to talking, and it turns out he tells me his wife was diagnosed about a year ago, and they'd tried all the usual treatments. Chemo. Surgery. But nothing was working, and now it spread, I think to her bones."

Cancer. Maria had cancer. Maria was dying?

Way off on all the fields, kids in polyester shorts and knee socks were running and kicking and missing black-and-white balls. Refs were blowing whistles. Mark was trotting along the sideline, taking notes. But Janek wasn't watching.

"So of course I told Johnny that I'd check on the Drugtrials database to see if there were any trials she could join."

"Is it—lung cancer?"

"Nah, you know, I'm sorry. I forget which kind. But I don't think it's lung. Lung cancer usually kills them pretty fast, doesn't it? And I think she has more of a fighting chance with her type. So anyway, Johnny told me last week that she'd gotten accepted into a trial, and they're gone. Just like that."

"Gone—where?"

Jack scratched the skin in front of his ear, squinting. "I think he said Texas."

"Texas? Where in Texas?"

"You know, I'm not sure. Maybe MD Anderson? That's a very respected cancer center. We looked into it for my dad, when he had prostate cancer. So are you good friends of theirs?"

Maria had cancer. All these weeks, in pain, maybe in terror that she was dying, and Eleanor had practically imagined her into a Nazi, because her father and grandfather had been pharmacists in Poland.

Was Eleanor a good friend of the Wysockis?

Slowly, she shook her head. "My son was pretty friendly with Tad— their son. But then—why didn't he tell me Tad wasn't at school last week?"

"You know, that kind of stuff we adults think is important, it washes over kids."

"True." Was it true? "Shit," she added. "Cancer."

"Yeah. I hope the clinical trial works for them." Jack patted her on the shoulder as he turned back to Dave.

Maria had cancer. Which probably explained the folding chairs at the soccer games that Eleanor had scoffed at, and why the Wysockis usually left so quickly. And why Maria had seemed so tired at CVS that other day. She was probably exhausted from chemotherapy, and drugs, and surgery, and more drugs.

Which also explained her perfect hair. The hair that was always exactly in place was a wig, because Maria's real hair had fallen out from the chemo.

Although not the kind of wig that Rose's old-fashioned grandmother had worn in Poland, before she was murdered at Treblinka.

Maria had cancer. Just like Chana.

"Wait—!" Eleanor actually tugged at his sleeve, and Jack jerked his arm a little as he turned around to face her. "Would anyone else have any information about where they went? How to reach them?"

Jack scratched at his ear again. "Maybe the coach. Why don't you ask him?" and he pointed, unnecessarily, toward Mark.

Yeah. Sure.

* * *

Eleanor stood on the grass, while Jack and Dave continued discussing their newest great stock discovery, and the wind shot pinpricks of shivers through her coat, and the referee's whistle shrieked, and the Hornets ran out onto the field in a blur of blue and white toward probable defeat, without their best player.

Tad and Maria and Janek and Konrad, gone without a trace. Like the Jews who were rounded up in Poland. Like the Jews that maybe Maria's grandfather the pharmacist had helped the Germans round up. Or maybe not.

How could Eleanor ever find out that truth?

She could try going to the Wysockis' house to speak with them, just in case they hadn't actually left New Jersey yet.

Or if they had already moved away, certainly they would have given a forwarding address to the post office. So Eleanor could write to Maria.

And what would she write? *Hi Maria, I'm sorry to hear you've got cancer, good luck, and by the way, what was the name of your town in Poland and what was your last name before you got married, because I'm wondering if your grandfather was a Nazi?*

Shit. How could a decent person even think of writing a letter like that to someone who might be dying of cancer?

But how could Eleanor just drop her search and forget everything her own mother had told her?

Okay then, could she ask Rose? Could she show Rose the phonetic sounds of the name of Maria's town that she'd scribbled down after the conversation at CVS and then, together, they could try to compare that with the name of Rose's town? Or possibly she could find an atlas of Poland, to see if there were two different towns with similar *Saw-khah*-names close by Warsaw. Rose might even laugh, because maybe there was another town near hers with a similar name, and while she was growing up people had constantly been confusing the two.

Well, no: Rose wouldn't laugh about memories from Poland.

Could Natalie help? After all, Rose had lived with Natalie and her parents for a couple of years, back when Rose was probably telling Chana her stories. Perhaps Natalie had overheard something?—No, Natalie had just been a baby then. Even brilliant Judge Natalie would not have been able to distinguish complicated Polish words when she was two years old.

Honestly, how could Eleanor think about such questions now? Maria might be dying.

Maybe it was pointless? Most likely, Maria's father had not been the Nazi pharmacist with the swastika armband who had gleefully handed the Germans the names of Rose's family and all the other local Jews. There were dozens of small towns in Poland that Maria's family could be from. Rose's town itself had at least two pharmacists. It would be too much of a weird coincidence.

But Eleanor would never know for sure.

Did it matter?

* * *

Without Maria or Mark to talk to, Eleanor stood by herself in the chill air, almost as far back at the fence as Konrad used to stand, hugging her arms around her coat, watching colors blur on the field. The chubby, curly-haired kid was Josh. The red-haired kid was Jack's son, Ben. Mostly, the colors seemed to hover near the Hornets' goal, and the cheers seemed to be louder on the other side of the field, so the opposing team was undoubtedly scoring more goals. The air was dead, weighted down by the gray clouds and the Hornets' lack of success. Adam was following at Mark's heels, up the sideline, down the sideline. At least Mark had the decency not to send him away.

And after this dreadful game, the even-more-dreadful pizza party loomed. How the hell would Eleanor get through that, crowded into a restaurant with Mark? She wouldn't, that was the solution. She would drop Adam off at the party, go somewhere by herself, and pick him up later.

Her feet were starting to ache from standing. Maybe she could sit down on the grass. But the grass was cold and even a little sharp.

It would be nice to have one of Maria's chairs right now.

It would be nice to be able to talk to Maria, right now.

"Maria wasn't even born back then. And your mother's alive now. That's what matters," Natalie had said.

Actually, Natalie was wrong.

Well, she was right *and* wrong. Yes, the fact that Rose was alive was obviously important. But that wasn't the only thing that mattered. Rose's stories mattered, too.

Those were the stories that made Rose who she was, and thus made Eleanor and Natalie and Kate and Adam who they were, and even Rose admitted that she'd always planned to share them with her offspring. And not only Rose's stories: The pharmacist's stories—whether or not he was Maria's grandfather—they, too, were the stories that made the Holocaust what it was.

And all of these stories needed to be talked about and passed on to the next generation. The villainy, as well as the heroism, as well as the ordinary life in-between. The Nazi pharmacist *and* Pani Helena *and* a couple of Polish teenagers kissing in some hidden corner of their *Sawkhah* town. People couldn't pretend it hadn't happened. Rose's daughter couldn't pretend she didn't think about the Nazi pharmacist, every time she saw Maria who might be the pharmacist's granddaughter. The same, probably, for any other group of people who had suffered harm from a different group: *What did your parents do to my parents when they tried to vote in Mississippi? What did your parents say when my parents were rounded up and sent to internment camps in California in World War Two?*

But inheriting stories through the generations was not the same thing as inheriting guilt.

That was the point that she and Susan and Natalie and Mark had missed, in all of their conversations. That was why it didn't matter whether Eleanor ever learned who Maria's grandfather was. The stories were the parents' and grandparents' stories, their sins and their heroism. Yes, their prejudices might get passed down along with their stories, and the younger generations had to learn to separate the prejudices and the racism from the stories. But they still needed to hear the stories

Eleanor would probably never see the Wysockis again. Hell, the world might end at midnight on December 31. She was working herself into a frenzy over nothing.

And yet.

Three was also a decent chance that the experimental trial would put Maria's cancer into remission and the Wysockis would return to New Jersey, after the trial was finished. Maybe Janek had only taken a leave from his job, rather than quitting outright. Maybe they owned their house and were merely renting it out for six months or a year. They could show up next fall, across the field at a soccer game one day. Or Eleanor might fill a prescription at CVS.

What would Eleanor say to Maria, then?

Can you spell out the name of your town in Poland?

I heard you went for treatment for cancer. I hope you're feeling better.

You know, I've been telling Adam some of my mother's stories about growing up in Poland; happy ones and sad ones. Maybe Tad and Adam could share their stories.

The sounds around her were different, suddenly. Louder. More shrill. There was clapping, growing stronger, on the sidelines close to her; on the Hornets side. The Hornets? A blue-and-white Hornet was streaking down the field as fast as Tad used to do, hurtling the ball along with powerful kicks toward the other goal. Except for the kid's brown hair, it was almost as though Tad had returned to save the day, the parents suddenly alive, Jack, Dave, Betsy, even Mark, jumping up, cheering with ridiculous hope.

THE END

Acknowledgments

So many people helped and inspired me—even, in many cases, when they didn't realize that my casual questions had an ulterior motive!

Thanks, first of all, to everyone who shared their stories about Poland and Polish anti-Semitism in the U.S. (or stories they had heard from others), including Lillian Calem, Ruth Franklin, Jean Kratzer, Leon Levy, Linda Motzkin, Jane Rosen, Nancy Schuman, Margaret Somerstein, Esther Widman, and my father, Edward Hawthorne. As well, Jolanta Postrzygacz and Ziggy Pelczyk were my wonderful guides on my visit to Poland in 2014, and Rita Baron Faust, Joel Levy, Necha Sirota, and Daniel Soyer filled in rich details about other countries under Nazi occupation, anti-Semitism, and Yiddish. Thanks, too, to Larry Fein: I "borrowed" a little bit of your tale of how your family escaped from then-Czechoslovakia.

Of course I knew from the start that this novel would demand tons of research about Poland. What I didn't expect was the need to learn about such a mix of other topics. Katherine Koch, Jennifer Napoli, and Vicki Sher helped me understand painting techniques, while Noreen Axon, Ben Kligler, Neil Motzkin, Kathy Robinson, and Jay Rubin patiently guided me through explanations of hip fractures, nose-piercing, and emergency medicine.

No editor would ever have read past Page 1 of my original five drafts. I am forever grateful for the advice and early readings of so many sensitive writers: my workshop friends Claire Dunnington, Julia Phillips, Alizah Salario, and Leigh Stein, and also my later readers Sarah Bruni, Richelle Gist, and Masha Hamilton. A special thanks to Sharon Harrigan for connecting me with my workshop-mates and for her advice and encouragement in general.

Anna and her family are nothing like the Wysocki family, but they unwittingly inspired this book when my son Joe was in a first-grade class with their younger son. Getting to know them a little bit spurred me to look deeply into my feelings about Catholic Poles in light of my family's narrow escape from Poland.

To my sister, Barbara Probst: Thank you for encouraging me to finally get off my duff and write.

To my agent, Sophia Seidner of Jill Grinberg Literary Management, and my editors, Kim Verhines and Jerri Bourrous at Stephen F. Austin State University Press: Thank you for your faith in me.

To Toshiya Masuda: Thank you for your artistic insight and efforts in creating the cover design.

And most of all, to my children, Joe and Mallory: This isn't exactly your family's history. But it is your inheritance.